PRIMEVAL VALLEY

EDWARD J. MCFADDEN III

SEVERED PRESS
HOBART TASMANIA

PRIMEVAL VALLEY

"So tomorrow we disappear into the unknown. This account I am transmitting down the river by canoe, and it may be our last word to those who are interested in our fate."

— Sir Arthur Conan Doyle, The Lost World

1

Tall evergreens creaked and swayed as a breeze redolent of pinecones and moisture pushed through the forest and up the river valley. Clouds of flies and gnats clogged the air, and the gentle sound of water falling over stones eased Gill's nerves. Birds chirped, and squirrels and chipmunks bolted in and out of the woods, looking to take a drink from the river but fleeing upon discovering human intruders.

"Look, da, a rainbow," Brian said. The three-year-old's pudgy little finger pointed at the sky.

Sunlight refracted off cool mist that rose from Clear River like smoke and arced lines of color spanned the gurgling stream like a bridge. Water rushed around Gill's waders as he snapped his wrist back and forth, pulling his fly from the water and flicking it back into place. Brian stood silhouetted beneath the rainbow, and sadness washed over Gill. The boy looked so much like his mother.

Steep mountains covered in Douglas fir, hemlock and whitebark pine filled the horizon, and rocks and sediment ran along the stream's edge. Mist snaked beneath the thick tree canopy, the forest a shadow world where plants and animals fought for every beam of sunlight. Midsummers in the Rocky Mountains are mild and pleasant when the snow and ice retreat to the mountain peaks.

Clear River bent sharply twenty yards downstream, and Brian stood in a shallow pool behind a line of stones, watching his father. A thick cloud slid by overhead. Brian's rainbow disappeared, and the boy's hand fell to his side.

Gill stopped fishing, his fly floating downstream. A chill ran through him and he shook himself, rolling his shoulders, but he couldn't shake the unease. The cube of ice in his stomach grew to a block, yet there was no cause, no visible reason to make him feel like he'd eaten a plate of Tijuana tacos. Gill stared at his son, whose attention was locked on something upstream.

The boy wiped blonde hair from his face and frowned, his expression passing from wonder to fear.

"Brian?" Gill said.

The cloud passed, and warm sunlight filled the dell.

Brian squealed, a whimper of terror muffled by fear of making noise.

Sweat slid down Gill's back and forehead, and he cracked his neck. Panic twisted him like a cyclone.

Brian lifted a trembling hand and pointed upriver.

Twenty yards upstream, the snout of an animal stuck from the tree break. Douglas fir packed the far shore, their thick branches encroaching to the water's edge. The beast's long jaws were open, and rows of white teeth stood out against bloody gums. Dark eyes the size of golf balls stared from within the shadows of the forest.

The animal's head twitched like a bird's, and it made a clicking sound Gill barely heard over the flowing river. Whatever the thing was, it was big and stood as tall as him.

A lizard-like head pushed past evergreen branches, bobbing side-to-side.

Gill searched the shoreline for his supplies. Their lunches and backpack sat on a rock and his Remington .22 leaned against a tree above the waterline forty-feet away. It was farther from him than the beast was from Brian.

The creature stepped from the forest into the river. Gill shook his head and blinked.

The beast moved to the center of the stream and rotated its long head to face Brian. The creature stood on two thick legs, one of which clawed at the river as if spoiling to run. Thin arms hung from a sleek torso, which was covered in tiny brown feathers. A patchwork of darker and longer feathers ran down the center of the beast's back out to the tip of its ten-foot tail. It took a step toward Brian, clicking and snapping its jaws, head bobbing.

That was enough for Gill. He started for his gun, slow at first, then picking up speed. The creature turned in his direction, but didn't move, its head shifting from Brian to him. Gill remembered where he'd seen a similar animal. It looked like one of the raptors from the Jurassic Park movies, but instead of grey leathery skin, it had tightly packed feathers and its head was thinner. Dinosaurs had been extinct for millions of years, so the thing had to be a mutant, a bastard spawn of an eagle and an alligator.

The beast took another step toward Brian, and Gill doubled his pace. Water sloshed and splashed, and the creature turned its full attention to Gill.

"That's it. That's it," Gill said.

The animal took two steps in his direction, jaws open in a tooth-filled smile. It clicked and chuffed, pushing through the water, tossing its head back like a horse.

Gill dove the last ten feet, turning his back on the animal as he lunged for his rifle. He grabbed the gun and spun around, bringing the stock to his shoulder.

The creature was gone.

Brian stood in the eddy, staring into the forest. Gill's heart pounded in his ears, and he got up and pushed through the river toward his son.

"You alright, partner?"

"What... what was that?" the boy sputtered.

"I'm sure I don't know. Come to me now. It might come back and there could be more of them."

Brian stomped through the water until he was at his father's side. He threw his arms around Gill's waders, and said, "I don't think I want to learn how to fish."

"Aw, don't say that. You just—"

The creature appeared from within the trees twenty feet away, its dark eyes appraising them.

Gill didn't raise his rifle, he was lost in the awe of seeing something that shouldn't be, one of those rare oddities that made you feel special for having seen it. The beast was damp with mist and sparkled in the sunlight. It raised itself to its full height, lifting its narrow head and nodding at them.

Gill pushed Brian behind him and lifted the rifle.

The creature stepped back into the dense forest, disappearing in the mist.

"If I didn't know better I'd think the thing was playing with us." Gill wanted Brian safe, so he could focus on... what? Shooting the creature? If he could take it alive... He remembered the teeth, the powerful legs. "Brian, go wedge yourself into that pile of rocks."

The boy stared up at his father, then at the boulders he pointed at, fear and betrayal filling the kid's face. "No. Stay with you."

Something screamed then. Gill knew it was a thing because human vocal cords couldn't roar with such ferocity and shrillness.

The primal wail was all Brian needed to push him into motion. The boy sloshed through the river toward the pile of rocks. Gill scanned the forest, but there was no sign of the monster. Brian reached the stone pile and was climbing toward his hiding place when the creature stepped from the forest behind the boy.

Brian couldn't see the beast and Gill decided not to alert him. If he knew the monster was behind him he might panic, and the animal would attack. Brian was almost to a gap between two large stones where the creature couldn't get to him.

Gill brought the rifle stock to his shoulder and put the beast in his sights. He took his eye from the scope. Brian had climbed in front of the creature, and if the beast moved, or he missed, or the bullet ricocheted off a stone...

The monster squawked and jumped atop a boulder. Brian froze, but didn't look back.

"Keep going son, you can make it." Gill was trying to convince himself. If the monster leapt twice more it would be on the boy.

Gill sighted the rifle and took a shot at the thing. He missed, and the bullet smacked a tree just as Brian slipped into his hiding place.

Air rushed from Gill's lungs. He pulled back the bolt and dropped another round in the firing chamber and jacked it closed. He fired again, but the beast was too fast. It zigzagged across the river, darting in and out of the trees.

The buzz of insects and the chatter of birds died away. Mist puffed from the forest as something moved within. Gill loaded the rifle and brought it up, searching for a target. Was there more than one? He felt exposed, standing in the river alone, gnats dive-bombing his head.

Gill bolted for the cover of the trees.

2

As soon as he entered the mist Gill knew he'd made a mistake.

Not only had he left Brian alone, but now he was blind. He walked into a wide fir branch, its tiny green leaves poking him like a thousand toothpicks as he pressed through it. Gill peered out at the river, but didn't see Brian in his hiding spot, which was good. He didn't see the creature either, and that was bad.

The beast could have taken off, or it could be ten feet behind him. Birds fought on a branch above, and flies and bees hummed like high voltage power lines, ringing in his head so loud Gill pressed his fingers to his forehead. He needed to get out of the forest. Back to Brian.

Gill brought up the Remington, panning it back and forth as he emerged from the evergreens. He eased into the river, looking over his shoulder, scanning the stream in both directions.

The raptor bolted from the forest in a blur.

Gill brought the rifle around and fired.

The beast slammed into him and the gun flew from Gill's hands, landing on a stone and bouncing into the forest. The raptor clawed at him with one of its seven-inch retractable talons, but Gill's momentum as he fell saved his life, the beast's swipe passing inches from his face.

He hit the water, landing on the rocky river bed. Pain spread across his back as the creature passed over him and crashed into the river. Gill rolled in the water, coughing and sputtering, fighting to distance himself from the beast.

"Dad? You OK?" Brian yelled.

Gill said, "You stay there. Stay there! It can't get you. I'm fine. You hear?"

No response.

Gill got to his feet as the raptor circled. The beast chirped and huffed, its teeth clicking as it opened and closed its long mouth. Its eyes never left Gill. He felt its stare, knew it was seeing every move, evaluating his strength.

Somewhere in the back of Gill's mind his dead father's voice rose above the panicked tumult, and the memory of a hike they'd taken when he was a boy came back to him as if sent from the beyond.

Gill and his dad were hiking in Rocky Mountain National Park and they'd come around a bend to find a massive grizzly bear standing on the path. Startled, the beast rose on its hind legs and roared, slime dripping from its tooth-filled maw. Gill remembered how he'd been thankful for not drinking all his iced tea at lunch, because only a tiny spritz of urine soiled his underwear. He recalled the fear like it was yesterday, just as he remembered his father's soothing words.

"Don't make any sudden movements. It's just as afraid of us as we are of him, and it's important not to show fear."

Then the old man did something that stunned Gill so completely he'd gasped.

His father charged the bear, yelling and screaming, waving his arms. The bear roared and bolted into the woods. "Just have to show them who's boss, that's all." Gill remembered thinking his father was the bravest man he knew. With his son's life in the balance, could he be as brave?

Gill ran toward the forest to get the rifle. The beast's eyes followed him, and it squawked, but held its ground. The gun lay just inside the tree break and he snatched it up. The raptor splashed in the river as it took a step forward. Gill slipped a hand into a pocket and pulled out a bullet. He slid back the bolt, ejected the spent cartridge, and slipped the .22 caliber shell into the firing chamber. The click of the bolt closing echoed over the river as Gill brought up the rifle.

The raptor attacked, charging and jumping into the air with its clawed feet forward like an eagle dive-bombing a field mouse. Gill lurched backward and fired. The shot went high and wide, but he managed to knock aside the creature's claws with the rifle as the beast came at him.

The raptor recovered quickly, and before Gill could get to his feet, the beast had him pressed into the river. Gill sucked in air as he was thrust underwater, the creature's short arms holding him to the riverbed, talons digging into him. Gill thrashed, pounding the raptor with the rifle and kicking it. The beast was strong, and it held him fast as its jaws smacked.

A loud caw came from the forest. The creature paused and lifted its head.

Gill knocked the raptor in the head with the rifle and freed himself. Another caw. The raptor's head jerked side to side, its eyes focused on the woods.

Gill inched backward toward the tree break. The beast wailed, opening its jaws and throwing its head back as it advanced, the call from the wild forgotten. Gill backed away, rifle held like a club. His shoulder ached where the raptor hit him, and he was losing his strength, tiny stars dancing in the air before him. That's when he remembered the fishing knife in its leather sheath.

The memory of the sheath brought a smile. People think of the strangest things when the adrenaline is flowing like wine. He and Abigale had gone down to Sonoma before Brian was born. A second honeymoon. They'd visited the four corners where Colorado, Arizona, Utah and New Mexico meet in the lamest tourist trap ever assembled. He'd wanted to leave, but Abigale and shopping had been an unstoppable force, yet it was he who had made a purchase.

Gill remembered the face of the young girl who'd sold him the sheath decorated in beads of various colors. She'd been so proud of her creation. It made him so happy to buy it from her.

He pulled the knife and his father's voice again mocked him from beyond. "What are you gonna do with that? Only you'd bring a knife to a dinosaur fight."

"Hey, you leave him alone," Brian yelled. He stood atop the pile of rocks, a baseball sized stone in his hand.

Panic ran through Gill. Brian was exposed, and it was his fault. Never taking his eyes off the creature, and keeping his voice steady so as not to frighten the boy, Gill said, "I'm OK son. Please go back to your safe place. Please."

The raptor inched forward, its talons clicking on river stones. Its mouth opened into a smile and the creature lunged for Gill.

The rock hit the beast square on the snout, and the raptor turned toward Brian. The boy stood perched atop a boulder, dirty-blonde hair blowing in the breeze, a broad smile running across his face. Then noticing the creature's gaze fixed on him, Brian headed back to his hiding place.

The raptor abandoned Gill and sprang across the river. Brian wasn't going to make it. The raptor was too fast.

Gill fumbled in his pocket for another shell, but there were none. He dug in his other pocket and found a bullet. He jacked it into the firing chamber and aimed the weapon at the beast.

The creature hopped onto the stone pile, lurched forward and pulled on Brian's foot with it snapping jaws. The boy held on, grasping at rocks as he climbed, but the strain was too much, and he fell backward into his attacker.

Gill fired and hit the animal's upper torso, blood splattering Brian's face. The beast's head jerked back, but it didn't release the boy's leg.

Brian cried in pain, and Gill screamed, a primal yell of fury, fear, and self-loathing. He'd allowed this to happen. He'd let Abigale die, and now he was going to lose Brian and it was his fault. He fumbled for another bullet, but his pockets were empty, the rest of the ammo in the backpack forty feet from where he stood.

The raptor jumped from the pile of stones and disappeared into the forest, Brian screaming and crying as he dangled from the creature's mouth.

3

Gill stood frozen in the center of Clear River. Water ran around his legs as his eyes filled with tears, the realization that the creature had taken his boy working its way slowly to the forefront of his brain.

Brian's strangled cries made him flinch and freed him from his paralysis.

Gill lurched through the river to the thin strip of shoreline where they had their supplies, stripped off his waders and hung them from a tree branch. He tore open the backpack and pulled out the box of shells. There were seven left. He loaded the rifle and stuffed the rest of the bullets in a pocket, zipped up the pack, and threw it over a shoulder.

The forest was grey beneath the thick tree canopy, and river mist twisted through the thick evergreens. The cool fog soaked Gill as he threaded through trees and shrubs, branches scraping his arms and face. Brown needles shed from the deciduous trees covered the ground, and the dead leaves crackled like breaking ice as they tumbled in the breeze. The beast ran through the woods. Tree branches creaked and snapped as Brian's screams drew Gill on, his path clear.

He burst from the forest into a clearing filled with boulders surrounded by tall grass and weeds. A path of bent vegetation led south toward the old mine. Gill crossed the field, traversing the large stones, but lurched to a halt when he saw a trail of blood.

The blood was thin, and pinkish, and he was no doctor, but it didn't look like human blood. He'd wounded the creature, and that would eventually slow it down as the beast's heart had to work harder, but he couldn't count on that. For all he knew the bullet may have passed through doing no significant damage.

An animal path led back into the dense forest and Gill couldn't tell if the raptor had gone that way. There was no trail of blood. The forest was quiet, and he no longer heard Brian's screams or the pounding of the animal's feet. Gill searched the ground for signs and, finding none, followed the path.

The deer trail plunged downward into a hollow that had a large puddle at its bottom. The dark brown water smelled foul, but Gill searched the damp mud around the water anyway. There were no tracks. No animal had been to this natural toxic waste pool recently.

Bile rose in Gill's throat as he ran on, the image of his son's bloodied body filling him with rage. If he lost the boy that would be it, he saw no reason to continue. When Abigale died, Brian had been Gill's anchor, this small boy who didn't understand why his mother was never coming home again. Taking care of Brian had gotten him through. Provided hope and a reason to go on. Without Brian, he had nothing.

He shook his head as he climbed out of the dell. He had to fight back the negative thoughts, they'd plagued him his entire life. He didn't see a glass half full or half empty. He saw a broken glass, shards piercing flesh, drawing blood and reminding him around every turn that good things weren't meant for him. Peace would not be his. Gill was so convinced of this it hurt his heart and losing Brian would break it beyond repair.

A wail of pain that Gill knew for certain was Brian echoed through the woods to the east. He'd gone the wrong way. He scolded himself as he turned and followed the noise, his heart hammering in his chest. Brian's cry was answered by a more primal snarl-bark.

He stopped when he discovered a thick trail of blood ending in a puddle the size of a dinner plate. The blood was the deep red of a human.

Something in Gill snapped then. The rubber band that held together his pathetic life, and the gears of his mind scraped and ground together. What he'd heard wasn't Brian being killed. There were no screams. No wails of pain. No. His boy was alive, he knew it as surely as he knew the sky was blue.

He stepped over the blood puddle and followed the trail to the side of a cliff face. Here the trail made a right and headed east toward the old ghost town of Winfield. Was the beast heading for the old mine shafts? If it was, then Brian was lost. The old mine was a maze of tunnels, some caved in, others filled with water, but it was said some were still passable.

He followed the cliff face until its end, where the trail of blood turned left into a field of boulders. Tall grass and weeds clogged the spaces between the giant rocks, but animal paths crisscrossed the area, and Gill followed the one that had a drip of blood every ten feet.

Then the trail of blood stopped. Just ended as though the beast had disappeared. Gill looked up, a premonition telling him the creature had climbed onto one of the boulders, but he saw nothing perched atop the stones. There was no sign of the creature at all.

Gill shouldered his rifle and dropped into a crouch. He was breathing heavy, sucking air into lungs that hadn't worked hard in a long time. Pain ran up his back, and his head pounded in rhythm with his heart. He wiped sweat from his brow with the back of his hand and cracked his neck.

He listened hard, the way they'd taught him in firearms training in the Army. Breathe, and slowly eliminate each sound as you identify them. The rustle of the wind, the buzz of insects, the bleat of crickets, the chirping of birds, all fell away.

Gill heard nothing. Not the beast. Not Brian. They were gone.

Thinking the creature had stopped bleeding, Gill traversed the area, following the path he'd been on. Soon he was running along a cliff face again and an old mineshaft with a boarded entrance appeared in the rock face. He paused to examine it. No boards had been pulled down, no blood, no claw marks or footprints. They hadn't gone that way, and that was a relief.

The cliff face tapered down to a twelve-foot natural stone wall, and a path ran through a cut in the stone. It was dark, and rocks and tall tufts of weeds and grass filled the tight gorge, a thin deer trail running down its center. He knelt to examine marks in the hard-packed earth.

Claw prints ran along the path, three dig marks from each foot caused by the beast's curved talons. Gill traced the gouges with the tip of his finger, and stared down the path, but it was dim and shadowy. Errant rays of sunlight pierced the greyness like klieg lights, and Gill avoided them like he was playing a videogame as he made his way down the path, but he didn't know why.

Thirty feet into the gorge the ground rose, but the path widened as the split in the mountainside grew. The beast's tracks climbed higher, and Gill lost the trail when the path disappeared into a tightly packed stand of Douglas fir trees.

Here he paused, panting hard, mouth dry as paper. Gill pulled a water bottle from the side of the backpack and took a long swallow. Water ran down his chin onto his shirt. The cool water felt good on his skin, and he cupped his hand and splashed some on his face.

A clicking and rumbling noise came from the forest, then the sound of breaking branches. Gill slipped into the trees, and the temperature dropped fifteen degrees. His skin was clammy, and his legs ached. He figured he'd gone two miles, and still he hadn't seen the creature.

No sooner had that thought fleeted through his mind when he saw the beast's tail sticking out from behind a tree. Gill shouldered the rifle, sighted the tail, and fired.

The bullet struck the tree, sending splinters flying.

The raptor bolted, zigzagging through the forest, a blur of brown and black. Gill loaded the rifle, but he didn't have a shot. The creature was moving fast and erratically, and there were trees in his line of fire.

Then it hit Gill like a truck: the creature hadn't been carrying Brian.

Gill lifted the rifle and worked his way through the trees, using them as cover. Ahead, a large oak had fallen, and beyond it the raptor hid within the trees' dying canopy, the brown-green leaves providing perfect cover.

Gill stopped and took a knee, peering through the thick evergreens. The beast moved, and Gill lost sight of it. His nerves pulsed, and he tried to shake it off, yet the unease persisted like the fading pain after an electrical shock.

A black eye peered through the foliage. It rotated as it blinked, but Gill didn't think the creature saw him. Then the eye was gone.

"Brian. Brian! Son, are you out there?" Gill said. He knew it could draw the creature to him, but he didn't care. He needed to hear his son's voice.

No response, except the rustling of the wind and the chirp of crickets.

A branch snapped to his left and Gill swung the gun and fired. A spray of wrens burst from the trees, chirping and squawking. He reloaded the rifle, and stalked through the forest, following the line of his gunshot.

Three loud concussion *booms* echoed in the distance, and Gill paused, taking a pull of water. Recently, companies looking for copper and other precious metals were revitalizing some of the old mines and opening new tunnels. The blasting had caused three avalanches up Mount Elbert's way, and several of the major ice sheets at higher elevations had cracked and broken apart. Gill shook his head. Many people had complained to the state about the blasting and what it might do to the ecosystem, but copper was copper, and the eagles and black bears didn't have a seat in the state senate.

The trees thinned, and the animal path widened. A red dot caught his eye and Gill bent to examine it. A splash of blood dripped over a white rock. He picked it up and sniffed it, like he was some master tracker and could tell the difference between human and animal blood by smell. He dropped the stone and went on.

Worry, fear and sorrow gripped him in their cold embrace, the idea that his son had been killed worming its way into his brain like a maggot. He pushed the toxic idea away, because he had no choice. His boy was alive. He was alive. He knew it.

Ahead the raptor stood atop a rise hiding behind a thick juniper bush, its head sticking out as it watched Gill work his way up the hill. The beast stepped from its cover, clawing at the ground, spoiling to attack. The raptor roared and came at Gill, who froze and brought the rifle to his shoulder.

The raptor zigzagged and hopped, flailing its head and shrieking. It bent low as it ran, head thrust forward like an arrow, arms dangling uselessly, powerful legs kicking-up rocks and dust. Its black golf-ball-sized eyes were locked on him, jaws cracked in a toothy grin.

Gill's hands shook. The creature was fifty yards off and coming on strong. Brian wasn't hanging from the beast's jaws, and that brought a moment of relief. He breathed, cleared his mind, and fired. The slug cracked off a boulder, spraying the monster with shards of stone.

The raptor didn't slow up.

4

When the raptor was twenty yards away it slowed and disappeared behind an emerald green juniper bush. Thrushes burst from the dense shrub and scattered the clouds of gnats that hung in the air like nasty snowflakes. The forest symphony came to a crescendo, as if the crickets and birds understood a confrontation was forthcoming. Daggers of sunlight sliced through the tree canopy, and woodchucks, ants, grouse, and squirrels skittered to the safety of their homes.

Gill sighted the rifle. If the bitch stuck out so much as the tip of its snout it would lose it. He trembled, and the sound of breaking branches spun him around. He scanned the forest, but the evergreens were a wall of green.

A roar and then high pitched clicking. Sweat dripped down Gill's forehead. He had become the hunted. Since time immortal predators have fought each other for territory, food and mates. As the scales of nature balanced beasts of all species, Gill realized he was in the raptor's world now.

The attack came from his right, a blast of talons and teeth as the raptor burst through the evergreens. Gill fell backward and brought up the rifle to ward off the blow and his finger slipped on the trigger and the rifle fired, sending an errant shot into the tree canopy.

Gill hit the ground and air rushed from his lungs. The raptor straddled him, talons digging into the ground on either side, its long jaws snapping and biting as Gill defended himself with the empty rifle. The beast came in for a bit, baring its razor-sharp teeth. Gill swung the gun like Babe Ruth and caught the animal on the snout. The raptor whined, and Gill rolled, coming to a stop next to a tree trunk and avoiding one of the creature's seven-inch retractable claws as it tried to disembowel him.

Gill vaulted to his feet like a surfer catching a big one. He slipped behind the tree he'd hit, fumbling in his pocket for a bullet.

The wind picked up and the evergreens scraped and sighed. The raptor didn't move. It watched Gill, its head moving like a chicken's, its right foot clawing at the earth. It chuffed and clicked as it took a step forward. A beam of sunlight lit the creature's face, and the beast blinked and shook its head.

Gill pulled a bullet free, fumbled it, and it fell to the ground. He reached for it and the raptor took two fast steps in his direction. Gill stepped back, falling in behind another tree. He brought up the empty rifle and dug in his pocket for a shell. Heart racing, nerves jumping like the FBI had just knocked on his door, Gill slid back the rifle's bolt. The click and rub of metal on metal made the creature take two more rapid steps in his direction. The beast was ten feet away. Slime dripped from its mouth, its eyes blazing with hunger.

Gill thought of the old westerns he'd watched with his pa as a boy. Fifteen paces, turn and draw. Except, he was locked in one of those stare down gun fights. The next move he made, the raptor would attack. Question was, did he have time to put the bullet in the chamber, close the bolt, and aim the gun before the beast was on him? If the thing got near him again, he wouldn't last long.

Fearing he was running out of time, and knowing he really had no choice anyway, Gill dropped the .22 caliber shell into its cradle and jacked the bolt closed.

The raptor was a blur as it launched itself, feet off the ground and forward, claws outstretched.

Gill swung the gun around and fired.

The raptor spun, the shot catching the beast in the torso above its right arm. But even as the creature reared back it whipped its thick tail, its tip catching Gill on the side of the head. He crumpled to the ground, tiny dead leaves sticking in his face, stars dancing before his eyes.

The raptor stepped back, dazed, blood dripping from the bullet hole.

A gunshot rang out, and the beast's head slowly rotated toward the sound.

Darkness encroached around the edges of Gill's vision, and he needed to vomit.

"You alright, dipshit?" his father's voice echoed in his head.

"Yeah, pa. I'm fine."

Darkness took him.

***

Gill came awake to the round face of Sheriff Nicki Sande. Her blonde hair was greying at the tips, but her bright blue eyes still sparkled. She looked down at him, eyes filled with worry. Sunlight lit her from behind and gave her an angelic quality. She put her hand on Gill's forehead, checking his temperature.

"Gill? You OK?" she said.

His head pounded like he'd drunk a fifth of Jack Daniels in one sitting. The bright light hurt his eyes, and he squinted under the harsh glare. Where was he? What had happened? Then it all came back like an avalanche, burying him in fear, doubt, worry, and sorrow. Brian. Oh dear God, Brian.

"Gill?" she pushed.

"I'm alright, I think. Where's Brian?" he said.

"I don't rightly know. Was he with you?"

Gill closed his eyes and took a deep breath. Where to begin? What had she seen? "Did you chase the thing down and kill it?"

"What? That bear? No, of course not. Why would I?" Nicki said.

"Bear? What bear?"

"Looked to me like you were getting attacked, so I fired into the sky and the thing ran off. Did you shoot it? I saw a trail of blood." Her eyes shifted to the ground. "No hunting bear, you know that."

Gill started when Officer Antonio "Ant" Vargas pushed through the evergreens. The big man said, "The blood trail disappeared into the forest. Just stops. The tracks are damn weird, too."

Gill sat up. "Did you see Brian?"

Ant looked at Nicki, who shrugged. "No, sir, should I have?"

Anger welled in Gill, his vision turning red. "What the hell do you think I was doing out here?"

"Why don't you tell us?" Nicki said.

"Me and Brian were fishing down by the river when we were attacked by..." Gill couldn't find the words. What should he call the thing? If he said it was a raptor dinosaur they'd think he was crazy. He decided to skip it for now. "I fought the thing, but it took Brian and I chased it up here past the eastern spur of the old mine."

"What thing attacked you? You mean the bear?" Nicki said.

"No, I don't mean a bear."

The three of them sat in silence for a time, and Ant took a handkerchief from his pocket, sat on a stone, and wiped his brow. Nicki paced in a circle around Gill, her hands moving in silent speech.

"What brought you up here, anyway?" Gill said.

"Ant and I were over at the Riverton place. Ms. Riverton thinks her chickens are getting taken by coyotes. We heard the gunshots, and since it isn't hunting season, we came to check things out."

"Gill, you're saying Brian was with you? And the bear took him?" Ant said.

"No!" Gill sighed. He was losing his patience and taking out his grief on these folks who were trying to help him. "I'm sorry." Gill got to his feet. "I need to go find my son. The longer we sit here the less chance I have to save him." He dusted himself off and started for the tree break.

Nicki reached out an arm. "Let us help you," she said.

"Well come on then," Gill said. He took a few steps and felt dizzy. He paused and braced himself against a tree.

Nicki rushed to his side to steady him.

Gill took her arm. This wasn't the first time Nicki had saved him from a fall. She'd been the one to tell him about his wife's death, and since then she'd gone out of her way to check on him and Brian, bringing meals, movies, just stopping over to see if they needed anything. Gill thought he could have feelings for her, but she was married, and he was... What? A widower? A widower who had no interest in replacing or forgetting about his dead wife.

"Sit down, pal," said Ant. The man's giant hands guided Gill to the ground, where he sat with his back against an oak.

Nicki said, "Ant, get the medics up here with a stretcher. I want him brought to general ASAP."

"No," Gill said, and he fought to get up.

Ant gently eased him back down. "Easy, buddy. Easy."

"No!" Gill brushed off Ant's hand and tried to get up again. Brian. He needed to help Brian. "My son, Ant, my son." Tears leaked from Gill's eyes, and he shook with fear and anguish.

"I'll go look for him. OK?" Ant said with a sidelong glance at Nicki. Gill knew that glance meant Ant was humoring him so he'd calm down.

The big man disappeared into the trees and Nicki called for the medics on her radio. She sat next to Gill and put her arm around him. "It'll be alright," she said.

Gill couldn't help but suck in her scent—perfume, soap, and leather. Guilt racked him as he felt himself getting aroused, and his eyes grew wide. He hadn't felt that urge since before Abigale died.

"So, now that you've calmed down, tell me about this bear," Nicki said.

Anger destroyed his calm. "It wasn't a bear. It was a raptor. You know what that is?"

She said nothing. Worry painted her face, eyes squinting, lips a thin line.

"Or something that looked a hell of a lot like one. The thing was a cross between an eagle and alligator and the damn thing was taller than me."

"Where's your gear?" she asked.

"My gear? What the hell..." Then he understood. "I haven't been drinking, if that's what you're thinking. Haven't had a drop in two weeks."

"That's great, Gill. Really. I'm so proud of you."

The warble of the ambulance siren sounded off in the distance as it made its way down county road 390 toward the old ghost town.

"Whatever it was we'll get this straightened out. You think on it. Maybe after you rest things will be a bit clearer," she said.

"Clearer? What? You think I'm delusional?"

"No. But you've been through a trauma. Brian is missing, and you're not thinking straight. You might have a concussion from the shot you took."

"I know what I saw, Nicki. It was no bear. It was like nothing I've ever seen."

Ant entered the clearing and said, "Nothing. No sign of him. Is it possible he headed back down to the river when you got separated?"

"What the hell are you talking about? The thing took him! He's not going to be walking anywhere anytime soon," Gill said.

The ambulance siren was close as the paramedics maneuvered down the old dirt road that led up to the abandoned mines. The siren fell silent, and a chill wind gusted through the forest.

Nicki and Ant said nothing as the paramedics found them and put Gill on the stretcher. He struggled against them, but he had no strength left. He was spent. Ant stared at him with pity, and Nicki looked away.

"Nicki. Please believe me. Check the scene. Trace my steps. You'll see the trail," Gill said.

She leaned forward and put a hand on his shoulder. "Don't worry. We'll find your boy." Her eyes shifted away from his.

Gill struggled to get off the stretcher, clawing and pulling at his restraints. Two mining blasts echoed through the mountains. He felt the prick of a needle and the world fell away.

5

The Reserve town hall fell silent as Gilbert "Gill" Philips entered. In a township of 2,019 people everyone knew everybody's business, but that's not what bothered Gill. It was the pity. It seeped from the assembled crowd like desperate animals looking to please their master. So much pity he felt crushed by the weight of it.

As he walked to the front of the room Gill noticed other types of stares. Anger. Confusion. Worry. His wife was dead, his boy lost, and everyone was looking at him like he was a shaken beer. Open at your own peril.

Gill understood the hostility. Small towns are cocoons, and anyone who threatened to rip that protective shell open was considered an enemy. Gill, with his crazy story and silly talk would bring the staties, and nobody wanted that.

His shoulder ached, and his head throbbed, but no worse than after a night of drinking. His night in the hospital was uneventful, but he got dizzy if he stood up too fast, or concentrated for too long, but the doctors said this was to be expected. The bear had given him quite the tussle, they said. The bear. This damn nonexistent bear. He'd have to stand up in front of all these people, many of whom he called friends, and tell them it wasn't a bear, despite the fact that he'd already told this to anyone who would listen.

Brian wasn't found despite a town wide search that stretched into the foothills. The staties had been called, but Sheriff Nicki Sande wasn't expecting anything to happen for a few days. One boy missing in the woods wasn't priority, and law enforcement knew certain indelible truths: the boy was either dead, or would wander out of the woods in a few days covered in bug bites and starving. Ninety-nine percent of missing children cases up Reserve's way were left to the locals to investigate. Nicki assured Gill the search for Brian would continue, and that's what the town hall meeting was about.

Reserve Hall sat 283, the extra odd seat due to an angle by a support column. The room was packed, and people stood in the aisles along the walls and filled the rear standing-only area. Sheriff Nicki Sande sat on a dais with Mayor Leppers, Deputy Sheriff Belinda Carmichel, and Officer Antonio "Ant" Vargas. A seat had been left vacant for Gill in the front row, and he turned to face his neighbors before he sat. He had more allies than enemies, but part of him knew that was due to the pity vote.

Had things been different and he the cause of the ruckus, he had no doubts they'd be carrying pitchforks. Small towns like Reserve could provide the best support system, but they could also be incestuous and hurtful when a silver fish swam upstream.

The rumble died away as Nicki cleared her throat.

"Thank you all for coming. I know you're concerned about Gill and Brian, and about the town's safety. Please be respectful of your neighbors and let them speak," Nicki said.

Silence. Outside, a woodpecker tapped a tree, and Gill heard Francis Coldburn's shallow breathing. The old doctor had served Reserve for forty years, but he'd slipped fast the last few months. Gill gave the old man his own version of a pity gaze.

"First and foremost, we have a missing child. How this came to be we will discuss here, as well as what our plan of action will be, but please keep in mind our primary purpose is to find Brian Philips."

Gill's friend, Clint Hyde, who sat next to Gill, put his hand on his shoulder.

"So I think it best to start the story at the beginning. Gill, would you mind telling everyone what happened?" Nicki said.

Gill closed his eyes and breathed deep, tossing his head side-to-side in an attempt to crack his neck. No luck. The pain persisted. He stood and looked around, all eyes fixed on him, some looking through him.

Gill shifted from one foot to another, his mouth so dry he thought his lips might crack. "Thank you to everyone for your help and assistance in the last twenty-four hours. I know many of you spent the night out in the woods searching for my boy, and for that I am eternally grateful."

A sniffle, a cough, shoes rubbing on the old wood floor, wind pushing through the open windows.

In a wavering voice that cracked every few words, Gill told his tale from first to last, leaving out nothing, but not exaggerating. He described the beast, but didn't call it a raptor or a dinosaur. When he got to the part where he told of shooting the creature, the room began to mumble.

Tracker Squirrel Redbone spoke-up first. "You hit the thing? Are you sure?"

"Sure as rain," Gill said. He told of how he'd fought with the creature and been knocked-out and of waking to find Nicki standing over him.

Nature guide Lydia Clamente said, "Why do you think the beast didn't finish you? It just left? Predators rarely do all the work and don't reap their reward."

"I fired a shot as I approached," Nicki said.

"And the beast was wounded," Gill said.

"So you say," someone from the back of the room yelled. The outburst was followed by too many agreeable mumbles for Gill's liking.

Nicki slammed her hand on the table, anger filling her face. Gill remained expressionless. "I don't see any reason Gill would lie, and until we have evidence otherwise, I won't allow him to be accused of anything. In fact, my report will support much of what he's said."

Nicki's husband Rajim said, "No disrespect, if you understand me, but I can think of several reasons why he might lie." Rajim looked at Gill and said, "Sorry." His dark black hair, usually curly, was matted to his head and he looked like he hadn't slept in days; red eyes, dark complexion, and a vein pulsing like it might burst next to a scar over his right eye.

Gill knew he wasn't sorry at all. Nicki's husband was no fan of Gill's. He'd made that clear many times, going so far as to tell Gill to stay away from Nicki. When Gill had told Rajim Nicki came to his house, the IT Manager had barked and stalked off.

"That's not helpful to—" Nicki said.

"No!" Gill shouted. "Let's hear my motive. I'm curious."

Rajim's eyes reddened and he appeared to shrink in on himself, folding up like melting plastic. "Don't mean nothing by it Gill, but you've been through some tough times and men stronger than you have snapped. Maybe Brian got hurt somehow, or killed, and maybe it was your fault, or you feel it was, so your mind makes up this elaborate fairytale to cover it up."

Gill lunged at Rajim, but didn't get his hands on him. Several people got in his way and held Gill back, guiding him back into his seat.

Nicki pounded on the table again. "That's enough of your theories, Mr. Kumar. One more wild speculation from you and you're out on your ass." She spoke with such derision her husband lowered his head. Nicki had kept her father's surname, which helped get her elected five times, four of which were uncontested. "I conducted my own investigation, and while not complete given the short amount of time, I did discover several things."

Silence in the hall. That woodpecker was going full tilt and it was making Gill dizzy.

"I found Gill's waders hanging from a tree branch right where he said he left them. Footprints were few because most of the action had taken place in the river, but—"

Several people coughed.

Nicki shot daggers from her eyes. "But, I found strange prints in the mud along the river and then again in the forest. Whatever attacked Gill had three talons on each foot, and the center one was longer than the other two. The markings in the dirt were clear."

"Strange footprints? That's all you got?" someone shouted from the back of the room.

"Next person to interrupt is out of here. I shit you not!" Nicki's face had gone red, and her left eye twitched.

"I found feathers that didn't come from any bird I've ever seen, and then there's the two types of blood." She paused to let that sink in.

The mayor asked, "How do you know that, Nicki? The tests aren't back from the state lab yet and won't be for at least four days."

"I tested both myself. You can buy kits online for five dollars and we always have a couple on hand just in case. I was able to match Brian's blood using his hospital records, but the other..." She looked pensively at the assembled town's folk. "My amateur kit came-up unknown host."

Deputy Sheriff Belinda Carmichel said, "Unknown? Is that odd?"

"Yeah," coughed Dr. Coldburn. He sneezed into his handkerchief, his red eyes blazing. "Nicki, you checked the results online for a match?"

Nicki nodded.

"Oh, shit," Dr. Coldburn said.

"What does this mean?" Rajim asked.

"It means, we have no idea what attacked Gill and took Brian," Nicki said.

Silence in the room.

"And there's more," Nicki said. She looked hard at Gill and he knew what was coming. "I found the puddle of blood that Gill described, and..." Her eyes went to Gill, then fell to the table.

Ant finished for Nicki. "It was the boy's blood."

Shocked intakes of breath and murmurs.

"Well that surly changes things," said the mayor.

"How?" Gill asked. "Reserve is in danger. That's all we need to know. We need to hunt this thing. Find my boy."

"What purpose would it serve to panic people? Mountain lions take livestock and pets all the time, and you remember the..." the mayor said.

Yes. Gill did remember the Humprey boy. Disappeared in the woods and they'd only found pieces of him.

"The mayor has a point, as much as it hurts me to say it," Lydia Clamente said.

"Brian is alive. I know it as surely as the sky is blue," Gill said.

"That may well be, but Gill, you're very close to this. I understand—" Mayor Leppers said.

"You understand nothing! None of you do," Gill said. He felt small as everyone weighed him, deciding which way to go.

People shouted and talked, and after an hour Gill had heard enough.

"I want this thing's head on my wall, goddamn it! I want my boy back. Why are we standing around? Each moment we waste lessens the chance I'll find him," Gill said. The word Gill left off, but was clearly on everyone's mind, was 'alive'. "I'll find him, alive."

"I'm concerned your obsession will put yourself, others and Reserve in danger," the mayor said. "We have to search, but I don't think the hunting party should be more than ten people. We can scour the woods around town while Nicki and her team tracks the beast."

"What team? I'm going," Gill said.

"Gill I'm not sure—" Leppers started.

Gill stood, his mind clouded with anger, the heat of hatred filling him. "I don't give a frog's fart what you're sure off. Try and stop me." Gill turned slowly and made eye contact with anyone who would look at him. More than half the people in the room couldn't even do that.

"But you're hurt, Gill," said Dr. Coldburn.

Gill said nothing. He felt that if he started yelling he wouldn't be able to stop until his head exploded.

"Given the situation, Gill, if you think you can make it you can come," Nicki said.

"I'm in," Rajim said.

"I don't think that's a good—"

"I'm coming," Nicki's husband said.

Rajim saw him as a threat. What a joke. Gill wasn't a threat to anything or anyone. He'd become a shell of his former self, and he knew it. On some level he'd made peace with it and was content to let others right the wrongs of the world.

"I'll organize search parties in and around town," Kyle Brady said.

Gill nodded at his friend.

"Who should go from the department?" Belinda asked.

"You should come with me and Ant, since he was there at the beginning and helped me conduct the investigation," Nicki said.

"An investigation in the barest sense. My prof at the academy wouldn't be proud," Ant said.

"We did the best we could with what we had in the time allotted," Nicki said.

"Do we have any volunteers?" the mayor asked.

The low rumble of the crowd filled the room. Gill looked out the window, frustration washing over him. The sun was already starting its descent to the horizon. They'd lost another day and Brian was further out of reach, but he wouldn't mourn. No. He wouldn't allow himself to let those types of thoughts creep into his head. Brian was alive. He knew it, even if the townsfolk doubted it.

"I'll go," Lydia Clamente said. "I've been a nature guide up this way for years. I can help you in the woods."

"Good. Thank you, Lydia," Nicki said. "Anyone else?"

Clint Hyde turned to Gill. "You want me to come? I've got guns and ammo."

Gill nodded. He didn't care about the guns and ammo, but wanted someone he trusted close. "Please, if you don't mind."

"Done."

"I'm in also, if you'll have me," Squirrel Redbone said.

"I was hoping you'd throw in with us," Nicki said. "We're going to need your tracking skills."

When no more volunteers came forward, Nicki said, "Officer Kate Fleming will join us and that makes nine. More than enough, I think," Nicki said. "Let's meet up at the end of the eastern spur at sunup. Bring any weapons you have, and I'll raid the department's armory. Tim, Joey, I know you guys have some fancy stuff. Any way we can borrow some?" Nicki said.

Both men nodded agreement, but said nothing.

"Questions?" Mayor Leppers said. When nobody spoke he said, "We're adjourned then, and may God help us."

"We're gonna need more than that," Rajim said.

Nicki shot her husband a look that could have wilted fresh lettuce and went to Gill. He sat unmoving, staring out the window. "Gill?" she said. "You alright? Need a ride home?"

Gill just looked at her. By morning Brian could be dead.

Seeing the anguish on his face, Nicki said, "I know it's difficult waiting around, but tracking the creature in the dark is a fool's game. You know that. We might miss an important sign."

Gill looked up at her. "Thank you for everything, Nicki. Really, I don't know what I would have done without you."

Rajim harrumphed and walked away.

"Gill, that night I should have... I wanted to..." Nicki looked at her feet.

"I know," Gill said. "I know."

6

When Gill arrived, the rest of the hunting party was waiting for him. Dusk settled over the forest as the sun inched over the horizon and shadows danced under the dense tree canopy. Two pickup trucks sat side-by-side, and one of them had a horse trailer behind it. Nicki's 2008 Crown Vic was parked on the shoulder of the road.

Gill brought his car to a stop and killed the ignition. He sat there in silence, peering through the windshield at the group of people who'd volunteered to help search for his son and hunt the thing that had taken him.

Nicki saw him sitting in the car and walked over. He powered down the window. "Hey, Gill. Everything alright?"

"Yeah. Just…"

"Yeah," she said. "We're ready to roll."

He got out of the car and went to the trunk and retrieved his backpack and rifle.

"We've got something better than that for you," Nicki said.

Gill said, "What's Lydia's horse trailer doing here?"

"She brought her donkey, Rhubarb. He's gonna carry the gear, supplies and food. He does it all the time when she takes out tourists," Nicki said.

"Morning," Clint said as Gill and Nicki approached. His friend had a Glock nine strapped to his leg and an AR15 slung over his shoulder.

"Hey," Gill said.

Nods and good mornings from the rest of the crew. Lydia was strapping duffle bags to Rhubarb, and the beast of burden didn't look happy about it. The donkey whined and brayed as Lydia tightened the straps that held their equipment, and then she stroked the beast and gave Rhubarb a carrot.

The police huddled together inside the tree break: Ant, Belinda and Kate. They were checking their service weapons and chatting. Squirrel Redbone sat by himself, staring into the dark forest.

"We got spare guns, and this is for you," Clint said. He handed Gill an M16. "It's old. Me and that baby have been through the shit, so don't hurt it." Modern soldiers used the M4 carbine, the M16 having been retired.

Gill took the weapon and caressed it. He hadn't held an M16 since his military days. "This full automatic? Or does it have the burst feature?"

Clint said, "You know your shit…" He looked at Nicki, then said, "Stuff. You know your stuff. It has the burst feature."

"Yeah, I remember the military saved a fortune in ammo costs when they went from full auto to the three-shot burst feature," Gill said. He slid back the bolt and put the rifle stock to his shoulder.

Nicki said, "We've got plenty of spare ammo and food. Enough for days."

Belinda, Ant and Kate joined them.

"We ready to go?" Ant said.

"Think so," Nicki said. "Let's start at the creature's last known location. Yeah?"

Nods and general agreement.

Car doors were locked, trunks slammed, and Rhubarb was given some oats and water. The sun was up and baking off the morning dew, and birds fought in the tree canopy. Small animals darted across Gill's path, fleeing from the line of invaders that traipsed through the forest like dwarves on a mission to steal a dragon's gold.

The party came to the spot where Gill had been knocked-out, and tiny red flags stuck from the ground marking blood drips. It looked like an ant's golf course, and the red flags trailed away into the woods.

"Squirrel, I want you on point with Clint. Lydia, follow-up behind them with Rhubarb. You and Squirrel are the experts out here, and I don't want to miss anything," Nicki said.

"Got it," Squirrel said. He led the group past the red flags and had only gone ten feet when he stopped to examine the ground. He harrumphed. "Can't say I've ever seen anything like this before. Lydia?"

The old nature guide bent over with considerable effort and stared at the footprint with narrowed eyes. "No idea what that is."

Those who'd never seen the footprint stepped forward to look, while Gill, Nicki and Ant held back.

"You see what I mean?" Nicki said. "Tell me that's a bear?"

Nobody spoke.

Gill said, "Believe me now?"

"It's not that we don't believe you, Gill," Belinda said. She was the only one in uniform.

"It's just hard to believe," Rajim said. He'd fallen in next to Nicki and he put a protective arm around her waist.

"The mind plays tricks. Especially during stressful situations," Ant said.

Gill said nothing. They were trying to sooth him, he knew that. They meant nothing by it, but anger still rose in him. He knew what he'd seen, as unbelievable as it may sound.

Squirrel followed the strange tracks past the dark black patch they believed to be human blood, and the group came upon more red flags identifying drips of blood. The sun rose in the sky, but the day was pleasant as the party made their way steadily upward. Several times Squirrel lost the trail and they were forced to backtrack, and at one point the trail disappeared altogether.

"Break for lunch?" Kate asked.

That suggestion was met with dropping packs and an excited bray from Rhubarb. They ate a fast meal of sandwiches, dried fruit and water. Gill saw Clint take a nip from his flask and for a moment he thought about asking for a hit. Ant and Rajim lit cigarettes, and Lydia wandered off to go to the bathroom. There was no checking of cellphones because there was no signal up this high. They had an emergency radio and had agreed to check in with Reserve at least once per day.

The party was back on the trail in an hour, rested and fed. They planned to trek until dark. The forest gave way to a thin river that babbled and sung as the clear water tumbled over stones. Fish leapt from the river, and mist hung in the air. There were several footprints in the mud along the riverbank, but Squirrel couldn't identify any of them, and the creature had left no tracks along the river in either direction.

"We have to assume it crossed. No?" Belinda said.

"I'd think," Lydia said.

Being careful not to slip on slime-covered stones, Squirrel led the hunters through the water. Rhubarb bucked and struggled, whinnying and chuffing, unwilling to cross the stream. Lydia whispered in the donkey's ear as she stroked his flank and the animal settled down and allowed itself to be led across.

Tracks led into the forest on the opposite bank, but to Gill they looked smaller, and each appeared to be different. The prints trailed into the woods as if a herd of giant chickens had pushed through the forest.

"These aren't from our guy," Squirrel said.

Gill said, "What the hell are they from?"

"Birds?" Squirrel said.

They found a new puddle of blood an hour later. They'd climbed a low cliff that cut through the mountains like a scar, and the trees had thinned. Nicki knelt next to the puddle and the crowd of hunters stood over her shoulder. She looked back at Gill and he saw in her eyes what she meant to say.

"Looks like human blood," Nicki said.

"If it's Brian's how'd it get here?" Gill said.

"Come again?" Nicki said.

"When I was attacked, Brian was nowhere to be seen," Gill said.

"That means nothing. The thing may have stashed the boy while it came after you," Rajim said.

Nicki shot icicles from her eyes.

"Or maybe the boy got away and the thing chased him?" Belinda said. She had her service pistol in her hand. Her eyes darted around and sweat dripped down her forehead.

Gill said nothing.

It was getting dark, the sun disappearing behind the Rocky Mountains to the west. When the sun went down it would get colder.

"Let's halt and make a fire," Rajim said.

Nicki ignored him, and so did the rest of the party. This was no place to stop for the night. They had no cover, nothing to protect their backs. They hadn't seen anything other than the blood in over a mile, and Gill was starting to think they'd lost the trail.

They made camp in a hollow, got a fire going, and ate in silence as clouds rolled in over the mountains. They were all exhausted, and one by one the party disappeared into tents for the night.

Gill's mind raced as he lay tucked in his sleeping bag. Nicki thought the puddles of blood were Brian's. Gill pressed his eyes closed so hard they hurt, and he was asleep in minutes, despite the ringing in his head and the sorrow that made his gut hurt like he'd been stabbed.

**

The second day started with rain, and dark clouds obscured the mountain peaks to the north. The team broke camp and packed-up their wet belongings and were back on the hunt by 8AM. The rain had wiped away any hope of following a trail.

"What the hell is that smell?" Rajim said.

Gill had heard Nicki and her husband fighting in their tent the prior night. They all had. Rajim had been feeling randy and Nicki was having none of it.

"Smells like an open cesspool," Lydia said.

"A what?" Kate said. Those were the first words Gill had heard the woman speak since dinner the prior night. Kate had been out of the Rockies twice and her world view didn't extend beyond the Reserve town line.

Lydia giggled. "Out east they dig holes and line them with concrete rings to hold waste from houses."

"No leeching fields?"

"No, they have those also," Lydia said.

"Can we table the discussion on shit storage until a more opportune time?" Rajim said.

The man was really starting to get on Gill's nerves.

"Let's go see what stinks. Beyond my husband, that is," Nicki said. She hoisted her pack and followed Lydia as she led Rhubarb into the forest in search of the sewer.

The smell of shit got stronger as the party came over a rise and the trees gave way to a small pond, no more than a depression in the land filled with rainwater. Tracks of animals big and small crisscrossed the entire area. The smell came from a pile of scat two feet around and a foot high. The rain had beaten down the light brown pile of waste, and sticks and bones stuck from the scat, and streaks of blood ran through the crap like strawberry syrup through vanilla ice cream.

Lydia and Squirrel examined the pile.

"Whatever this came out of is big," Lydia said. She covered her nose with her hand, trying to ward off the smell, and by the look of horror on her face, she failed.

"Over here," Squirrel said.

Beneath a tall Douglas fir many tracks like the ones they'd seen prior crisscrossed the area. The prints were half the size of the bigger beast they were tracking, and the trail led into the forest away from the watering hole.

It was getting colder as they went higher into the Rockies, and snow appeared in patches on shady hillsides. Rinker Peak rose to the north, and Mount Elbert, the highest peak in the Rockies, stood like a sentinel to the northeast. Both peaks were covered in dark clouds that looked like smoke.

A mournful cry stopped Gill in his tracks. The sound made him think of a dying whale; deep and solemn. The wail got louder and sharper and suddenly ceased. The breeze brought the scent of the dung pile mixed with evergreen. Gill thought of the little green tree air-fresheners he bought at the gas station for ninety-nine cents.

Gill pushed past Nicki, his M16 held out before him. His son was out there waiting for him to come find him. Doubt gnawed at Gill as he flicked the M16's selector from single shot to burst.

7

Late afternoon on the second day out from Reserve, the party came across a disemboweled half-eaten moose. It was covered in a thin layer of frost, but maggots still feasted and squirmed in the rank flesh. Dark blood covered the ground and the scent of rot and decay filled the air. That smell every living thing understood and disliked. Entrails spilled from the crushed ribcage, and most of the meat had been stripped away. One of the great beast's antlers was broken off and stuck from the ground.

"Mountain cats," Squirrel said.

"I don't know about that," Lydia said. She examined the broken antler. "This was bitten off. Never seen a mountain lion do that before."

The land fell away before them into a shallow bowl filled with hemlock and spruce. There was a chill in the air, and patches of snow had become more frequent on the shaded hillsides. Gill estimated they were around 8,000 feet above sea level. His ears popped, and his breath was getting short.

"Look here," Nicki said. Ant and Kate stood with her.

Gill gasped when he saw what they were staring at. It was one of Brian's sneakers.

"Dear God," Lydia said.

"Don't think he can help," Rajim said.

"What's that supposed to mean?" Gill said.

Clint and Ant moved between the two men.

"What? You gonna try and cold-cock me again?" Rajim said. "You're lucky my kids were at the town hall."

Nicki put a hand on her husband's chest. "You're out of line," she said.

Rajim sighed and rubbed his eyes. "I just meant religion is bullshit. OK?"

Gill bent and lifted the tiny blue sneaker. He sniffed it and examined it like the shoe was a fifty-carat diamond. "No blood." He stood. "Look around this clearing. Something happened here to distract the raptor."

Rajim sighed and Squirrel coughed, but nobody spoke.

"It's carrying Brian, and it comes across this mountain lion kill, and it gets distracted and eats," Gill said.

Nicki threw him a bone. "Brian is injured, can't run, loses a shoe."

Gill knew they were reaching, and to hear Nicki stretch that rubber band further made his heart sing. "The beast finishes eating, continues on."

"You figure the... raptor is bringing Brian back to its babies?" Squirrel said. Realizing how that sounded, he added, "The thing would want to keep him alive then. Could be a good thing."

Gill rocked back as if punched.

"Sorry Gill, I didn't mean to—" said Squirrel.

"That's why we're on this thing. We'll get Brian back before the creature gets to wherever it's going," Clint said. He threw Squirrel a look that said 'think before you speak' and stalked off into the trees.

"I didn't mean anything by it Gill, I just thought..." Squirrel said.

There was no right way to say it, and Gill knew that. Squirrel and some of the others thought Brian was dead, gone, and a mutant bear was carrying the fresh meat to its young. He couldn't give in to that idea. Couldn't let that reality seep in for fear of it becoming true. Squirrel, for all his insensitivity, was probably right. The raptor was bringing fresh live meat back to its babies. The thought made him sick and hopeful at the same time.

The party worked their way down the incline into a gully and then up the slope on the opposite side. Cold mist hung in the forest as chilled air coming off the patches of snow mixed with the warmer ambient air rising from the lower elevations. An owl hooted, and in the distance the sounds of a nasty cat fight reminded Gill there were many dangerous beasts in the woods. Coyotes barked and howled at night, and the party had to fire warning shots to scare the aggressive animals off.

The forest grew thin as they climbed, and it got colder. It was August 19th, but Gill figured they'd passed 10,000 feet. A thin blanket of snow covered the ground and made it slippery. Rhubarb the donkey huffed and whined, and the poor beast slipped and almost fell twice, his hard hoofs sliding on slick stones.

Dusk came on, and Gill was thinking of dinner stew, when a screech and wail sent a shiver through him and his nerves jumped.

"What the hell was that?" Lydia said.

"Whatever it was sounded wounded," Nicki said.

"You think?" Gill said.

"What do you think it was? Your monster?" Rajim said.

Gill bit his lip. He didn't know how much longer he'd be able to take the man's constant taunts before he kicked the man's ass. Looking around at his fellow hunters, Gill saw the frustration on their faces and it was clearest on Nicki's. Jealousy was one thing, but downright boorishness didn't sit well with anyone regardless of the motivation.

Gill stepped toward Rajim, and Clint and Ant moved quickly to his side.

"It's cool. No worries," Gill said. He got as close to Rajim as he could, their faces inches apart. "If we're gonna work together we have to get along. Whatever your problem with me is, and I think it has more to do with your relationship with your wife then it does me, I suggest you get over—"

Another violent howl and answering cries that sounded like an odd form of speech.

"Look, I don't give a rat's ass what you—" Rajim said.

Rajim was thrown to the side as a creature the size of a large turkey with a mouthful of teeth sprang from the trees. Rajim fell to the ground, avoiding the beast at it sailed over his head and skidded across the snow. It came to a stop and whipped its head around, baring its teeth.

Ant drew down and fired, hitting the creature in the chest and knocking it backward. The creature sprawled against a stone, righted itself, and took two steps toward Rajim. The beast slowed, jaws flexing, head jerking side-to-side. Blood leaked from the chest wound, and the animal's glassy eyes rolled back in its head and it pitched over, a puddle of blood soaking the snow around its corpse.

"That answers the 'what the hell was that' question," Squirrel said.

Nicki and Ant held their guns out before them as they approached the dead beast. It spasmed as the creature's brain sent out a few dying pulses, and Gill jumped. His heart was racing, and pain lanced his lower back like it always did as the adrenaline fled.

"This looks like a smaller version of what attacked Brian and I," Gill said. He stood behind Nicki and Ant.

Tight feathers covered leathery skin, and three talons protruded from each claw, and they matched the smaller prints they'd found. The raptor's large eyes stared vacantly at the sky, its mouth hanging open revealing rows of teeth in a narrow jaw.

"This is what the big heads think a *velociraptor* looked like," Kate said. "They're much smaller than what we see in the movies."

"There are several types," Nicki said.

"This leave any doubt, Rajim?" Gill said. He couldn't help but let some sarcasm drip into his question.

Rajim said nothing and walked off into the trees.

"Anyone else question Gill's story now?" Nicki said.

"Is it possible this is what attacked you? Sometimes proportions are skewed during stressful encounters," Lydia said.

"Not possible," Gill said. "The thing I fought, toe-to-toe, was taller than me. Granted, I get what you're saying, but in this case it's just not true. I know what I saw."

A line of thick trees blocked the way to the north, with a deep gully to the west that ran along the deer path they'd been following. Squawks and wails came from the woods, and it sounded to Gill as though a fight was in progress. Hissing barks and shrieks of aggression rose above breaking tree branches.

The creatures came from the trees like a flock of angry eagles, their coordinated attack bee-like, all the bird-lizards focused on their prey. The cloud of beasts yelled and cried as they came at the party like a toxic fog filled with teeth.

Ant was the first to react, and he drew his gun and fired into the swarm of raptors. When his six shots were done he reloaded, and this woke the rest of the hunters from their paralysis.

Clint aimed his AR15, and Gill pulled his M16 from his shoulder, but by the time he brought his weapon to bare on the creatures it was too late. The beasts were among them, chomping and clawing, and if Gill fired he might hit one of the searchers. For a minute nobody fired, and the delay let the animals get in close.

Kate and Lydia struggled, but went down. Both women kicked and clawed to keep the animals from biting them. Kate got her gun up and shot the raptor hovering over her in the head. The beast's skull exploded, splattering Rajim with blood, brains, and bone.

Seeing Kate's success, Lydia fought to get to her gun, but she didn't have a chance. Gill opened up with the M16 and three bursts peppered the raptor with bullets and it fell away. Gun smoke filled the air, and Gill spun around, looking for a new target, but the creatures were everywhere.

"The trees," Ant yelled. "Take cover in the trees."

Nicki, Rajim, and Squirrel stood back to back, guns before them. Several of the creatures surrounded them, mouths dripping with slime, hunger filling their eyes. The raptors chomped and bit, but seemed afraid of the guns.

Gill was knocked backward as a raptor lunged at him, claws first like an eagle, razor-sharp talons ready to gorge him. Gill fired, and spun on the ball of his foot, spinning around and sighting the gun on the crowd of beasts surrounding Nicki and the others. Before the raptor Gill shot hit the ground, he let loose with four more bursts of three, gunning down the creatures that surrounded Nicki.

Rhubarb whinnied and bolted into the forest.

Someone screamed. It was Belinda. Gill had almost forgotten the woman was there. One of the raptors was clamped on her leg, thrashing its head like a shark, trying to rip the leg free.

Nicki stepped forward, placed the tip of her gun against the beast's head, and blew its brain all over the white snow. Blood splattered on Belinda, and she fell back, grabbing at her leg wound. Blood geysered through her fingers, and she wheezed in pain.

The creatures regrouped and were together at one end of the clearing, sizing up the party.

"Screw this," Clint said. This time he used his Glock, and the gun barked as he moved it in a wide arc, bullets spitting out at the rate of two shots per second. Raptors dropped, and when the gun clicked empty, Clint slammed a new magazine home. Several of the beasts turned tail and disappeared into the forest, but not the two alphas.

The biggest of the group darted at Gill, zigzagging across the clearing like an alligator. Guns popped and snapped, and one of the beasts went down, but the second reached Gill and speared at him, mouth open, wet eyes focused.

Gill shot the beast between the eyes and it crashed into him, knocking Gill backward onto the ground. Blood dripped on his face, as the beast chomped and bit as Gill fought the creature off with the M16. The raptor pressed him to the ground and reared back, preparing to take a bite. Gunshots rang out and the raptor's head disappeared in a spray of blood and dinosaur brain.

The headless beast went limp, and its corpse fell onto Gill. The commotion died away, and it was getting dark. So very dark.

8

Gill shielded his eyes from the sunlight. Ant and Nicki pulled the dead raptor off him and Gill sat up, dazed. "Did that just happen? Or am I asleep?" he asked.

"Oh, it happened," Nicki said.

The ground lay littered with dead raptors, and the surviving beasts scattered into the forest, yipping and snarling as they went. Belinda lay on the ground moaning as she grabbed her right leg. Blood poured through her fingers and Nicki and Kate went to assist her.

Rhubarb wandered back into the clearing, the donkey's glassy eyes bulging from its head. Lydia went to the beast, stroked its flank and whispered in the donkey's ear.

Gill rubbed his eyes and let his head fall into his hands. How had things gone so wrong so fast? He pulled Brian's sneaker from a jacket pocket and sniffed it. The scent of powder mixed with laundry detergent filled his nostrils and brought him to a happy place. A place where his son hadn't been dragged into the woods by a giant lizard that shouldn't exist.

"Everyone OK?" Ant asked.

"If I can be OK after getting attacked by lizard-turkeys with three-inch teeth, then yeah, I'm good," Rajim said.

"That's not helping," Clint said through grinding teeth.

Gill got to his feet. Nicki was cleaning Belinda's wound and Kate was digging through one of the bags strapped to Rhubarb looking for the first aid kit. When she found it, she pulled it open and took out gauze, two large compression pads, and medical tape.

When the wound was as clean as she could get it, Nicki said, "Can I get a nip off someone's flask to sterilize the wound? There's no rubbing alcohol in the first aid kit."

Clint pulled his silver flask from a pocket and handed it over. Nicki unscrewed the top, sniffed, and said, "Scotch?"

"Jack Daniels," Clint said.

Nicki took a pull and offered the flask to Kate, who refused, then she poured some of the brown whiskey on Belinda's wound. The woman clenched her jaws and let out a cry that sounded like air escaping a punctured tire.

Nicki handed the booze back to Clint, who took a nip and offered the flask to the onlookers. Gill took a swig of the offered Jack. He didn't want to be slow to react, but his nerves were jumping so fast he doubted he'd be able to help anyone in his current state. He capped the bottle and handed it back to Clint.

"How bad is it?" Belinda forced out.

Nicki had finished bandaging the wound, and said, "Can you stand?"

Clint and Kate helped her up, but the officer screamed when she put weight on the injured leg.

"Not good," Rajim said.

Everyone in the party stared at Rajim, and Gill wondered how Nicki had ended up with the asshole. Life took strange paths, he knew that better than most, but whatever twisted path had led Nicki to fall in love with Rajim was beyond his understanding. They had nothing in common, and the man showed his wife little respect, despite the fact that everyone in Reserve not only respected her, but counted on her. To that the amateur psychologist in his head said, feelings of inadequacy cause all kinds of stresses that manifest in odd, yet predictable ways.

"What are we going to do?" Squirrel said. "If we don't get after those things we'll lose them, though I reckon they're leaving a clear trail."

"Where would they be going?" Lydia said.

"This is nuts. You want to continue? Are you batshit?" Rajim said.

Nicki said, "Can I have a word. Sweetie." That last word was said with such derision even Rajim appeared to notice he'd gone too far. The husband and wife stepped into the trees, and muffled arguing and yelling could be heard. Nicki was the only one to emerge.

"You kill him?" Lydia asked.

"Not yet. I told him to take a walk and cool off," Nicki said.

"That a good idea? Being alone with those things around?" Ant said.

Nobody spoke, and Gill thought he saw Lydia and Clint smiling.

"Rajim is right about one thing. Belinda can't go on even if the rest of us decide to," Nicki said.

"If we go on? I am going on. There's nothing in the world that could stop me," Gill said. On some level he knew he was being irrational, but he would die trying to find his boy. It was as simple as that, but that didn't mean the rest of the group felt the same way. Sure, they wanted to get Brian back, but if it meant losing their own lives Gill didn't know how far his friends would take things.

"First things first," Nicki said. "Belinda's situation aside, who thinks we should continue?"

All hands went up.

"Rajim's not here, but it looks like his vote wouldn't matter anyway, so let's assume we're continuing the search. We have to. Just wanted to make sure you all felt the same way."

Gill stepped into the center of the group. "Thank you. Thank you all. I know this is getting more dangerous by the minute, but I can't tell you how much I appreciate your help. I owe you all my life," Gill said.

Birds chirped and the gusting wind rattled tree branches and swirled the dusting of snow.

"Who's gonna stay back with Belinda?" Kate said.

"I think it's more than that," Nicki said. "I think Belinda needs medical attention. She needs to go to general, so I think that will take at least two people. We can build a stretcher."

"I think I've seen enough," Lydia said. "But I don't think I can carry the stretcher."

Gill sympathized. As he got older he couldn't do many of the things he'd been able to do in his youth, and Lydia was pushing sixty-five. The woman was clearly shot from the trek into the mountains. If they were attacked again who could protect her? They'd been lucky because the creatures weren't used to guns and people, but next time that wouldn't be the case.

"I'll go," Ant said. "I've had just about enough of this shit." He held up his two-way radio. "I tried calling base, but got nothing. I can fill the mayor in, maybe head back up here with another team."

"That sounds good," Nicki said. "Who else can go with them?"

Gill searched the faces of his friends. Nicki wasn't going anywhere, she was their leader. Kate and Clint were strong, good shooters, so that left Squirrel.

"Squirrel, do you think you can handle helping Ant?" Nicki said.

"You won't have any tracking ability then. I know the path is clear now, but that could change," Squirrel said.

The small man had a point.

"I'll go on," Lydia said. "I'm tired, and I can't fight well, but I know these mountains better than any of you." She pursed her lips and appeared to make a decision. "I'm staying."

"It's settled then," Nicki said. "Ant and Squirrel will bring Belinda back to town and the rest of us will continue. Agreed?"

General nods and agreement.

The party spent the next half-hour getting ready to continue the hunt and making the stretcher. When they were done they laid Belinda across branches that barely supported her weight. Ant wasted no time, and before the party started its climb, Ant and Squirrel had disappeared into the forest with the injured deputy sheriff.

Rajim returned as the party was preparing to leave. "What'd I miss?" He seemed to be in a much better mood, glassy eyes gleaming.

Nicki filled her husband in. Everyone else ignored him.

"At least we may have settled a scientific argument," Lydia said.

"I'll bite," Rajim said.

"It's long been theorized that raptors may have hunted together," Lydia said.

"And how the hell would they know that? And you think those things were dinosaurs? Has everyone gone crazy?" Rajim said.

"I know what I saw," Nicki said. "Whatever doubt there was is gone."

"And to answer your question, there is some proof *velociraptors* hunted in packs," Lydia said. "In China there are fossil footprints showing these creatures walking together, and there are preserved fossils showing more than one raptor attacking a triceratops."

"Doesn't sound like our new evidence is needed," Gill said.

"No. No, it is. The fossils I mentioned are it. Those two. There is no other proof... was no other proof they hunted in packs," Lydia said.

The hunters followed the *velociraptors'* confused footprints into the forest. The tree canopy was thick, and beneath it a chill breeze iced Gill to the bone. He'd brought winter clothes with him, but it was too warm to put on his thick jacket, and too cold not to wear it, so he left it unzipped and let it hang off his shoulders when he got hot.

All the creatures were going in the same direction as a pack. More proof of what Lydia had been talking about. Gill wished he'd paid more attention to the National Geographic documentaries he'd seen about dinosaurs, because other than knowing what a few species looked like because he had a young son who loved playing with dinosaur action figures, he knew next to nothing about what they were up against. If he could get half an hour on the internet...

They trekked the rest of the day and didn't stop to rest. The party came across an occasional drip of blood, or the remains of a small animal the creatures had stopped to kill and eat. Gill was no expert, but based on what he saw it was clear to him the beasts had a destination. They were staying together and moving fast. They'd seen no sign of the larger raptor.

They came over a small rise and Nicki yelled, "Look!"

In the distance, climbing up the opposite side of a thin valley, was the pack of *velociraptors*. They didn't appear to notice the party as they pushed on into the woods, the animal path they followed taking them into a crack in the mountains.

The sun fell below the horizon and Nicki called a halt for the night, and the party spent an uncomfortable evening eating stew, keeping watch, and huddled in sleeping bags.

When Gill awoke on the third day out from Reserve his tent was covered in a thin layer of snow. The sun was out, but overnight the winds had picked up and the temperature dropped. Gill rubbed his hands together and went in search of coffee.

Nicki had a pot going on a camp stove, and she sat alone staring at the white mountain peaks. Gill thought she looked beautiful.

"Sleep well?" he said.

She scrunched-up her face and her eyes narrowed. "I suppose."

No fighting had been overheard in Nicki's tent the prior night. There had been no sounds at all.

"He's just scared of losing you, that's all," Gill said.

Nicki nodded, but said nothing.

Rajim joined them, and then Clint. Lydia and Kate were tending to Rhubarb, getting him water and giving him oats.

By 8AM the hunters were climbing a steep slope, following the raptor tracks, when they found a blood-covered shred of Brian's shirt. The blue flannel with white and grey stripes stuck from a snow bank, and Nicki did her best to distract Gill so he wouldn't see it, but was unsuccessful.

Gill dropped to his knees, examining the torn fabric. "He's still alive. I knew it," he said.

Nicki put a hand on Gill's shoulder.

The howl of a coyote made everyone look to the mountains. Paw prints of various sizes and shapes covered the area.

"Over here, Nicki." It was Clint.

Nicki broke away from the group, and Gill followed her. "Why don't you stay—"

"I'm coming with you," Gill said. He picked-up his pace and moved past Nicki.

A bigger piece of Brian's shirt lay beneath the bows of an evergreen. The blood on it was dry, and the fabric was stiff and covered in dust and a thin layer of frost.

Gill broke down, all the emotions of the last three days spilling from him. He wept and buried his face in his hands. "No. No," he said over and over.

Nicki knelt beside him and put her arm around him. "It's OK, Gill. This doesn't prove anything."

Clint kicked snow over the fabric.

"Look at this shit," Rajim said.

Twenty-feet away a large raptor lay dead, blood covering its open jaws, the wound from Gill's gunshot scabbed over. Patches of feathers were missing from the beast's hide, as if the *velociraptors* had tried to eat their larger brother.

"Looks like our guy," Nicki said.

Gill stood and pulled Clint's Glock from its holster on his leg.

"Hey," Rajim said.

Gill emptied the Glock into the dead raptor, squeezing the trigger like a man possessed. When the gun clicked empty, Clint took it from his hand.

"Guess that's it then," Kate said.

"It? Not even close. Brian is alive. I know it. I'm gonna find out where these things have taken my boy and get him back, then kill every last one of them."

9

Gill kicked the bullet riddled raptor. He was screaming, but all he heard was the static of fury, his head filled with an image that was driving him mad; his son alone in the dark, bleeding and hungry, wondering why his father hadn't rescued him. Gill crumbled to the ground, all energy expended. He wept, the feeling of loss so great he wished he was dead. What did he have to live for?

Brian. Revenge. He'd save his boy if it was the last thing he did and slaughter the beasts that had taken him. No parent would ever go through what he had.

Gill got up and headed for the woods.

Nicki stood in his way. "Whooh Gill, holdup."

Gill pushed her aside. "Don't tell me to hold up. I have to find my son. Hold up? For what?"

Rajim pushed Gill. "Keep your hands off my wife."

"I don't think—" Nicki said.

Gill sprang at Rajim, tackling him. Rajim struggled beneath Gill as the older man pounded the younger, punches landing on Rajim's head and face. This went on for two minutes as Rajim screamed and fought to free himself.

Normally the herd stops fights, even fights that appear necessary, but none of the hunters stepped forward to help Rajim, or pull Gill off. Once Rajim's face was bloodied, Nicki put her hand on Gill's shoulder.

"Come back," she soothed.

He heard his wife's voice in his mind, the calm way she used to speak to him when he was angry, or depressed. How he missed her.

Gill stopped swinging on Rajim and got up, looked around, and collapsed onto his ass. He rubbed his eyes and started to cry again.

Lydia and Kate tried to comfort him, but Gill shook them off, got up, and stalked into the trees. He needed to be alone to think, to reason things out and decide what to do. Was charging into the unknown really the right thing? It was the only thing. As long as hope remained that Brian was alive, he would continue the hunt.

"Hey," Nicki said. She pushed through a line of dense Douglas fir.

"Do you think it's a good idea to be here with me? Alone. Won't Rajim get his panties in a bunch?" Gill said.

"I don't really care what he thinks. If it wasn't for Kiki and Fred, I think…"

Gill understood. Having kids changed everything, and Rajim and Nicki had two. Kiki was in high school and Fred junior high. "Rajim cares about you, that's all."

"Really? Because I'm having trouble seeing it," she said.

"Usually this type of stuff is a manifestation of bigger issues. Listen to me, amateur psychologist."

"You might be an amateur, but that doesn't mean you're wrong."

Gill said nothing.

"How are you?"

"How do I look?"

"Like a man who's afraid to lose the person he loves most."

"I just don't know, Nicki. When I lost Abigale, I had Brian to focus on. Feeding him, making sure he had clean clothes, and felt loved and secure. I had to keep Abigale's memory alive, for him. Show him the pictures. The videos. He needs to know. I love him so much it hurts."

Nicki bit her lip, which was her tell that she didn't know what to say.

"It's OK. Don't worry about me."

Her cheeks reddened. "Not that easy."

Gill's face got hot. He cared for this woman more than he could admit. She was married with children, and whatever feelings he had meant nothing. He couldn't act on them even if Nicki wanted him to. It was bad enough his family had been ripped apart and destroyed, he wouldn't be the cause of another family's destruction.

"What do you plan to do? Keep hunting these things? Maybe we should go back and get help?" Nicki said.

Gill breathed deep, and cold air filled his lungs and brought focus and resolve. "I'm not stopping until I find Brian," he said. "If you want to go back and get help I understand, but I won't be joining you."

She sighed. "That's enough for me. Let's go get the others and get moving."

Gill smiled through his grief. Even after everything that had happened she was still looking out for him, trying to protect him and do the right thing.

Rajim and the rest of the crew mumbled, but nobody protested when Nicki informed them they were moving out. The mid-day sun beat down on them and Gill stripped-off his jacket. The dusting of snow was gone, but drifts remained on the western side of hills and boulders. Squirrels and chipmunks darted about, but Gill saw no larger animals. With the snow gone the tracks of the *velociraptors* were harder to follow, but the path was still clear. It wound up into the mountains, the elevation rising with each step. The insects had taken a break when the weather turned chilly, but the sun brought the revival of the gnats and black flies. They buzzed Gill's head as he trudged forward, head down, eyes focused on the ground, thoughts filled with the events of the last four days. So much had changed, yet so much was still the same. He felt alone.

The party stopped for lunch and pushed on. Gill knew they were getting close because every few moments a guttural screech would tear through the stillness. Cries so shrill they hurt his ears. He checked his M16, looked to the sky, and wiped sweat from his brow.

The forest thinned to a spattering of sparse pine trees, and a light dusting of snow covered the shaded evergreen leaves. Challenger Peak rose before them, and for the first time Gill realized how far they'd come. The three-and-a-half-day march had brought them fifty miles to the north, and judging by the temperature and skyline they were up at least 12,000 feet. The air was getting thin, and Gill noticed Lydia struggling to breathe.

Gill inched-up next to Nicki. "Hey," he said.

She turned to look at him, then searched for her husband. Rajim walked several paces ahead, a towel held against his bloodied face. When she saw Rajim hadn't noticed Gill, she said, "What's up?"

Gill turned to look at Lydia, who led Rhubarb the donkey over the rock-strewn mountainside. "You notice she's having a tough time? Maybe we should send her back? I don't think we really need her anymore. Path looks clear as fresh water to me."

"Yeah, maybe, but she's a grown woman. I can't make her do anything."

Gill nodded and fell back. He'd done what he could, but of course Nicki was right.

The hunters came over a rise and passed through a densely packed section of forest. Douglas fir and spruce grew into each other, packed so tight Gill didn't know how they got water and sunlight. His mind flashed to the scene in the 'The Lion, the Witch, and the Wardrobe', where the young adventurers push through fur coats that change to pine trees as they pass through the wardrobe.

The party broke free of the forest. A vast ice sheet with a crack running down its center stretched into the distance, velociraptor tracks leading straight across it. The sun glare was blinding, and with no trees to placate the wind, it tore across the open plain. Swirling snow and dirt clogged the air as Gill inched his way across the ice.

He didn't see the sinkhole until he was almost upon it. The ice sheet had collapsed because of the crack, revealing a deep depression that fell away to a center point like a giant colander.

The raptor tracks led down into the sinkhole.

"This doesn't look too good," Nicki said.

Gill jumped over the edge of the hole and made his way toward the bottom.

Ice tinkled and popped, but Gill didn't care. He brought up the M16 and scanned the area as he went, hoping to see one of the little shits poke its head out, but the creatures were nowhere to be seen.

"Gill. Gill!" It was Nicki. "For shit's sake."

"No, Nicki, don't—" Rajim was cut off by a booming crack of ice.

Gill looked back and saw Nicki standing on the rim of the sinkhole, a giant crack in the ice opening to her left. Warm gas that smelled like rotten eggs escaped the crack and puffed out over the ice. When it was clear the ice wasn't going to cave-in, Nicki continued to where Gill stood.

At the bottom of the depression the ice had fallen away and a hole ten feet around opened into darkness. Claw and bite marks lined the hole's edge, and a foul stench rose from the opening, wet and thick. The echoes of raptors screeching and yelling rose from the hole.

Gill knelt and looked in. Rock and ice lined the walls of a tunnel.

"So, what the hell do you make of this?" Nicki said.

"Come back up here. It's too dangerous down there." Rajim yelled from the top of the sinkhole. He sounded concerned, but not concerned enough to follow his wife into the depression.

Answering Nicki, Gill said, "No idea, but it's clear this is where the things came from. They must have some kind of shelter below this ice sheet. I bet all the recent blasting caused the crack and the hole to open."

Nicki waved her hand in front of her nose. "Whatever that gas is, sure smells bad."

"And it's warm. Strange shit," Gill said. He stood and shouldered the M16.

"What now?" she asked.

"We go down there," Gill said.

Nicki bit her lip.

"Let's go tell the others," Gill said.

He and Nicki climbed out of the sinkhole. Snow drifts and piles of cleaved ice lay in drifts along the southern side of the hole, and the ice glistened in the mid-day sun. There were no animal tracks. Gill heard no birds, or wolf cries, or the bleat of crickets, or the buzz of insects. He thought that odd. It was much colder high in the mountains, but the sun and summer heat still warmed things to a point that wildlife should be enjoying the respite from the deep freeze, yet all was quiet, as if living things had decided to avoid the area.

When Gill reached Rajim and the others he wasted no time. "I want to continue on right away. We're wasting time," Gill said. "I heard them down there. They're close."

"Gill, I don't know—" Kate said.

"You don't know?" Rajim said. "I know. I know Gill's obsessed. All he sees is false hope and revenge and I'm not dying for that, and I won't let my wife, either."

"Rajim, nobody asked you to come," Nicki said.

"And I've had just about enough of your attitude," Lydia said.

Rajim looked at the older woman, but said nothing. Gill figured even an asshole of Rajim's magnitude had been taught to respect his elders.

Clint said, "We need to be cautious here, Gill. You saw what these things can do."

"We can post guards here while someone goes and gets reinforcements," Kate said.

"The proper equipment," said Lydia.

"Screw that. We should seal this hole and the damn things won't be able to get out," Rajim said. "Sorry, Gill, but that's what's best for Reserve."

"Sorry? What's best for Reserve? You want to give up on Brian? Screw you." What he didn't express was he grudgingly had to admit Rajim had a point. Seal the exit and the creatures would be done. Problem was, he wasn't done, and he wouldn't be until he found Brian and all the raptors were nothing but bones.

Nicki pulled out her two-way radio and tried to call base. When she got no response, she said, "Figured I'd try." Cellphones barely worked in Reserve thanks to the lone cell tower, but up in the mountains 12,000 feet above sea level phones got no service and radio signals were often weak.

"Maybe some of us should head back? Tell the mayor what we've found and warn the rest of the town," Kate said.

If Gill and the hunting party failed and were killed, Reserve wouldn't know of the threat the beasts posed until they attacked again, and then it would be too late. Bringing in the staties and the FBI would take time. They'd have to convince them, which wouldn't be too difficult given all the cellphone pictures they had of the raptors, both big and small, and Brian was still missing.

Shadows were getting long, the temperature dropping, and soon twilight would embrace the mountains. A cry rose from the hole at the bottom of the depression, and as if in answer a loud *pop* reverberated across the ice sheet.

"Maybe we should wait until morning, either way," Nicki said.

Nobody responded, but Kate and Lydia shook their heads, and Clint looked despondent. Rhubarb the donkey nickered and tossed his head making his vote clear. The beast had to be hungry and cold.

Gill couldn't take any more of the paralysis by analysis. He knew what he was doing, and if nobody wanted to join him that was their problem. He wasn't waiting until morning. He wasn't waiting at all.

"I'm going. The rest of you can do what you want," Gill said.

He shouldered the M16 and started down into the sinkhole.

10

Gill inched toward the hole at the bottom of the depression in the ice sheet, testing the thickness of the ice as he went. The tunnel below was dark, and when he shined his flashlight into it he couldn't tell how far down the floor was. The raptors had gotten out, so the walls were climbable.

He pulled a hundred-foot coil of rope from his pack and tossed it on the ground. Then he pulled his hunting knife, knelt, and started carving a half-circle in the ice to make a ballock to secure one end of the rope. He chipped away the ice until the half-circle was three inches deep with a three-foot diameter. Gill tied off a loop on one end of the rope and fitted it into the groove in the ice he'd created. He tied his backpack onto the other end of the rope and lowered it into the hole.

"Gill, don't do this alone," Clint yelled. "Let's talk about this for a minute." He stood with the others on the rim of the depression.

He ignored his friend, flipped onto his belly and grabbed the rope tightly with both hands. He wiggled backward, his legs dangling into the opening. The ice was slick and cold, the chill working its way through his layers of clothes.

As he dropped in Gill wrapped one leg around the rope to stabilize himself, then pulled a flashlight from a pocket. He panned the light around the tunnel and saw that the floor was fifty feet or more down, but blocks of ice and rock protruded from the walls providing natural steps. Claw prints marked the natural steps, and drips of blood trailed away into darkness.

Gill lowered himself, scanning the tunnel as he descended. The walls appeared to be an odd mixture of dirt, ice, and stone. The place looked old, and Gill found that he was sweating.

When he reached the bottom, he stripped off his coat. The thermometer on his knife handle said it was sixty-two degrees. How could that be? He was in a tunnel made half of ice, beneath a massive ice sheet, 12,000 feet above sea level. If it wasn't cold here, where would it be cold?

Gill heard the chatter of voices and looked up to see Nicki and Lydia's faces staring down at him. The rope was set. If they wanted to follow, all they had to do was climb down. He hefted his pack, slipped it over a shoulder and checked the M16, sliding the clip out to ensure it was full, then slamming it back home.

The floor was covered in a thin layer of dirt and was slippery. Gill almost fell as he took his first step. The raptor tracks disappeared down the tunnel and Gill flicked on his flashlight. The tunnel was more of a cavern. Huge icicles hung from the ceiling, and the cavern's sides pushed out in all directions. The chamber looked to be a depression in the mountains roofed over by the ice sheet.

Gill followed the tracks and the cavern narrowed.

"Gill?" The echo of Nicki's voice rolled down the tunnel.

He stopped. It sounded like she was close, down in the passageway with him. He turned back and saw a flickering flashlight beam coming at him, so he waited.

They'd all followed him. In a way, he wished they hadn't. Now he felt responsible for them and would have preferred not to have anyone's life in his hands. He was also tired of the debates that accompanied each decision. He was hunting until he found Brian. No further discussions were necessary.

Nicki, Rajim, Clint, and Kate joined him.

"Where's Lydia?" Gill asked, though he could guess the answer.

"She's staying with Rhubarb," Nicki said.

"You think she could've made the climb down?" Rajim said.

No matter what the man said it always sounded like a challenge. "Yeah, I think she could make the climb," Gill said.

Rajim started to speak and Nicki cut him off. "Can we put this adolescent bullshit on hold until we're out the tunnel filled with creatures looking to eat us?"

Gill knew better than to answer her, but as expected, Rajim didn't. "What? I'm not allowed to talk now?" He'd cleaned most of the blood off his face, but Rajim's shirt was stained red from the beating he'd taken.

Nicki sighed, but said nothing.

Gill had enjoyed kicking the man's ass. He wasn't a fighter and could count on one hand the number of fights he'd had in his life, but once he got going he had crazy strength.

The party continued deeper into the tunnel following the tracks. The scuff marks in the dirt and ice were going in both directions. Flashlight beams reflected off the ice and stone creating rainbow daggers in the darkness. It had gotten hotter, and Gill was stripped down to his t-shirt and his knife thermometer said it was seventy-one degrees.

"What do you make of this heat?" Clint said.

"Must be some type of thermal vent in here," Gill said.

"Volcanic?" Rajim said.

"There's been no volcanic activity in these parts for millennia," Nicki said. "But who knows, though, right? With climate change? The Earth's average temperature rising could have been a contributing factor in the ice sheet cracking."

"Releasing the raptors," Gill said.

"Come on, dude. You're still clinging to that dinosaur shit?" Rajim said.

"Clinging to shit? What, are you blind?" Gill said.

"I don't know what I saw. To say these things are dinosaurs, which have been extinct for... what? Seventy-million years or something like that? Just because we don't know what they are doesn't mean they're dinosaurs," Rajim said.

"Call them whatever the hell you want. It doesn't change anything," Gill said.

"What I want to know is how the damn things can even exist," Clint said.

"Me also. Given the winters and seasonal temperature fluctuations I don't see how lizard-like animals could survive up here. They can't fly, so migration is out of the question," Nicki said.

"And somebody would've seen the things flying around," Rajim said.

All this was true, but it didn't solve anything or provide any answers.

Clint said, "Maybe the dinosaurs were frozen when this part of the world was flat. You know, like crytopics."

"Cryonics," Gill said.

"Yeah, like flash frozen, and now that the planet is warming up they defrosted. Or maybe eggs thawed," Clint said.

"That's a stretch," Gill said. "There have been instances where very simple organisms have been frozen and revived, but there has never been a complex lifeform revived from a frozen state."

"Water expands when it freezes and that causes major problems. Destroys the brain and damages most tissue beyond repair," Nicki said.

Rajim harrumphed, but said nothing.

The tunnel changed from a mix of dirt, rock and ice, to mostly rock as it turned downward and brought the party deeper under the mountains. The floor was no longer flat, but rounded, lifting at the edges in a casual arc that made the tunnel a tube. It bent and curved like a stream of hot water had bored through ice. Gill smiled through his grief at the thought of his younger self pissing a hole in Clear Creek Reservoir. The sound of dripping water filled the cave, and moisture trickled down the walls as the heat coming from below warmed the tunnel.

The hunters came around a wide turn and met a wall of ice. It clogged the tunnel, except for a hole just big enough for the raptors to crawl through.

Gill examined the hole that had clearly recently been formed when the ice wall began melting.

"You think the big one could get through that? The hole is pretty small," Nicki said.

"I don't know, but what I do know is animals fit through spaces that appear impossible," Gill said.

"If the thing's head can fit, its body can fit. At least that's normally the way it goes," Clint said.

"Really? You think that big bastard got through here?" Rajim said.

"I do," Clint said.

"The real question is, can we fit?" Gill said.

"What? You—" A look from Nicki shut Rajim down.

A low chittering sound emanated from the hole. Like a thousand cockroaches scuttling over stone.

"What the hell do you make of that?" Kate said.

Nobody responded.

Gill stripped off his pack, thrust it through the hole, and stuck his head in. It was pitch black, and he brought up the flashlight.

The tight tube stayed the same as far as he could see, the thin tunnel taking a sharp turn right fifty feet ahead. Gill put down the light and pulled the M16 off his back. From a crawling position, he held the flashlight against the gun barrel with his left hand and used his right for the trigger. He army crawled through the tube, gun before him, the light blinding as it reflected off the walls.

The clicking sound got louder, and Gill jumped when the first cockroach thing crawled over his leg. It was three inches long and had green eyes and long antennas.

"Gill, you alright?" Nicki called.

"Yeah," he said. He brushed the bug off and continued on.

The cave changed into a waterslide, and Gill slipped and fell, sliding down the tunnel and coming to rest on a pile of bones littered with the cockroach bugs. He screamed, rolled off the pile and brushed off the creatures. He shone the light around, and the cave was once again a mixture of rock, dirt and ice. All of it was covered with giant roaches.

He called out to the others. "I'm through. Be careful, there's creepy crawlies in here."

Gill waited as the light in the tunnel grew and one by one his companions fell out of the tube onto the bone pile.

"Geez-us," Rajim said. "You could have warned us about the drop."

"Yup."

The tunnel turned up and got hotter. More and more of the bugs appeared, and Gill almost threw up his lunch thanks to the crunching sound the party made as they walked.

The smell of rotten eggs filled the air again, and Nicki said, "The warmer it gets, the stronger that smell gets."

"Smells like sulfur," Clint said.

More cockroach bugs appeared as the tunnel rose, and soon they filled every surface. The scraping of their legs reverberated in the cave along with the sound of crunching shells.

"This is getting nasty. You figure the things flee when the raptors come through?" Nicki said.

"Who knows, but they're sure as shit back now," Rajim said.

"Oh shit," Clint said. He was trailing up the rear.

"What—" Gill spun to find two huge cockroach bugs bigger than ponies. Their pincers were a foot long and they clicked up and down as the creatures came on.

Clint drew down his Glock and blew both the bugs apart. The gunshots rang out through the tunnel, and a large crack appeared in the cave's ceiling.

"Easy," Gill said. "Loud noises might bring this whole thing down."

All the bugs scattered like birds after a backfire, disappearing into cracks and holes, and within thirty seconds there were no bugs to be seen, but the sound of scraping legs still filled the tunnel.

"Um, Gill, there's more," Nicki said.

A group of the large cockroach-things came at them, mandibles snapping, clawed feet scuttling along the floor.

Gill looked down the tunnel, then back at the giant bugs, and yelled, "Run!"

11

Gill slipped on a section of ice and went down, arms cartwheeling as his feet shot out from under him. He hit the ground and air rushed from his lungs. Rajim grabbed at him and tried to help Gill to his feet as he rushed past, but Gill shook him off. The bugs were clicking and snapping their way through the tunnel, and Nicki ran past him, slipping and sliding as she went. Gill got to his feet, arms outstretched for balance, and like a train building speed, he ran.

As if fate had abandoned them the tunnel turned upward, the floor tilting twenty degrees. Nicki fell and tumbled into Rajim, who went down and slid into Gill, who braced like a defensive lineman and stopped them all from careening into the approaching bugs.

Clint opened-up. Carapaces cracked and shattered, legs flew, and the sound of crying insects pierced Gill's head like a nail. Clint was a machine, firing with discipline and accuracy, picking off each giant cockroach as it came forward.

The walls and ceiling of the tunnel cracked and moaned as the sound of gunshots sent soundwaves into the rigid ice and stone.

Clint stopped firing. Gun smoke filled the cave, and the brass shell casings that littered the ground glinted in the flashlight beams. No more king cockroaches came from the darkness.

"We should head back," Kate said. The young police officer looked harried. Dark bags blackened the pale skin beneath her eyes, which were red as cinders.

The party was sleep deprived, angry, hungry, and frustrated.

Nicki said, "Things are getting real. What the hell were those things?"

"Mutants. God damn mutants," Rajim said.

Gill was starting to think the pain-in-the-ass might be right. And what was that bull-shit of Rajim trying to help him during the retreat? What was the shitbag up to? "I'm going on, but if you guys want to go back, I totally understand," Gill said.

"I'm with you," Clint said.

"Me also," Nicki said.

Kate sighed.

Rajim grabbed Nicki gently by the elbow and turned her to face him. "For real? You've got two kids. Grandkids are going to need you. Reserve." He let her go and put up his hands. "Me. I need you."

Nicki bowed her head.

"He's right, Nicki. Listen to Rajim. This is my fight, not yours," Gill said.

"I appreciate the macho bullshit. I do, not being a wiseass. I know it's coming from a conditioned place, and from love. That said, thing is, it's my fight too. I know Brian, Gill. I know him well." She turned away.

"But orphaning your children won't help anyone," Rajim said.

Gill nodded.

"I'm going on and I don't want to hear any more about it," Nicki said.

"It's getting cooler in here. Let's go," Clint said.

The party continued up the steep tunnel, the temperature dropping as they went. Odd striations marked the cave walls; yellow, red and crystal, and water no longer dripped from the icicles and stalactites protruding from the ceiling.

Smaller tunnels appeared on both sides of the cave, and they twisted upward in every direction. Some were big enough to crawl through, and Gill thought of giant roaches burrowing their way through the dirt, stones, and ice. Screeching and yelping could be heard further down the main tunnel and this spurred the hunters on.

The trail was unmistakable; claw marks, scat, and drips of deep red blood. Gill brought up the M16, holding the flashlight next to the barrel like a sight. He swept the light side to side and saw the backs of his companions as they moved through the cave. The party went on for what felt like an hour, but was only fifteen minutes, when they came around a wide bend in the tunnel.

A large crack in the mountainside filled with light marked the end of the cave.

The exit grew bigger as Gill went on. The pack of *velociraptors* bounced off the walls ahead, the nasty creatures backlit by the open cave mouth. They hissed and squawked, pulling and tearing at each other, trying to be first, strongest, fastest.

Clint and Nicki fired, and the *pop* and *snap* of the gunpowder expanding made Gill remember his own weapon. He opened-up, the old service rifle on burst. Three shoots in fast succession fired from the M16 each time Gill shifted his aim, and raptors fell like swatted flies.

"Hurry now," Rajim said. "Let's finish them and get out of here." He trailed behind and hadn't fired a shot.

The cave entrance loomed large as the party got closer, the giant opening filled with evergreen forest, blue sky, white clouds and... What was in the sky? Something glittered in the sunlight like diamonds.

Gill slowed when he reached the cave mouth. The raptors disappeared into a forest below, screeching and hollering, sending birds scattering from the dense woods. Gill's heart hammered, his neck and back hurt, and he was sucking air. He bent and put his hands on his knees.

The hunters stood on a precipice that jutted from the eastern mountainside of a narrow valley that stretched into misty clouds in all directions. The land fell away steeply from the cave mouth, a spattering of evergreens filling-in to become a dense forest. Steep snowcapped mountain peaks rose to the sky in every direction, and half the valley was covered with a roof of ice. The ice-drift curled off the taller western peaks in a gentle arc and it was clear the valley had once been fully covered. Rough edges of cracked ice marred the eastern peaks, and below, where the giant chunks of ice would have fallen, a lake stretched to sheer cliffs to the north and west.

"Holy shit," Rajim said.

"Yeah," Clint said.

Gill walked to the edge of the precipice and peered down the steep hill. "We can make it down easy," he said.

"I know I sound like a broken record, but shouldn't we go back?" Kate said.

"Back? We're right on their tails. After seeing this you want to go back?" Gill said. He was so tired of debating everything he wondered how the group had gotten as far as it had.

"This… we…" Rajim said. "Nobody foresaw this lost world. Who knows what lives in those woods."

Color fled Nicki's face. She looked around at the hunters, worry lines creasing her face. "He's got a point, Gill. This is unlike anything ever discovered. A true primeval world. Shouldn't we get experts? Scientists?"

Gill didn't answer. He'd had enough of talking and he'd had enough of these people. He pulled his backpack straps tight and started down the hill toward the woods below. Gravel, sand, and dead leaves shifted and spilled down the hillside as he followed the raptors. The beasts' screeching and calling could still be heard as the animals tore through the forest.

When Gill reached the bottom, he found Clint with him, but the rest of the hunters watched from the rock ledge above.

"Clint, you don't—"

Clint drew his Glock, slipped out the magazine to verify it was loaded, and slammed it back home. "Yes. Yes I do," he said.

Gill put his hand on his mate's shoulder. "Thank you."

Gill and Clint followed the raptor tracks into the forest, and the sunlight angling through the opening in the ice roof eased under the thick canopy. Evergreen trees grew into each other, their thick branches filled with green needle leaves that poked and scraped at them as they pushed through the woods following the trail of broken branches. Squirrels and chipmunks cleared out as the two companions cut a path through a forest that had probably never been seen by a human. Sparrows and warblers flitted in the trees, and pine cones and brown needles covered the ground. The temperature was mild, but not colder than in the tunnel.

"What's the temperature in here?" Clint asked.

He looked at his knife thermometer and said, "Sixty-six degrees."

"Get out. How can that be? We're 12,000 feet up."

"Don't know, but it doesn't matter. Whatever is causing the unusual temperatures is probably what lets this place survive."

Clint shook his head. The older man's hair was grey, his face red with blotches from too much alcohol, his voice raspy from years of smoking. "I don't know, man. That's some thin shit."

Gill nodded. It sure was, but he didn't care.

The evergreens ended, and a thicket of hemlocks clogged their way. The raptors had disappeared like rabbits into bushes, and there was no way to follow them without crawling on the ground, which Gill had no intention of doing. There was no sign of Nicki and the others. They hadn't followed.

"Sure would be nice to have a chainsaw," Gill said.

"There's a hand saw and axe out there with Rhubarb, for all the good it will do us," Clint said.

"We'll go around. If we—" Clint froze.

Gill followed his friend's line of sight and saw what had stopped him.

A small finger, severed above the knuckle, sat on a pile of brown pine needles, muscle and gristle sticking from one end.

Gill knelt and picked it up. It was Brian's. There was no doubt.

The slap and thump of meat being torn from bone made Gill lift his head. Tears leaked from his eyes and he felt dizzy, like his entire world had just run down the drain. Brian was gone. He knew that now, the severed finger breaking the protective cocoon he'd built around the possibility that his son was alive.

"Look here," Clint said.

Ten feet away a pool of blood filled a depression in the ground. It was the deep red of human blood.

Gill lost it and crumpled to the ground, weeping wildly. What would he do now? He had nothing.

Clint put his hand on his friend's shoulder and said nothing.

Gill had no hope left and realizing that made him feel horrible. He'd endangered his friend, Nicki, the entire party, all for nothing. All because he refused to accept what had been clear to everyone else for days.

Brian was dead.

They buried his finger and marked the spot with a cross made of conifer branches. Gill cried, Clint patting his back as tears leaked from his eyes. Gill said, "Thank you for coming this far. I re—"

The ground trembled, a faint rumble that felt far off.

"You think we should head back?" Clint said. "I hate to push you, but if you think we're done here…"

Rumble. Rumble. The vibrations were closer together and picking up speed.

"Yeah, we're done," Gill said. He slung his M16 over a shoulder.

"You know what that rumble sounds like?" Clint said.

He did, but Gill didn't want to think about it.

A mighty roar tore through the silence and Gill jumped. The primal scream echoed off the sheer mountain cliffs and reverberated over the valley. The insects stopped buzzing, the birds fell silent, and even the wind seemed to die away as silence filled the valley.

Rumble. Rumble. The sound of thunder. Trees swayed, rocks tumbled, and Gill and Clint stood frozen, curiosity and fear rooting them to the ground.

A giant lizard-like head pushed through the line of evergreens to the east. Dark glassy eyes the size of baseballs scanned the area. Massive jaws slid open, and slime dripped from between three-foot teeth. The long snout jerked right, then left, and the beast threw its head back and let out another earsplitting cry that let every living thing in the valley know who was boss.

Gill and Clint stood frozen like spiders when the lights are turned on, adhering to the oldest myth: if you stay still it won't see you. Unfortunately for Gill and Clint, that idea was indeed a myth.

The giant lizard stomped its huge feet, giant claws tearing up the ground. The beast screamed again when it saw them, pausing and cocking its head to the side like a confused dog. It inched forward, tiny arms dangling from its torso, thick muscles rippling beneath black and yellow striated skin.

"What the hell do you make of that?" Clint said as he slowly backed away, terror filling his face.

"Clint my friend, that's a *tyrannosaurus-rex*," Gill said.

12

Tyrannosaurus-rex, king of the apex predators, stepped from the trees into sunlight. Gill's breath caught. The T-rex was the big kahuna, the real deal. Gill rubbed his eyes, but it was still there. The great beast reared back on its thick hind legs and stood twenty feet tall, its massive tooth-filled head balanced by a fifteen-foot tail. The theropod dinosaur had ruled what was now the western United States, which was an island continent known as Laramidia sixty-five million years ago when the T-rex, along with all its buddies, went extinct.

Yet here the thing was. Looking at Gill and Clint like they were cheese puffs. The dinosaur lifted its right leg and stomped with such force the ground shook. It bent low, bringing its head down, opening its huge jaws, and made nasally clicking sounds like the beast was gargling.

Clint slipped his Glock from its holster, and Gill brought up the rifle, sighting the creature's head. The beast was three hundred yards away, and Gill didn't think a few bullets would do much damage. Muscles bulged from the T-rex's torso and legs. It would have to be a head shot, an accurate one, and maybe more than one. If he could put a bullet in the dinosaur's open mouth or an eye that might bring it down, but Gill didn't think that was possible. The beast swayed constantly, jerking and shaking its head.

The T-rex took a step, and the ground shook. It took another step, then another.

Gill fired a warning shot into the air. He didn't want to enrage the animal, but perhaps the gunshot would give it pause. The ancient creature had probably never seen a human being and would be unfamiliar with guns. It could be the first shot ever fired in the primeval valley.

The wind picked up, and Gill thought he heard Nicki calling his name, but when he listened hard he heard nothing but the singing of the evergreen leaves clicking against one another and the distant rumble of giant beasts as they moved around in the forest.

Gill's shot stopped the T-rex, and it rose to its full height. Large folds of skin tightened, and small arms clawed air. The massive monster sucked in a breath and opened its mouth.

The T-rex smiled at him.

With an agility that surprised Gill, the dinosaur leapt forward using its hind legs, pushing off like a rabbit. It landed with a thunderous explosion of dirt and dust, head forward and almost touching the ground. It cried out as it charged, the sound echoing off the steep rock walls and filling the valley.

Gill and Clint fired, but the gunshots didn't slow the beast. Clint hit the animal several times, as did Gill, but neither man managed to get an eye. Blood seeped from wounds on the animal's upper torso, but like a bee sting on a bear, the bullets served only to anger the T-rex.

When the dinosaur was a hundred yards out, Gill's M16 clicked empty. The spare clip was in his backpack, and he didn't have time to get at it.

"Go ahead. Make a run for it. I've still got a few shots," Clint said.

Gill didn't wait to be told twice. He looked toward where they'd found Brian's finger, felt his sneaker in his pocket. He'd thought so much about death recently, even wished for the abyss to take him, but now that the adrenaline was flowing, survival instinct took over and he double-timed it into the woods, leaving Clint behind like a bad date.

The T-rex came at Clint, who stood legs spread, Glock held in both hands. He squeezed off shots until his gun clicked empty and then he turned and fled after Gill.

The T-rex fell in behind Clint, chasing him down as his friend threw himself forward in a panicked run that made him look as though he might fall at any moment.

When he went down, Gill screamed.

The giant dinosaur skidded to a stop and bent over Clint, who was scrambling to get back on his feet. The creature opened its massive jaws and snapped at Clint, who rolled away as the jaws clamped closed.

When the T-rex pulled back to make another thrust, Clint vaulted to his feet and ran between the beast's legs. The T-rex, unable to catch Clint in its mouth due to the angle, lifted one of its giant feet and tried to stomp Clint as he ran past. The beast missed, but the ground shook, and Clint went down again, sprawling in the dirt fifty yards from the cover of the forest.

"Come on!" Gill screamed. Then he remembered the spare magazine in his pack and pulled it out. He dropped the spent magazine and jacked the new one home, but before he brought the rifle to bear, Clint was running past him.

"You OK?" Gill said as he ran after him.

The T-rex roared in its frustration and pressed its head into the trees, trying to get at Gill and Clint.

"I'm fine. Come on. Back to the tunnel," Clint said.

"Yeah," Gill said. His bloodlust had fled, and he felt tired. So very tired, and he no longer wanted to fight. To kill. He was done and wanted to mourn his dead son.

The two friends wormed their way into the tight forest, working east toward the cave mouth. Surely Nicki and the others had heard the commotion and would be prepared to help them. If they were still there.

The ground shook, but when Gill looked over his shoulder he saw nothing pushing through the trees and heard no breaking branches. Maybe it was going away and leaving them be.

The top of a Douglas fir to Gill's right disappeared between a row of teeth. The T-rex stood above them, the tree sticking from its gaping maw. It dropped the evergreen and roared, slime dripping from the beast's mouth onto Gill's head.

Clint dodged left and Gill went right, disappearing under the bows of a dense evergreen. He ran blind, branches whipping his face, the sharp spike leaves pricking him like a million tiny knives.

Gill broke free of the forest and the mountainside loomed up before him, shrouded in mist.

"Gill! Here! Gill!" It was Nicki. She stood with Rajim and Kate on the precipice. Gunshots rang out as his companions fired at the T-rex. The beast slowed and turned to the north, stomping along the tree line, sniffing the ground, tail stiff, tiny arms bouncing off its torso. It stopped, shifted its massive weight, and chomped at something Gill couldn't see.

The dinosaur's jaws closed with a crack, and Clint burst from the trees, rolling on the ground and vaulting to his feet. Clint ran toward him, and Gill realized he was standing in the open, mouth gaping, and hadn't moved. Clint ran past, and the T-rex howled and turned itself around. Its tail got caught in the trees, and for an instant the beast was stuck. It shook and stomped. Trees fell, and dust rose into the mist.

Clint came back for Gill and shook him by the shoulders. "Gill! What the hell are you doing? Let's go."

Clint's urgency ended the work stoppage in Gill's legs, and the two friends sprinted around boulders and hemlocks, and up the steep incline toward their friends.

The T-rex bellowed and shook its head, but it didn't pursue them. Several gunshot wounds leaked blood on the dinosaur's chest, legs and head, and Gill figured the beast had given up. There had to be better food around then their skinny asses.

As if reading his mind, Clint said, "What the hell has that bitch been eating to get so big?"

"We're not hanging around to find out," Gill said.

Clint watched Gill's back as he climbed the incline to the precipice. Nicki threw her arms around Gill, then less enthusiastically around Clint.

Rajim said nothing, but looked like he'd just sniffed spoiled milk.

"I thought we lost you that one time, Clint," Nicki said.

"You saw?" he said.

"We had a decent view from up here. Specially with these." She held up her binoculars.

"What the hell is that thing?" Rajim said.

"What the hell do you think it is? It's a dinosaur," Clint said.

"That's not possible," Rajim said. "Not possible."

"And yet you just saw it with your own eyes," Nicki said.

"I don't know what I saw," Rajim said.

Gill let an exasperated sigh escape his lips.

"Screw you, Gill. This crazy shit almost got us killed," Rajim said.

To that, not even Gill had a response.

The party gathered their stuff, packed up, and plunged back into the darkness of the tunnel. They lit torches this time, not for light, but safety. If the giant bugs attacked, the party would burn them to cinders. The torches popped and crackled as they walked, black smoke filling the tunnel. The temperature got warmer when the tunnel turned downward into blackness.

With Rajim and Kate listening, Gill told Nicki about what they'd found in the valley, and what he thought it meant.

"I'm so sorry, Gill." She was crying.

Gill wanted to put his arms around her, tell her everything was going to be OK. But he couldn't, and it wasn't. Things would never be OK again, not for Gill.

Nicki wiped her forehead with her shirtsleeve, and said, "You see anything out there that would explain this heat?"

Gill shook his head. "We didn't see much."

"How can the place be?" Rajim said. "And the... animals."

"Have you seen nothing?" Kate said. "It's clear this entire valley once had an ice roof. Could've been that way until recently."

"So? That explains why it wasn't discovered, but what about everything else? You telling me these things have lived here for millions of years? In an unbroken chain? In a naturally sealed environment?"

"If I've learned one thing, it's that nothing is impossible. Unlikely, maybe," Clint said.

Water dripped from the ceiling, and the party stepped around a large puddle. A few of the little cockroach bugs scuttled around and these smaller creatures had green markings on black carapaces. Long antennas scanned the area around the bugs, serving as eyes as its pincers looked for food. Gill's torch went out, and he flicked on his flashlight.

Gill pulled a protein bar from his backpack and ate some.

"Wouldn't have any more of those, would you?" Nicki asked.

The hunters hadn't eaten since breakfast, and that seemed like a lifetime ago. Was Lydia still waiting with Rhubarb at the tunnel entrance? How were Belinda, Squirrel and Ant doing as they made their way back to Reserve? It was a three-and-a-half-day trek back to town, and they had to carry Belinda.

"I'm sorry, Gill," Clint said.

"For?"

"About your boy, and for… not getting the fuckers," he said.

"That wouldn't bring Brian back," Gill said. He reached in his pocket and felt his son's sneaker. He turned it over and over in his hand, felling the rubber and cloth, remembering the boy who'd worn it. A tear slipped down Gill's face.

"You OK?" Nicki said.

"I don't think so," Gill said.

"You've had no time to mourn. To say goodbye," she said.

Gill said nothing. He needed to deal with his grief. If he wanted to live, there could be no more hiding.

The party came around the wide bend in the tunnel and the passage was blocked by the ice wall. Gill couldn't see the hole they'd crawled through, but glowing eyes stared back at him from the darkness like a cartoon.

The scraping sound got louder, and Gill trained his flashlight on the ice wall.

A pack of *velociraptors* blocked their way.

13

The raptors moved up the tunnel toward Gill and his companions, screeching and hissing as they came. In the dim light their eyes glowed, and Gill instinctively took a step back, slipped on the wet floor, and fell on his ass. Rajim lifted him to his feet and pulled him back down the tunnel the way they'd come.

Anger rose in Gill as he watched the *velociraptors* bounce off the cave walls, slowly picking-up speed as they gained confidence. His hatred had returned. His urge to kill these creatures. To splatter their little brains all over the ice and stone. He wanted to take a piss on their corpses.

"Be careful not to—"

Gill opened up with the M16, peppering the beasts as they came on. Clint and Kate followed suit, and the sound of gunfire boomed in the confined space.

Nicki was yelling, but Gill didn't hear what she was saying. Didn't want to hear. Bloodlust filled him as he thought of the tiny sneaker in his pocket. The sneaker his son had worn less than a week ago. All the sorrow came rushing back, the pain and loss, it overwhelmed him, and he let the gun drop to his side.

Clint drove forward as everyone else fell back. He fired methodically, dropping raptors like he was hitting metal ducks at a carnival. Bullets hitting meat, death cries, and furious yelps and snarls filled the cave and turned to static in Gill's head.

Clint was in a fog. Whatever battle he was reliving, or score he was settling in his mind, there was no stopping him. When the AR15 clicked empty the magazine dropped, he jammed another home, and resumed firing.

A loud crack reverberated through the tunnel, and everything paused for an instant. The raptors stopped, looking to their front runner for guidance. Gill looked up and a large crack spidered across the ceiling. Chunks of ice fell, and water streamed like a garden hose from the holes.

Gill backed away, keeping his eyes on the raptors, who had determined there was no danger and had resumed their advance.

Clint was on point, firing at the beasts as they came on. Gill and the rest retreated. Dead raptors clogged the tunnel, but a cloud of the creatures still attacked. Clint's gun clicked empty, but when he reached for another clip, he found he didn't have one. As if the beasts somehow sensed his vulnerability, the raptors doubled their pace.

Gill's friend of ten years stood his ground. Clint dropped the AR15 and pulled his Glock. "Come get it!"

"No!" Gill lurched forward, intent on helping his friend, but was dragged backward by Rajim.

"Gill, there's nothing you can do," Nicki said.

"Let me go," Gill said. He jerked his arms free and bolted toward Clint, but came to a skidding halt a moment later.

The raptors had reached his friend, who fired wildly and infuriated the beasts. One of the raptors bit Clint's left arm, and he screamed. Another severed the arm. Blood spurted from Clint's shoulder as the raptor fled with its prize.

Clint swung the gun wildly with his remaining arm, blood and gristle spilling from his shoulder, bullets smacking the walls. He staggered to one knee, gun held out before him. Two *velociraptors* attacked at once and knocked him over. The Glock barked and one of the beast's heads blew apart, but the other clamped down on Clint's left leg, and tore it off.

Gill brought up the M16, but didn't fire.

Clint screamed as he disappeared under a mound of *velociraptors* as they ripped him apart. It no longer mattered if he hit his friend, and Gill fired, aiming at the raptors as they fled with parts of Clint's body.

Gill screamed, and Rajim and Nicki tugged at him to follow. The cave rumbled, and more water poured from the ceiling.

"We need to get out of here," Nicki said.

The remaining *velociraptors* fled like rats under a spotlight. The floor of the tunnel trembled, and rocks and chunks of ice fell from the ceiling.

Kate didn't move. She stared into the darkness, her gun still held out before her.

Gill wanted to help her. Tell her she needed to run. To escape, yet he understood there would be no escaping from what had happened here. No respite from the sorrow. The realization that his best friend was now dead along with his family brought on such sorrow Gill had the urge to sit on the cold floor and cry.

"Let's go!" Nicki was in his face. She pushed and hit him, trying to shake him from his paralysis, but Gill was gone, off on the playground with Brian.

Rajim slapped Gill across the face.

Gill shook his head, then raised his fists, then lowered them.

The mountain sounded like it was coming down. More rock and ice fell from the ceiling.

"Come on," Rajim said.

"We need to help Kate. She's—"

The cave ceiling collapsed, and everything went black.

Rubble fell on Gill and he went down, rocks and ice pelting him. He covered his head with his arms as he was buried alive.

The rumble ceased, and the bang and smack of rocks falling stopped. Gill was twisted like a pretzel, but he could move. He shifted his position and emerged from the rubble. He picked-up his flashlight and panned it around.

The tunnel leading out was gone. The ceiling hadn't collapsed, the entire cave had. There was no longer a ceiling, but blackness that stretched to nowhere. The way back to the lost valley was covered in stones and chunks of ice, but it was passable. Nicki and Rajim dusted themselves off.

"Everyone OK?" Nicki asked.

"Yeah," Rajim said. He and Nicki had been further down the tunnel where the cave hadn't totally collapsed.

"I've got some nasty bruises, but I think I'm OK," Gill said.

Then he remembered Kate.

"Kate!" he called into the pile of rocks. "Kate!"

No response.

"Kate," Gill said, but there was no strength left in his voice. He sank to his knees and wept. Clint and Kate were dead. His obsession had killed them.

"Kate," Nicki said.

No response.

"This cave-in is pretty bad. Maybe she's on the other side and can't hear us?" Rajim said.

"Maybe," Gill said. He had to take hope where he could find it.

"What now?" Rajim said. "Should I try and dig through?"

Nicki shone her flashlight on the gigantic pile of rock and ice and shook her head. "There's no way we can clear that without the aid of equipment or dynamite, and that could cause more damage. It collapsed where the ice wall was. The one we climbed through. Must be a crack in the eggshell somewhere and water dripped through. Never good for a sealed system."

As that thought settled in his mind, Gill's anger fled and was replaced with fear and worry. Fear for a life he hadn't wanted a few short hours ago and worry for the wellbeing of Rajim and Nicki. If Kate was dead her blood was on his hands, as was Clint's. If he hadn't been in denial about Brian, insisted on hunting the beasts, even after it was no longer practical to do so, Clint and Kate might be alive.

"This is all my fault," Gill said.

"Not all of it," Rajim said.

"You couldn't predict what we'd find in that valley or know the structural integrity of a cave that by all accounts shouldn't exist," Nicki said. "Wasn't your fault the things took your son."

"All the same, they're all gone, yet here I am."

A loud *pop* echoed through what was left of the tunnel and a large stone fell from the portion of the ceiling still intact.

"We better get out of here," Nicki said.

"To where?" Rajim said.

"Where the hell do you think? It's not like we have any choice," Nicki said.

Rajim's face twisted in the flashlight beam, and his gaze shifted between the collapsed tunnel and the passage that led back to the primeval valley. "What about rescue? If we leave the area and they come looking, they'll miss us."

"You got eyes," Gill said. "If we're rescued, I don't think it will be through here."

Rajim harrumphed, picked up his bag, and threaded his way through the debris.

The party walked in silence for two hours before the exit appeared in the distance. Unlike earlier in the day, there was no sliver of light, no clouds or green trees. Cockroach bugs scuttled about, but Gill didn't see any of their bigger brothers.

They exited the tunnel into the cool night air. Stars shined through the opening in the ice roof, and the buzz of the insects was so loud Gill couldn't hear Nicki when she spoke to him.

"What?" he said.

"Stay here for the night?" she shouted.

The valley below was pitch black, but Gill didn't need to see to understand the danger. In addition to the static buzz of insects, the sound of breaking trees, the cries of predators and prey, and the wet sound of meat being ripped from bone filled the valley.

"Yeah, let's make camp over there behind the large boulder," Gill said.

The precipice was thirty yards across and twenty yards deep, with a line of boulders along the mountains edge where they'd fallen. The decision was made to forgo a fire until they understood the valley better, so they erected their tents, ate a cold meal, and tried to sleep.

Gill volunteered to stand guard because there was no way he'd be able to sleep. In addition to the cacophony of sound, and the chunk of ice in the pit of his stomach, he didn't feel comfortable closing his eyes, let alone going to sleep.

He rubbed his eyes and leaned the M16 against a stone. In the morning they'd have to take inventory, see what they had. Gill shook his head as the idea of survival brought back the anger. Sorrow washed over him. It was bad enough that he'd lost his family, but now thanks to him, Rajim and Nicki's children might be orphans. Kate's parents would never get over her loss, and the thought of telling her mother brought bile up Gill's throat. Nobody would miss Clint much, except him. He settled against the mountain face, out of the breeze, and the constant insect noise rose in a crescendo.

14

Gill was awakened on the fourth day out from Reserve by a light rain. He'd fallen asleep on watch, but he'd been lucky. Everything was quiet. He stretched and looked around camp, making sure all the tents were where he left them. He heard Rajim's snoring, and the soft puff of Nicki's breathing. Their tent had been silent the prior evening.

The forest below was subdued. No animals screeched or barked, the birds were perched beneath the dense tree canopy, and the rain had driven away the mist. He was starving, but decided to wait for his companions before breaking out the food.

He retrieved his backpack and spilled the contents out on the floor of his tent out of the rain. He glanced at his watch, and it read 6:19AM. The pitiful inventory of items made him frown.

He had a box of twenty hollow point 9mm parabellums, five protein bars, a bag of beef jerky, a sweatshirt, two t-shirts, an extra pair of underwear, a set of long johns, field glasses, blood pressure meds, dead cellphone, water bottle that when charged produced water from the humidity in the air, a roll-up solar panel to charge the water bottle, a hundred feet of Infinity rope, and a disposable lighter. The food wouldn't last long, and even if he and the others were lucky beyond belief it would be several days before rescuers could reach them.

He pulled his dead radio from his belt. With a little work Gill thought he could recharge the radio with the solar panel, but he didn't know what good that would do. They were at least 12,000 feet above sea level in a cleft of mountains that would block the signal, but the device had an emergency beacon function and maybe he could get to higher ground. That would have to wait until it stopped raining and the solar panel could catch some sunrays.

He stuffed everything back in his backpack, except the box of shells. He reloaded one of the Glock's magazines with fifteen bullets, then took the remaining shells and partially loaded the backup clip. Twenty bullets. He hoped Nicki and Rajim had some ammo or getting food was going to be difficult.

The patter of rain stopped, and he went outside. Sunlight broke through the clouds, heating the moisture and creating thick mist that hung over the valley like a shroud. He took out his binoculars and scanned the valley floor, but saw nothing through the thick mist.

"Hey there," Nicki said. She was crawling from her tent, her hand on her back. "Bedroll sure isn't like my king back home." She disappeared behind a stone, presumably to relieve herself. When she returned she held something. "Why didn't you wake me to take a watch?"

Gill looked at the ground. "I may have… may have mind you. I may have dozed off for a few minutes."

She smiled.

"If a few is equal to half the night," he said. "What you got there?"

"Oh, yeah. I just found this." Nicki held up a turtle shell about a foot long and six inches wide. "We can use it to cook our gourmet dinosaur stew."

They chuckled, and that sound brought Rajim from his tent. He glared at Gill and went to his wife and tried to give her a good morning kiss. Nicki looked at the ground and turned away and the kiss landed on her cheek.

Awkward silence.

"Anybody hungry?" Gill said.

"Starving. What we got?" Rajim said.

"Not much. Did you guys do an inventory of what you have?" Gill said.

"Not yet," Nicki said. "But you're right. We need to start rationing right away."

Nicki went to retrieve her backpack and Rajim followed like a dutiful puppy.

The mist was lifting and dissipating in the sun, and Gill turned his field glasses back on the valley.

The slit in stone the party was calling a valley was nothing more than a gap in the mountains. Gill estimated it stretched no more than fifty miles end-to-end, and ten miles across. A large lake sat in the northwest corner, its dark water lapping against the mountain face. An evergreen forest filled much of the valley floor, and several large grass patches stood out like spots on a green leopard. At the foot of the mountains large boulders and hemlocks clogged the ground, but above, Gill saw many cave openings. Some looked large enough for people to go into, others were much smaller, even too small for the *velociraptors* to squeeze into.

A head stuck-up through the tree canopy.

"What the hell is that?" Rajim said. He'd come up behind Gill and was staring into the valley.

"It's big, whatever the hell it is. Think it's a mutant?" Gill said. He couldn't help but poke the man.

Rajim started to say something, but when Nicki arrived his lips sealed into a tight red line.

Gill told them what he had.

"I don't have much," Nicki said when Gill was done. "Thirteen bullets for my Colt, hunting knife, some clothes, and empty water bottle, and some bric-a-brac. All the food I brought is gone, except a pack of spearmint gum. I don't assume pictures of my kids could be used for much.

"What about you?" Nicki said to Rajim.

"Not much better. I've got half a sandwich, three candy bars and one power bar. No water. Hand axe. One hundred feet of regular rope. What the hell is Infinity rope? Who are you? Gill and his magic rope and Jack and his stalk?"

"You're a riot, Alice. A Real riot," Gill said.

Nicki laughed.

Rajim's face twisted.

"What else you got?" Gill said to break the tension.

"I've got eight rounds for my .22, some clothes, and what did Nicki call it? Some bric-a-brac?" Rajim said.

"Damn. We're screwed," Gill said. Rajim had something he wasn't telling. Gill would bet his life on it.

"Yup," Nicki said.

"All the camping supplies and food stuff was strapped to Rhubarb," Gill said.

Something wailed in the forest below, a guttural cry that ended with a squeak that sounded like metal being rubbed on glass. The companions looked out on the valley, and several shapes moved about in the clearings.

"Looks like everybody is waking up," Nicki said.

"So... about breakfast?" Rajim said.

"Your half sandwich is perishable, so we should split that and drink the water," he said.

"Makes sense," Nicki said.

"The three of us are going to split half a salami sandwich?" Rajim said.

"I see no choice. Until we get orientated, make a fire and see what food might be available, we can only eat what we have," Nicki said.

"But I'm famished," Rajim said.

Gill added, "Me also. Rajim has a point."

Nicki's mouth fell open.

"What? He's right. If we're going to accomplish anything today, we need to expend energy. To do that we need to burn calories, so we need to eat. I suggest you two split the sandwich and I'll eat half a protein bar."

Nicki nodded.

"And what is it you expect to accomplish today?" Rajim said. The détente had passed.

"We have to search the valley for another way out," Gill said. "What else is there?"

"Search the valley? Are you nuts?" Rajim said. When Nicki glared at him he stammered, "Not nuts. Sorry. But Gill, take a look around. Do you really think it's smart venturing into those woods?"

"Like I said, what else is there?"

"We hunker down up here on this ledge. Away from everything down there. Wait for rescue," Rajim said.

"We've been over this," Nicki said. "No one is ever getting through that tunnel again without explosives, and I don't think we want to be here if they start blasting the side of the mountain."

"Where will we get food? Water? We're almost out of both," Gill said.

Rajim said nothing.

Gill said, "Look, I get it. Seems crazy wandering around a world that appears to be filled with prehistoric animals that want to eat us, but if we're to have any hope of survival we can't stay here."

"We can use it as a home base," Nicki said.

Rajim's face brightened.

"That might work," Gill said.

"What if they send a helicopter for us?" Rajim said.

"How will they know where to find us?" Nicki said.

"The others could direct the authorities to the tunnel mouth and it shouldn't be hard from there," Rajim said.

"True," Gill said. The sun was shining, and all the mist and moisture burned off. "Plus," he continued, "I'm gonna charge the radio and send out an emergency signal."

"It will never get out of the valley," Rajim said.

"We don't know that and what do we have to lose by trying?" Nicki said.

Something howled in the jungle below and the companions paused in their conversation.

A gentle breeze brought the scent of pinecones, shit and rotten eggs. Clouds floated across the opening in the valley's ice roof, and birds of all sizes came and went from the sheltered valley. Gill's stomach rumbled. They needed some real food.

"I like my base idea. We can build a permanent camp up here while we search the valley for food and water," Nicki said.

"And search for a way out," Gill said.

Rajim nodded, and with that settled the party went about preparing for a hunting trip into the lost valley.

Gill unrolled the small solar panel and laid it on a flat stone facing the sun. He took the back off the radio, and removed the battery. Black and red wires connected to a small transformer, which Gill removed from the radio. He attached the black wire of the solar panel to the transformer and on to the battery, then did the same for the red. There was no way to know when the battery was fully charged. With everything set, he covered the battery with leaves to keep it cool and dry.

Nicki and Rajim moved their tent between two large boulders, and Gill thought that was a good idea, so he did the same.

"You think we should build a fence across the hillside, so nothing can get up here?" Rajim said.

"I don't think so," Gill said.

"Why?"

"I'm thinking we should blend in as much as possible. We don't want to stand out and draw curious guests," Gill said.

Rajim nodded.

Nicki fainted an hour later. Nothing serious, but she fell hard and just missed hitting her head on a stone. Gill reached her before Rajim, and the two men fighting to lift Nicki to her feet would have been comical in other circumstances.

"Are you OK?" Rajim said.

"What the hell happened?" Gill said. His heart was racing and his back ached, as it always did when stress wrapped its loving arms around him.

"I got light headed. You smell that?" she said.

Rajim ignored her question, and said, "You passed out because you're thirsty and starving."

Gill ran to his tent and got a protein bar. "Eat this while Rajim and I go find water," he said.

"We what now?" Rajim said.

"We need water. Food can wait, but we need water now," Gill said.

"That lake looks a long way away, and who knows what lives in it?" Rajim said.

"I haven't seen a single dinosaur… mutant… go to the lake to drink. There must be watering holes in the forest, probably a spring or two gushing from the mountainside. We can always do a little climbing and collect snow," Gill said.

"I'm fine. I can come," Nicki said. As she tried to get up her face turned white as milk and she sat back down.

"Rajim, take her to your tent so she can lay down. I'll get some weapons ready. We can hunt while we search for aqua."

Rajim nodded.

Gill checked the M16 and surveyed the valley again. Some of the stuff Rajim said made sense as his mind reconciled what he'd seen so far with Rajim's paranoia.

Time to eat some pride. "Rajim, you might be right," Gill said.

Nicki's eyes grew wide.

"Until we have more time to observe and get our bearings, maybe we should just climb to the nearest snowline," Gill said.

"Let's grab anything that can hold water," Rajim said.

The lost world would have to wait.

15

Nicki coughed and wheezed as Gill and Rajim collected anything that could hold water. In a backpack they stowed Gill's twenty-four-ounce solar bottle, and Nicki and Rajim's twenty-ounce stainless steel bottles. To that they added an empty soda bottle Nicki found stuffed in her pack, and the torn-out bladder from a pocket of Rajim's backpack. It had a zipper and wasn't water tight, but it would serve if they were careful, and it could hold packed snow. They also brought the shell Nicki found and hoped to melt snow onsite to maximize the amount of water they could carry. To that end Gill argued they should haul a bundle of dried wood, some kindling and Rajim's hand axe.

"This is getting complicated," Rajim said.

"You got a better idea?" Gill said.

Rajim stared down into the valley, then up at the snowcapped mountain peaks and went to get his axe.

Gill shouldered the M16 and picked-up the pack. "We'll be back as soon as we can," he said.

Rajim gave Gill the stink-eye as he kissed his wife on the forehead. Gill hadn't seen them kiss on the lips in days. Some evil, jealous part of him rejoiced in this and that led back to his fantasy and attraction. Of all the people in Reserve he ended up trapped with Nicki... and Rajim. Their history. His feelings. He felt stretched, and he was tired. So tired.

"Which way you going?" Nicki asked.

Gill was tired of arguing so he looked to Rajim.

Rajim's right eyebrow arced. He lifted his chin and examined the mountains above their position.

There was no snowline until the peak, other than a few sparse drifts in notches on the sheer cliff face. To the north the steep cliffs continued out of sight around an outcrop, and to the south a slope threaded upward alongside the rockface.

"South until we find a way up? Looks like there might be icicles on some of those outcrops. If we could break a couple of those off we'd be set," Rajim said.

Gill didn't look at Nicki, because he didn't want Rajim to see their shared surprise. "Good idea. Let's go," he said.

Gill and Rajim spent four hours of their first day in the valley traversing large boulders, avoiding patches of tall grass, swiping at gnats and flies, and working their way upward toward the frost line. The sand

and gravel he and Rajim walked on was loose in spots, and more than once both men slid backwards as the sands shifted.

"Damn, Gill, you bust one?" Rajim said.

He hadn't, but the rank stench of rot, decay and shit riled his gag reflex.

"What do you make of that smell? It wasn't this nasty in the tunnels," Rajim said.

Gill kept his speculation to himself as he concentrated on working his way up a steep section of hillside. Animal trails wove through the boulders that had splintered off the mountain and stuck from the ground like forlorn teeth.

Gill crested the hill and stopped to catch his breath, bent over, hands on knees.

Rajim finished his climb. "There we go," Rajim said.

"What?"

Rajim pointed to an outcrop of stone jutting from the mountainside. Icicles hung where water had dripped, and they looked substantial. "If we can knock a few— whooh, we got company."

Several dinosaurs stood at the far end of the hilltop. At first Gill thought they were boulders, but when one moved, he considered bolting.

The beasts looked like six-foot armadillos. Their armored heads bobbed up and down as they ate the tall grass that grew around boulders. The creatures didn't appear to notice them.

"I think those are *ankylosaurs*," Gill said. "See the armored back and the club at the end of the tail? That was for defense."

"They're hiding up here from the T-rex," Rajim said.

"I'd think so. The big beasts can't get up here. I wonder where they get their water from?" Gill said.

Rajim didn't hear him. He was transfixed by the dinosaurs. He took several hesitant steps toward them, eyes wide.

"They appear to be plant eaters, but that doesn't mean they won't get spooked. Be careful, they look heavy," Gill said. He'd seen bulls a third the size take down cowboys.

Rajim ignored him.

The crunch and chomp of the beasts eating filled the glade, but the dinosaurs froze as one when the alpha of the pack saw Rajim and went rigid.

The creature's big black eyes rolled as it searched the area for an escape route.

"Looks like the way we came is how they get up here," Gill said.

Rajim stepped forward, eyes locked on the dinosaurs.

The beasts had wide, low heads, with two curved horns pointing backward and two down. A hooked beak covered its mouth and four thick legs supported a sausage-like torso. The creatures' long tails ended in a club, knobs and plates of bone covered their backs, and their skin appeared to be covered in scales. The beasts swayed and moved like cows, and the alpha brayed, sounding like a horse in pain.

"Rajim, I wouldn't go too close," Gill said.

"What? They're lettuce eaters." Rajim was only fifty yards from the creatures, who stood watching him.

"How much do you think those things eat a day?" Gill said.

"No idea, but I've been wondering where all these things get their food," Rajim said.

"Small populations."

"Maybe." Rajim was about twenty yards from the biggest *ankylosaur* when it stomped like a bull ready to charge. Two of the smaller beasts peered from behind their protector.

Gill didn't like what he was seeing. "Mommy is getting nervous. I think we should—"

The biggest *ankylosaur* charged, bounding forward like a hippo. The ground shook, and the pack followed their alpha. Gill ran, not worrying for Rajim, or anything else. He wove in and out of boulders, tripped on a vine, and went down. Rajim helped him up and they ran on, the sound of the creature's heavy footfalls spurring the companions on.

The path forked, one way led higher into the mountains, the other plunged back down the way they'd come. Gill headed up, disappearing into a thin band of mist that separated the snowline from the warmer climates.

The pounding of the *ankylosaur*'s feet faded and Rajim caught up with him. Gill asked, "You alright?"

Rajim nodded as he caught his breath.

"Looks like they gave up," Gill said.

"They… didn't… look very agile," Rajim said between breaths.

"Well look at that," Gill said.

An ice flow much larger than the first one they'd seen ran down the rock face, ending in a giant ice cube that could provide a year's supply of water.

"Sweet," Rajim said. He took out his hand axe and started chipping ice as Gill collected it. Without the constant hum of the insects, every strike to the ice block echoed off the mountainside like a speaker. Gill didn't like the idea of announcing themselves, but what choice did they have?

"Should I get the fire going? Start melting this stuff? If we're lucky we might get back to camp before dark," Gill said.

Rajim didn't answer and Gill looked up from his work to see why.

The commotion had brought another native.

A six-foot bird-like beast appeared, head jerking side to side and up and down. It stood atop a rock, and half jumped, half flew toward them, its short arms acting like gliding wings. It looked like a deformed ostrich. The half-wing-arms ended in three-fingered hands, and the beast balanced on two hind legs, which were stout and muscular. Brown and black feathers covered the entire creature, and it yipped as it came forward.

Gill brought up the M16 and sighted. The creature showed no sign of halting its charge, but Gill held his fire.

"Gill," Rajim said. "Behind you."

A second beast slipped from the foliage. Gill shifted his position so he could see both dinosaurs, and moved the gun back and forth between the two animals.

"What are you waiting for?" Rajim's rifle was still slung over a shoulder.

Gill flicked the firing selector from burst to single fire. He eased his finger down on the trigger and the head of the dinosaur coming at him jerked backward. The beast's body continued to run, then stopped and fell over, spurting blood.

The second creature paused, its gaze shifting between its dead partner and the invaders. Figuring it wouldn't do much better than its friend, the remaining beast jumped onto a boulder, and glided out of sight.

Gill panned his gun around, nerves jumping, pain lancing his neck and back.

The ice he'd chopped off was melting into the ground, but slowly. It was fifty-one degrees. Gill went back to work, but this time he was more careful with his strikes, making sure each impact yielded a nice chunk of ice to minimize the noise.

"What about the fire?" Rajim said.

Gill sighed. He wasn't sure drawing attention to themselves was smart, but weren't they safer up high away from the big boys? Gill shook his head and tried to crack his neck. He was being simplistic. A microprobe could take them down. A small spider. Who the hell knew what dangers big and small threatened to catch them around every turn?

The dinosaur's corpse lay across the clearing and it occurred to Gill that he'd just provided the group with some meat. "Do you know how to butcher that thing?"

Rajim's eyes went to the ground, and he shifted his weight from foot to foot. "I've carved the Thanksgiving turkey, and I've carved a roast beef, but beyond that…"

"Can you handle the fire?"

"Yeah. Yeah." He looked over his shoulder, eyes darting about.

"Keep your rifle handy and eyes up."

Rajim nodded.

Gill pulled his hunting knife and went to the fallen dinosaur. For a big animal it didn't have much meat on it. Its legs and arms were pure muscle and bone, and there wasn't much on the torso. Gill sniffed the air. As soon as he cut the animal open the smell of blood would bring all kinds of problems. He sheathed his knife.

"Hey, I'm gonna wait to cut this thing until we're ready to leave. Don't want to ring the dinner bell."

"Yarp," Rajim said. He was stacking the firewood they'd brought into a neat t-pee.

As soon as the fire was going, Gill placed a big chunk of ice in the turtle shell and placed it at the edge of the fire. The ice began melting at once, and within minutes the shell was overflowing with water. Gill and Rajim drank deep, then put more ice in the shell.

When they'd drunk their fill, and all the containers were full, Rajim kept watch as Gill sliced meat from the fallen dinosaur. The strips of red meat looked like flank steak as Gill peeled it from the beast's rib cage and shoulders.

"We can smoke that stuff to preserve it," Rajim said.

"Not here we won't. Takes time and we need to get back."

Rajim nodded.

Gill put the melting fire out, loaded up and began the arduous task of trekking back to Nicki.

16

Nicki finished her bottle of water with one long pull then commandeered Rajim's. Minutes later she had stomach cramps and doubled over, vomiting. After a gagging fit, she sat on a stone and caught her breath. "I feel better now. Thanks. Thank you both," she said.

Sunlight slanted into the valley as the sun set, and a rainbow crossed the divide between the eastern and western mountains. Gill thought of Brian standing in the river beneath the rainbow, smiling, his hair tossing in the breeze. Sorrow swept over him, and he saw Brian's finger lying on the ground in his mind's eye, dripping blood.

The guttural wails and cries of fighting animals rose from the forest. It was feeding time and every species, big and small, fought for dinner.

"So how'd you make out? Other than finding water, I mean," Nicki said.

Rajim told their story, and Nicki said nothing, but she glanced at Gill twice as if checking to see if what her husband said was true. "See here," Rajim held up the bundled meat as evidence.

"Guess we're lighting a fire whether we think it's smart or not," Gill said.

"I wonder what the smell of roasting meat will bring?" Rajim said.

"At this point I don't really care. I'm starved," Nicki said.

"Why don't you go lay down while Rajim and I prepare dinner and a fire?"

Rajim threw Gill a dirty look, and said, "Yeah. We can handle this... honey."

Gill almost laughed. Nicki had been giving her husband the cold shoulder for a couple of days, and there was no thaw in sight despite Rajim's best efforts to apply heat.

Gill and Rajim watched Nicki enter her tent.

"I've been meaning to ask. What's the deal with you and firing your weapon? Do you need me to show you how to use it?" Gill asked. He knew Rajim would get mad, which was why he waited until Nicki was gone. He didn't want to embarrass the man, but what good was a gun if you didn't use it when needed?

Rajim harrumphed. "I'll get wood," he said, and disappeared into the field of boulders.

Dusk settled over the land as Gill made a ring of stones and butchered the dinosaur meat into thin strips. The meat looked OK, but he knew they were taking a big chance eating the flesh of the dinosaurs. Who knew what parasites they carried? He'd cook the meat well-done.

Rajim returned and darkness enveloped the valley as Gill got the fire going. They kept it small, and only burnt dried twigs to keep smoke to a minimum. The aroma of cooking meat he couldn't do anything about. Gill stretched the meat on tree branch skewers, and Rajim and Gill held them over the fire, turning them and keeping the dino steaks from burning. Fat dripped onto the red-hot wood and sizzled. The smell wasn't exactly steak on the BBQ, but it was close. Gill's mouth watered, as did his eyes from the smoke.

"Hey there, smells good." Nicki had crawled from her tent. In the firelight Gill saw her red cheeks, the dark bags beneath her eyes, and the scratches and dirt on her face. Despite all this, she looked much better than she had that afternoon. She rubbed her hands together and sat down next to the fire.

Rajim handed her his water bottle, and she drank deeply. "I forgot to mention," Rajim said, "I've got a little surprise." He pulled a pint bottle of tequila from an inside pocket of his jacket.

Nicki laughed.

Gill said, "Probably not a great idea. We're real short on water and alcohol dehydrates your body."

Nicki laughed again. "Gill, you've got to loosen up."

A stab of pain pierced Gill's stomach. He looked at Rajim who wore a smug self-satisfied smile. Maybe Nicki was right. He was always worrying. Trying to plan. For what? He had nobody to take care of anymore. Who really cared what he did? Whether he got out of the valley alive?

"Gill does have a point, though," she said. "Can't go crazy."

"Right. Can't over do it because…. why again?" Rajim said.

"Because we need to be sharp so we can get back to our kids," Nicki said.

A roar came from the valley. It sounded like a big one, maybe the T-rex.

Gill said, "Looks like this is done." He took a bit of meat off the end of his stick, chewing it as if it was filled with razorblades. He nodded. "Not bad."

"Taste like chicken?" Rajim said.

The three companions laughed, and the sound rolled across the precipice, and Nicki put her hand over her mouth. It was so easy to forget where they were, the dangers. This wasn't a camping trip, and the three of them weren't friends. Gill didn't know what they were.

"You believe it's only been four days since we left Reserve?" Nicki said. She pulled meat off her stick and fat dripped down her chin.

"Feels like four months," Gill said.

"Aye," Rajim added.

They ate in silence. It was in quiet times like these that Gill's mind was his worst enemy. When he was talking, or working, or otherwise occupied he didn't think about Brian. Or of the night Nicki had come to his house to tell him Abigale was dead. Alone in his sleeping bag at night, with the walls of his tent pressing in on him, and the blackness sucking away all hope, he thought of his family, what might have been, but mostly he tormented himself with what would never be. Brian would never go to High School, never know the love of a woman, or have kids. He was gone, all the indelible strings of his life severed.

The fire popped and shot sparks into the sky.

"You think we should do a quick patrol around the ledge? Make sure our cooking meat isn't bringing unwanted guests?" Gill said.

Rajim looked put-out, but nodded. Gill figured the man may have learned a lesson earlier in the day with the *ankylosaurs*. Things may not always be as they appear, and danger comes in many forms and not all of them are obvious.

"I'll do it," Gill said. He finished his piece of meat and retrieved the M16. "Be back in ten." He strode from the ring of firelight into the darkness and paused, letting his eyes adjust. It was chilly, and he pulled his jacket tight about him.

Being careful where he stepped, Gill threaded between the hemlocks and boulders, gun arcing back and forth. Things scuttled away in the blackness, but nothing bigger than a squirrel. A snake hissed as it slithered into a mound of grass, and birds shrieked when Gill bumped a hemlock and a cloud of tiny wrens sprayed from the greenery like flies.

He saw no threats, and when his circuit of the ledge was complete he returned to his seat by the fire. Nicki and Rajim were already drinking. He sighed. When in Rome. "Gimme that," he said.

Nicki handed Gill the bottle of golden liquor and he took a short pull. The alcohol burned his throat and warmed his stomach. He felt lightheaded, and the fire danced higher and brighter.

"See anything out there?" Nicki said.

"Naw. Nothing to worry about. We're hidden behind boulders, so the beasties may smell us, but they'll have no way of knowing exactly where. We're high up," Gill said.

"I wish Kiki and Fred were here," Rajim said. "I mean, I don't wish they were... you know what I mean."

"I do," Nicki said without taking her eyes off the fire.

Gill felt that pain creep over him. The pain of his son's loss that he knew would never leave and would torment him for the rest of his days. He wanted to tell his companions that, but he said nothing.

He handed Nicki the bottle and she took another pull. Her cheeks were deep red, and her eyes burned like cinders. She was already half drunk. She said, "You look worse than the night..."

There it was again. The night. The event that would tie Gill and Nicki together whether Rajim wanted it or not.

"I'm sorry, Gill. I..." She took another pull of tequila and stared at the ground.

Rajim took the bottle and tipped it to his lips. Gill could tell Rajim wanted to ask a question, but the look on Nicki's face was clear as air: shut the hell up.

Gill broke the silence. "It's OK. I don't know what would have happened that night if you hadn't been there. I don't know what I would have done."

This time Rajim just couldn't contain himself. "And what exactly did happen that night?"

"Rajim, now's not—"

"No, it's OK, Nicki. It feels better to talk about it sometimes."

"Is this one of those times?" she said.

Gill looked to the sky, the stars blinking down at him. Abigale and Brian both urged him on as if the memories of his family would bring them back to life in the telling. "I was home with Brian, who just an infant. He was wailing and screaming, and I was so bad at getting him to sleep Abigale hardly went out. On this night she'd gone out with friends, and I was dancing, singing, reading books, making funny noises. Nothing worked. The little guy was screaming so loud I thought he might hurt himself. I was stressed beyond belief."

"I can relate," Rajim said. "Kiki wouldn't go down for anyone except Nicki."

"When Nicki knocked on my door I looked through the decorative glass and saw it was her. I knew right away something bad had happened. Not a stretch, right? Cop shows up at your door at 10:30 on a Friday night and it's safe to say they're not selling raffle tickets for the benevolent association fundraiser," Gill said.

Nicki took the bottle of tequila from her husband and took a pull. "I was going to call first, but I just couldn't do it." She sniffled and wiped tears from her face. "I wanted to call you. To break the news that way because I knew facing you would be the hardest thing I'd ever done, but I couldn't."

She passed the bottle to Gill who took a lame swig.

"What did you tell Brian?" Rajim said. His voice was filled concern, and in that moment, Gill didn't hate the man.

"The truth," Gill said. He took another drink and passed the bottle. His vision was getting blurry and his stomach ached from the meat and booze. "I told him his mother collapsed while walking to her car. That a blood vessel in her brain broke, and that she'd gone to Heaven to see grandma and grandpa. I went catatonic and if it wasn't for Nicki taking care of Brian and me, I…"

Nicki took a swig of tequila and searched for the bottle's cap.

"Not yet," Rajim said. He took the tequila from her and took a long pull before handing it back to Nicki, who capped it. "Did they ever find out exactly what happened?"

"Not really. Freak thing," Gill said.

"Her funeral was the saddest gathering I'd ever been to," Nicki said. "Abigale was such a wonderful woman. The ways of this piss-poor world." She kicked at the dirt in front of her and got to her feet.

"God's plan, they said." Gill tried to tell himself he wasn't bitter.

"God? Screw God if his plan includes taking a mother from her twenty-month-old son," Nicki. "How can people thank God for helping them find their lost keys, but are OK with him allowing children to be raped?"

"I'm not su—"

Rajim barked a snore as his head fell forward onto his chest. He sagged like a fallen tent, his breath coming in ragged bursts as he slept.

Nicki laughed. "Never could hold his liquor."

Gill said, "Wish I could fall asleep that easy."

Nicki kicked her husband gently and he came awake with a start. "Let's go rockstar, tomorrow's another day."

Gill shuffled off to bed, where he laid in his sleeping bag staring at the green neoprene ceiling and waiting for sunrise.

17

Gill's second day in the valley started under the grey of an overcast sky. Thick mist hung over the forest below, and other than the titter of birds and the buzz of insects, all was quiet. He was first up, and he retrieved ice and melted it over a small fire. When he returned to camp with his bounty, Nicki and Rajim were awake.

"Morning," he said as he handed them their full water bottles.

Both drank deep and thanked him. Rajim even wore a smile.

"What's on the agenda today?" Nicki asked.

"Search," Rajim said.

Gill nodded.

"All three of us?" she said.

Rajim nodded.

Gill said, "Not to be an alarmist, but wouldn't it make sense if one of you stayed up here?"

"Why?" Rajim said. Though he still had half a smile the tone of his voice revealed his suspicion.

"I know why. The kids?" Nicki said.

Gill nodded.

"What?" Rajim said.

"It's relatively safe up here on the ledge, but down there the risks increase exponentially," Gill said.

"Who will look after Kiki and Fred if we both die out here? Granted, that is still a possibility, but shouldn't we do everything we can to avoid both of us being in the same dangerous situations?" Nicki said. "You remember Jody Crastorlly? Her parents flew separately when they went away without the children."

Rajim sighed. "That's just nuts. I don't think we should split up. Haven't you ever seen any horror films?"

Gill chuckled. "He has a point. We're stronger together than apart."

"And we'll never survive if we act out of fear," Rajim said.

Another good point, but Gill said nothing.

"What's up with the radio?" Nicki asked.

Gill had forgotten about the charging battery. He went over to the stone where the solar panel was laid out and disconnected the battery and hit the tiny battery charge button. One green light out of five. "This thing is hardly charged," he said.

"So it's working?" Rajim said.

"Slowly, and without full power the signal may not be as strong. I say we let it sit until fully charged," Gill said.

"You mean just leave it here?" Nicki said.

"Who's gonna take it?" Rajim said.

Gill reconnected the solar panel, and hid the radio next to the stone in a tuft of grass and smoothed the solar panel out over the stone. "That should be fine until we come back to get it," he said.

"Was the battery hot?" Rajim asked.

"A little, but I think it will be OK."

"What do we bring and what do we leave?" Nicki said.

"We don't know when we'll be back up this way. Might be a day or two, so I think we need to bring everything. The food, tents, anything we can stuff in our packs," Gill said.

"So much for maintaining camp," Rajim said.

"We have our supply of firewood," Nicki said.

That was a small consolation, but there was no other choice. They might find someplace better to make camp, a cave, or another place that proved better shelter and protection. The companions folded their tents and broke camp, and by 9AM the three weary travelers started down the slope to the valley floor.

They walked the path Clint and Gill had followed when they'd arrived in the valley the first time. Their boot prints marred the loose dirt and foreign tracks crisscrossed the path. Tall tufts of devil's grass sprouted around the boulders and hemlocks, and hedgehogs peered out at the party with shiny black eyes as they passed. The cloud cover was breaking up and it looked as though it wouldn't rain. Wisps of mist rose from the forest as the temperature went up and the fog baked off.

Gill stripped off his jacket. He figured they'd descended about a thousand feet into the valley and the temperature had risen at least ten degrees.

"That damn smell again." Rajim took off his jacket and wrinkled his nose.

"What I don't understand is the temperature. I know it's summer, but it's never this warm up this high," Nicki said.

"I'm more worried about what we might be breathing," Gill said.

A bellow sounded from the forest, followed by a bark-wail that reminded Gill of a hurt puppy.

"Doesn't seem to hurt the wildlife," Rajim said.

The party reached the valley floor and saw Gill and Clint's footprints leading into the forest. Tall Douglas firs stood like a wall to the north and west, the mountain face to the south.

"How should we do this?" Gill said.

"Walk the perimeter?" Rajim said.

"Makes sense," Nicki said. "Keep the mountains to our backs."

"Except over by the lake. The water runs right up to the cliff face," Gill said.

"One problem at a time. We can search the rest of the valley before we need to worry about that," Nicki said.

The party went single file along the valley's edge, skirting boulders and thickets of brambles and hemlocks. The scent of the air shifted as they walked, leaving behind the sulfur-shit smell and transitioning to pure rankness.

They hadn't gone far when they came across a huge pile of scat. Sticks and broken bones stuck from the three-foot pile of waste, and streaks of green grass and other vegetation gave the brown sludge some color.

Nicki put her hand over her nose. "Dang, that's nasty."

"Wouldn't want to meet the beast that pushed out that deuce," Rajim said.

"I think I already have," Gill said.

"The T-rex?" Nicki asked.

"What else have we seen that's big enough to push that out?"

Nicki and Rajim didn't respond.

An animal path led away from the cliff face, a mix of big and small prints, some with three talons and others with four. "I think we should follow these tracks," Nicki said.

"Whatever for?" Rajim said.

Gill answered for her, "It looks like a well beaten trail. There must be something... water, probably. Why else would so many of the animals come this way?"

Rajim looked at his wife, anger below his attempt at a blank expression.

"You guys want to wait here?" Gill said.

Rajim sighed and pushed past Gill, heading away from the sheer mountainside and disappearing into a tangle of hemlocks.

Nicki looked at Gill, but said nothing. Then she followed her husband.

Gill didn't move, frustration eating at him. He was tired of Rajim's passive aggressive bullshit. Nicki and Rajim had issues with their marriage that had nothing to do with him... specifically. Yes, he had feelings for Nicki, but he hadn't acted on them. How did Nicki feel about him? The evidence was mixed. She seemed to side with him when it came to important things, but stayed with Rajim on all the low risk decisions, as if appeasing her husband. Maybe she was. It was really none of his business.

As predicted, the party found a small watering hole, no more than a dirty puddle, and also as predicated, it was a popular spot. Tracks of various sizes marked the area, but no animals drank as the party approached.

"Guess we're loud," Nicki said.

"You think?" Rajim said.

"What are the odds no animals would be here? Haven't seen any other spot to drink except the lake," his wife said.

"We need to tone it down or we're going to meet our big friend again," Gill said. "You think we should drink this stuff?"

The water wasn't bad or the beasts wouldn't be drinking it, but as US citizens, Gill and his friends were used to crystal clear water. The puddle looked like mud.

"I'm not. I've got water left," Rajim said.

"Me also," Nicki said.

Gill bent and sniffed the puddle. It smelt like unwashed socks. "Yeah, I'm gonna pass for now also. We can always come back if we need to. Boiling the stuff might help."

They left the watering hole behind and threaded through a thin stand of evergreens that brought them up against a sheer cliff face that rose into the sky three hundred feet. They headed west, and soon were forced to head away from the valley's edge due to an outcrop of stone.

The companions came upon an open glade filled with grass and stunted trees. Four creatures stood at the far end of the clearing, two large and two small. The beasts chattered and brayed, but they hadn't seen Gill and his friends. Gill hid behind a low thicket, peering around its edge to watch the family of dinosaurs.

The beasts had crocodilian heads, and stood on two legs like the T-rex, but weren't as big. Yellow and green striations covered black leathery skin, but it was hard to see any detail. The creature's back rose like a sail, and thick bones could be seen running through the skin.

"I think those are *spinosaurs*. Brian had one in his toy set. The card said it was one of the biggest carnivorous dinosaurs to ever live and was equal in size and strength to the T-rex. And it could swim," Gill said.

"And those small ones are kids. If mom and dad catch a whiff of us, we're dino-chow," Nicki said.

The three companions tip-toed away, never taking their eyes off the four *spinosaurs*.

After a time, they came around the outcrop of stone and worked their way back to the edge of the valley where they continued the search.

Gill wasn't hopeful. All the caves they'd seen were small for *velociraptors*, and Gill saw no claw prints leading into any.

They did, however, find water running down the mountainside in thin rivulets as the ice above melted. Capturing the water wasn't easy, and it took an hour to fill the water bottles. Gill sat on a stone and watched the water drip into his bottle, taking a drink from it every few minutes and emptying it.

"What do you make of those?" Nicki said. She stood next to him and pointed at a series of holes in the mountainside to the south-west.

"Caves, but I don't see how we'll get up there," Gill said.

"I've got rope," Rajim said.

"They're high up, so the beasts can't escape through there, but we might be able to," Nicki said.

"Let's check it out when we get closer," Gill said.

They trekked for another hour, and the sun passed noon and disappeared behind the broken ice roof. They stopped and ate some cooked meat, drank some water, split up to take care of bodily functions, and were climbing a steep incline toward the tunnels they'd seen by 2PM.

It was hot, and the scent of sulfur and scat was thick. Clouds of yellow-brown gas filled the air like smoke, and the companions gagged and covered their noses with their hands. The closer they got to the edge of the valley the thicker the yellow fog got, until it was impossible to see ten feet ahead.

"I think we should stop." Rajim's voice was muffled by his hand.

"Why?" Gill said.

"Why? Look around. We don't know what this stuff is. It could be poisonous," Rajim said.

"I don't think so. I feel fine. In fact, I feel great," Gill said.

"And it doesn't appear to hurt the dinosaurs any. If the stuff was—"

"Holy shit," Rajim said.

The curved bones of a giant ribcage broke from the yellow fog and surrounded the party.

18

Gill brought up his gun, staring into the yellow mist as if it might attack him. The curved rib bones of a long dead animal encircled the party as they pressed on. He felt good, better than he had in a long time. His breathing was crisp, and his legs and eyes no longer hurt. Something scuttled over his feet. He jumped and knocked into Rajim, who grabbed one of the thick bones to stay on his feet.

The ribcage ended, and bones lay scattered about. Some of the skeletons were complete, like the beast's body had gone undisturbed. Others were broken as if their final moments hadn't been peaceful, or their corpse had been gnawed on and torn apart.

When Gill reached the cliffside he could hardly see. The gas was dense, and he swiped his hands in front of his face, clearing the fog.

"Oh boy," Gill said.

"What is..."

Yellow gas and steam poured from vents at the base of the mountain like an AC on full blast. It reeked of rotten eggs, and Gill was sweating, tiny droplets slipping down his back into his ass-crack. His undershirt was soaked, and he glanced at his knife thermometer which said the ambient temperature was eighty-four degrees.

"Well, now we know why it's so warm up here," Nicki said.

"And where the smell is coming from," Rajim said.

"Thermal vents," Gill said. "They usually appear in areas of geological upheaval, like around volcanoes."

"That doesn't make sense," Nicki said. "It's very unusual for them to be in the mountains, especially this high."

"What do you make of the gases being expelled?" Rajim said.

The closer Gill studied the yellow fog piping from the vents the more color he saw. Greens, blues, and browns mixed like a depressing rainbow, and pinpricks of light reflected off minerals and flecks of other solids in the gas and steam.

All around the vents, animal skeletons of all shapes and sizes lay strewn about. Some looked to be dinosaurs, others were unrecognizable

"You think the beasts came here to die?" Nicki asked.

There were many examples of animals going to a specific place to die: whales, elephants, and other species, including dinosaurs. Gill seemed to remember reading someplace that some of the best digs for dinosaur bones were boneyards believed to be places where the prehistoric beasts went to die, thus leaving areas with an abundance of fossils of various species. Gill said, "I don't know. It's possible."

"Or did they come here to try and live?" Rajim said.

"Come again?" Gill said.

"Maybe they knew on some instinctual level the gas might help them," Rajim said.

Gill hadn't thought of that, but it was possible. Hadn't he felt better for breathing the odd mixture of elements? "Maybe," he said.

"I think Rajim might be right. All my pains seem to have disappeared," Nicki said.

"I was afraid to say anything for fear of you thinking me mad," Gill said. "But I think breathing the gases has helped me also. I had a terrible headache that disappeared as the yellow fog got thicker."

"Do you think that's what preserved the creatures up here?" Nicki said.

"Who knows? We've been through this, right? Maybe they were frozen and thawed, or their eggs or DNA were," Rajim said.

"Whether they were frozen, or their DNA, or who the hell knows? Life finds a way," Nicki said.

"Stop with that old school bullshit. Life don't find anything. The creatures in this valley are alive due to a series of unusual circumstances that we will never unravel. The ice roof, the temperature shifts, these vents, the general warming of the Earth. Even if we had the tools and a team of top scientists, it would still be next to impossible to piece together the sixty-five-million-year timeline," Gill said.

"Plus, whatever happened, or is happening, was most likely the result of several generations of adaptations," Rajim said. "These beasts may be dependent on the gas."

"The raptors that got my son didn't appear affected," Gill said.

"It might take time," Rajim said.

The vents ran at the base of the mountain for half a mile, and as the companions walked, Gill's mind drifted. Was it the gas? He felt great, but also a bit lightheaded, like he'd drunk too much or taken a hit off a joint. The yellow fog lessened as they moved away from the vents.

A chill ran through Gill. His t-shirt was damp with sweat, but the temperature dropped as they got further from the vents. They entered a few crags in the mountainside, but they all terminated within a few feet, or narrowed to the point where the party was unable to continue.

By lunchtime they'd gone a couple of miles around the edge of the valley and the caves that were their destination loomed above. They ate a fast meal of smoked dinosaur meat and drank the last of their water, but this was no longer a problem. Thin streams of water flowed down the mountainside in many places, and filling their bottles was easy.

The cliff face below the three tunnels was smooth, not so much as a ledge.

"Who's gonna climb that?" Rajim said. By the tone of his voice it was clear that person wouldn't be him.

Gill had dabbled with mountain climbing in the past. He lived in the Rocky Mountains, but he was far from a pro. He wouldn't even consider himself proficient, so he hoped Nicki and Rajim had more to offer.

As usual, hope didn't live up to its name. Not only didn't Rajim climb, he was afraid of heights.

"Even if I manage to get a guide rope in place you're not coming with us?" Gill said.

Rajim stared at his wife, but said nothing.

"I think I can get up there with a guide rope. But free climb? Not on your life," Nicki said.

Rajim stared at him, eyes blazing.

Gill sighed. It was up to him then. Rajim tossed him his coil of rope and Gill fed it through his fingers, creating a loose pile at his feet. Then he tied one end to his belt, bent down and picked-up a handful of dirt, and rubbed it in his palms as if getting ready to bat in the World Series.

"If I fall and die, speak well of me," Gill said.

Nicki chuckled.

Rajim harrumphed, as if that was the best possible outcome.

Gill climbed atop a large rock leaning against the mountainside. He reached for a handhold, slipped, and looked back at his companions, smiling. They watched him, Nicki's face painted with worry and Rajim doing his best to hide a thin smirk. He tried again, and this time found purchase and pulled himself up.

The climbing was slow as Gill was very careful. He tied off a safety line on vegetation clinging to the mountainside whenever he could and that slowed things down. He was halfway to the tunnel entrances when he realized soon the sun would go down and the valley would fall into dusk. They hadn't thought this out very well, but he'd gone too far to stop. His muscles cramped, and he was thirsty, hungry and tired. He stopped several times, stretching and letting the rope take some of his weight. It creaked and popped, and he dropped a few feet when a section of the mountainside gave way and just missed hitting him in the head.

After an hour of climbing Gill pulled himself into the tunnel. Darkness spilled from the cave, and he drew out his flashlight and shone it into the tunnel. Grey rock striated with silver and gold disappeared around a bend.

He tied the rope off on a rock and threw the other end down to Nicki and Rajim. With the guide rope, Nicki was able to scale the mountain much faster, and after a few scrapes and falls she arrived in the tunnel. She was nervous, but relieved.

Rajim had a harder time. The man struggled to climb each foot, his fear of heights crippling him. But Gill knew there was no way Rajim would leave Nicki alone with him, and he and Nicki watched as Rajim fought his way up the mountainside. When he reached the top, he rolled over the edge into the tunnel and said, "Showoffs."

Gill decided to let that go, and didn't taunt the man.

The tunnel twisted and turned randomly. There were no stalactites or stalagmites. The walls were mostly smooth, as if the cave had been drilled from the stone with a bent drill bit. Veins of gold and silver and other metals Gill couldn't identify ran through the stone, and in places the walls were wet. Insects, centipedes and the mini-roaches with green eyes scuttled about, but paid them no mind. They trekked for over an hour when Gill said, "Do either of you have any idea what direction we're traveling in now?"

"Good luck with that," Rajim said.

Gill paused to take a drink of water, panning his flashlight down the tunnel. Nothing could be seen except the grey walls and the patch of blackness in the distance.

Gill glanced down at his watch: 4:51PM. "This thing doesn't look like it's going to end anytime soon. You think we should go back?"

Rajim started, his flashlight falling to the floor and scattering the bugs. "Back? This is the best chance to get out of here that we've found."

"Agreed, but I think I know what Gill is worrying about. Night is coming. We hardly have any supplies. This tunnel could take days to investigate," Nicki said.

"What are you suggesting?" Rajim said.

"We go back, camp on the ground for the night, and set off fresh in the morning," Gill said. "We rushed in here, and didn't think about how long we might be in the tunnel. If the path out takes days to traverse as it twists through the mountains, what will we eat and drink? Provisions need to be prepared and packed. Torches in case our batteries fail, and other things I haven't thought of yet." Gill's father's voice echoed in his head. That stern voice that guided him when nothing else would. Sometimes a step back is two steps forward, his father had often said. He hadn't understood what that meant when he was a boy, but now it was one of the principles that shaped his life. He said, "Pushing onward for the sake of pushing forward is a fool's errand."

Nicki nodded.

"I'm heading back. You guys do what you want," Gill said. He turned and headed back the way they'd come.

Muffled bickering and whispers filled the tunnel, then "Gill. Wait up."

Gill turned to see Nicki's flashlight beam bobbing in the darkness. Behind her was Rajim's.

Wind whistled through the tunnel, and to Gill it sounded like laughter. He dug in his pocket and felt the cool rubber of Brian's little sneaker. His eyes watered as he thought of his son, turning the shoe over and over.

When they reached the end of the tunnel, Rajim sighed and cleared his throat as he watched his wife mount the lead line and start her belay back to the ground. Rajim went next, and soon Gill stood alone in the cave mouth, staring out across the valley as dusk settled over the land.

Two great beasts wrestled and fought in the clearing before the lake, and their cries and yips filled the valley. He grasped the rope, and carefully belayed down the side of the mountain, pushing off slowly at first, then picking up speed as he got comfortable.

"See, that wasn't so bad, and with the lead line in place, climbing back up will be easy," Gill said.

Nicki and Rajim said nothing as the three companions ate the last of their dinosaur meat, drank their water, and settled in for the night. Unlike the prior night, there was no merrymaking or tequila.

They made camp within a ring of boulders out of the wind, and Gill lay alone in his sleeping bag, his stomach a frenzy of worry. When he heard Nicki snoring, and the patter of Rajim's footfalls as he walked around camp, he closed his eyes and tried to sleep. Despite his angst and worry, he fell off in moments.

19

Gill slept fitfully. His family came to him in his dreams, which always began in a pleasant way, but ended with his wife dead and his son ripped apart. He'd woken sweating and disorientated, and for an instant believed the last nine days had been nothing but a dream. Then he saw the green neoprene stretched overhead and heard the cries of the beasts of the valley. Depression and sadness choked him.

It hadn't gotten better as everyone said it would. Gill wondered if he'd ever be able to sleep well again, but didn't really care. He found comfort in the pain. He was supposed to be in pain, what other state was there? The idea that he didn't deserve to be happy, or joyful, or have feelings for another woman made sense to him, and guilt clogged his mind when he pitied himself. In those moments, he wished the *velociraptors* had taken him as they had Clint.

He crawled from his tent to find Nicki filling their water bottles. She stood at ease by the mountainside, holding a stainless-steel bottle under a trickle of water.

"Yo," he said. "Sleep well?" He'd asked out of politeness, because he could plainly see she hadn't. Dark bags below her eyes, the way she leaned against the cliff face, her posture that of a deflated balloon, all accented her weariness.

"Not really, you?" she said. Rajim's loud snore punctuated the question.

"Rajim didn't have any issues," he said.

"Don't be so hard on him. He's just jealous of…"

"What exactly?"

"Why, you of course."

"Me?" Gill's laughter was forced. "I can see that. I am in an envious position. Wife dead. Son dead. Retired Army unemployable techie with no job prospects and trapped in a valley with prehistoric monsters that shouldn't exist. Yeah, I can see how that would appeal to people."

"Not that. It…"

"What?" It was Rajim.

Gill and Nicki's heads jerked toward the sound. Rajim was standing outside his tent, watching them, eyes narrowed. "What?"

Nicki looked at Gill, and said, "Nothing. We were just chatting."

"Yeah," he said. He dragged his pack out of the tent and got a power bar, their last, and started eating it without offering any to Nicki and Gill. When Rajim came to take one of the full water bottles, Nicki pulled it from his grasp.

"You can get your own," she said, and went to drop her tent.

"Nice. See what you did?" Rajim said to Gill.

With each passing second Gill saw the confrontation between himself and Rajim drawing closer. Clearly the man blamed him for the problems he and Nicki were having, and it was only a matter of time before his frustration overflowed.

A wail echoed through the forest. Gill got the M16, made sure it was loaded, and called out to his companions. "I'm going hunting."

"OK," said Nicki. "I'll get a fire going so we can cook and smoke the meat."

Gill shouldered his gun and headed down the slope that led to the forest. Despite the morning sun, thick mist still hung like a blanket under the tree canopy, and visibility was poor. Tiny green birds with streaks of yellow and brown fluttered about, and rodents and other small creatures darted about the forest floor, scattering like roaches when Gill came near.

A high-pitched trilling filled the woods, and Gill followed the sound. Three ostrich-like dinosaurs pecked at the carcass of an unrecognizable animal, screeching and snapping at each other.

A fight broke out, and while two of the beasts wrestled and bit at each other, the third continued eating.

Gill knelt behind a hedge of bushes and eased the M16 off his shoulder. He flicked the firing selector to burst and sighted the head of the chowing animal. He breathed deep, easing his nerves. He eliminated the sound of the wind, the rattle of tree leaves, and the buzz of insects. He closed his right eye and pulled the trigger.

Three shots severed the dinosaur's head from its long neck. Blood pulsed from the beast's neckline, its head hitting the ground with a thud. The headless creature ran around the clearing, spooking the other two before it slowed, and toppled over. The other two scattered into the trees.

Gill shouldered his rifle and went to the fallen animal. He needed to gut and dress the dinosaur before its internal organs spoiled the meat. He pushed the dead beast onto its side, and using his hunting knife, slit the beast's chest open. He was pulling organs out, his hands covered in blood, when he heard the rustle of tree branches behind him.

"Hey, look—" Gill froze, and if he could've disappeared, he would have.

The thin lizard head of a *spinosaurus* stuck from the trees, its dark eyes watching him, jaws slightly open, revealing a smile of teeth. The dinosaur bent low and sniffed at the ground, as if searching for Gill, who didn't move.

The beast threw its head side to side, stomped its feet and roared. The *spinosaurus* wasn't as big as the mom and dad he'd seen the prior day, but it was bigger than the younglings. The dinosaur stepped forward, half out of the trees. Its sail-like back vertebrae was caught on tree branches that had momentarily stopped its progress. The *spinosaurus* shook and wiggled, freeing itself, and Gill used the time to crouch behind the fallen carcass he was butchering. Realizing hiding behind blood covered meat might not be the smartest move, he backed toward the forest.

The *spinosaurus* squawked and pounded its right foot. The ground trembled and Gill brought the rifle up and fired, catching the beast in its right leg as it sprang at him, mouth snapping.

The beast missed, reared up and screamed, blood pumping from the wound in its leg. It bent low, jaws opening as the white gleam of teeth came at Gill.

He dropped and rolled, and the *spinosaurus*'s jaws snapped closed with a deafening crack. Slime dripped from the beast's mouth onto Gill's face, but he didn't move. He was a dead branch, an old bone, a pile of leaves. The spino wouldn't see him. It would move on.

For a moment it appeared that Gill's fantasy might come true. The great beast lifted its yellow and green head, eyes rolling away from him. It squealed as if in pain, and took a step back, and that's when the dinosaur saw him.

The spino roared, and Gill rolled and didn't stop until he hit the prickly leaves of an evergreen. He laid under its protective branches for a heartbeat, sucking in breaths, sweat dripping into his eyes. The top of the tree disappeared, and Gill had a flashback to his encounter with the T-rex.

As if on cue, a mournful wail echoed over the valley and the *spinosaurus* paused, lifting its head and sniffing the air. Gill vaulted to his feet and ran deeper into the woods, running wildly through the thick forest, tree branches scraping his face and arms, pain lancing his back. There was no sound of pursuit and Gill slowed, looking over his shoulder, the memory of his fight with the T-rex coming back in stuttering bursts. The T-rex had gone around the forest and cut him off. Was that how the beasts hunted within the confines of the forest? Chase their prey onto a known path and catch them at the other end?

Gill backtracked and found that the animal hadn't gone around, but instead stood eating his kill. It took the great beast two bites and a week's meat supply was gone. Now he'd have to keep hunting. He eased back into the forest, tripped over a branch and stumbled. Gill fell into an evergreen and branches snapped and swayed.

The *spinosaurus* turned in his direction. Its jaws fell open, and it made a clicking sound. He brought up the M16, then thought better of firing. It would take several shots to even have a hope of putting the huge creature down, and it was a risk.

He turned and ran, cutting through the trees and doing his best to take random turns to throw the beast off. The sound of breaking trees followed, and this time when he looked over his shoulder he saw the beast struggling through the woods after him.

The forest thinned, and Gill searched for a place to hide. The dinosaur would be free of the dense forest in moments, and he'd be exposed. Evergreens dotted the clearing, and large flowers with yellow and red firework tops provided a pleasant smell to push away the constant scent of sulfur and scat.

There was nowhere to hide, and he wouldn't make to the far side of the clearing before the *spinosaurus* caught him. As he ran, he felt the bulge of Brian's shoe in his pocket and rage rose in him like a tide. The beasts had taken his son—not this specific animal—but what was the difference? Brian was gone, and Gill's emotional pendulum swung yet again. He wanted nothing more than to kill every beast in the valley.

Gill stopped running, turned and dropped to one knee. He brought up the M16, and waited, heart hammering.

Snapping branches and the titter of fleeing birds preceded the *spinosaurus*, and when it burst from the forest Gill held his fire. He wanted it to come at him. Come in close so he could aim for the beast's forehead and eyes.

The creature turned its massive head as it searched the sparse trees, and when it saw Gill, it bent low, bringing its head almost to the ground. It sniffed and shook like a dog trying to dry off. Blood still trickled from the beast's leg, and Gill saw bone poking through the yellow and green skin.

The *spinosaurus* came at him, and Gill flicked the M16 to single shot and fired.

The bullet hit the dinosaur in the right eye and its head jerked back as if punched, but it recovered and came on. Gill fired again. And again. And again.

The fourth shot blew the side of the beast's skull apart, and the dinosaur ran on for a few seconds, slowed, then toppled onto its side with a crash and a cloud of dust. The *spinosaurus* lay still, and its last breath pushed the rank smell of rot into Gill's face.

The creature lay twenty feet from where he knelt aiming the gun. He breathed rabidly, the fog of battle still upon him. The dead animal spasmed, and Gill fell backward, startled. He sat there, waiting, but the dead animal didn't move again.

Gill got to his feet, and leaving the beast where it had fallen, went in search of his companions. He could come back and retrieve meat if there was any to be had. The *spinosaurus* looked to be all corded muscle, but food was food.

He threaded through the forest, making for the edge of the valley marked by the sheer cliff face. He saw his yellow and brown rope hanging from the lowest of the three cave entrances. They might have escaped by now if they'd kept going.

When Gill reached the spot where he'd left Nicki and Rajim, he couldn't find them, and there was no sign of where they'd gone. Their packs were gone, supplies and water bottles. Gill leaned against the mountainside. "Great. Just great."

20

Gill sat with his back to a stone, staring into the forest and listening for his companions. He felt vulnerable, and he was tired, hungry and thirsty. Loneliness seeped over him like a fever, and the tips of his ears grew hot. The pit of his stomach was cold, and angst snaked into him like a worm. He'd heard no gunshots, no cries or wails of beasts. Perhaps his friends had heard the commotion of his fight and ventured into the woods to assist him? They could have passed in the dense forest.

He got to his feet and searched the area. There were many footprints, but it was impossible to tell new from old. The tracks crisscrossed and disappeared into the forest in several spots. He'd have to follow each trail if he hoped to find which direction his friends had gone. There was no blood on the ground, so whatever had caused his friends to move on hadn't hurt them. If Rajim and Nicki had gone in search of him, wouldn't they return here? To his last known location? What if they'd been run off and were being pursued? They might need help. Gill sighed and rubbed his forehead.

A roar echoed off the mountains, and a shrill cry beckoned back. How long should he wait? Nicki and Rajim couldn't have gone far, he'd only been gone an hour.

Gill was in the middle of his second search of the area when a gunshot rang out in the distance. The shot had come from the east, but in the narrow valley soundwaves bounced around. It sounded no more than a mile away. Gill headed back to the cliff face. Once beneath his rope, he eased the M16 from his shoulder and made sure it was set on single shot. He fired into the air. The shot silenced the trilling insects and chirping birds, and as if the kings of the valley had to prove they wouldn't be intimidated, a series of squawks, grunts and primal roars replied.

He leaned his gun on a boulder, and drank some water.

An hour later his companions still hadn't returned, and he was starting to worry. They'd surely heard his shot. Was there a reason they couldn't come? Gill was considering going to his original search plan when Nicki and Rajim strolled from the forest.

"Thank the man upstairs," Gill said.

"He had nothing to do with it," Rajim said.

"What happened?" Gill said.

"Happened?" Nicki said. "We went to look for food. I thought maybe we'd find acorns or some green stuff."

"We thought you'd be gone for a bit. We heard your gunshots and figured you were doing well," Rajim said.

"Everything OK?" Nicki said.

"I had another close call. *Spinosaurus*. Thing tried to bite my head off, but I got it," Gill said.

"Any meat on something that big and muscular?" Rajim said.

"That's why I came back here. I need help craving this thing up. We need to hurry before the meat goes bad," Gill said.

"You didn't gut it?" Nicki said.

Gill sighed. "I was shaken, and I came back looking for you guys with the intention of heading right back there with you, but when I got here, and you were gone, I decided to fire a warning shot and wait. The thing is big," Gill said.

"Look what Nicki got," Rajim said.

Nicki held up three grouse and a rabbit, all gutted and skinned and ready for cooking.

"Nice. Some real food," Gill said. "Surprised to see the grouse with all these predators around."

"There's a lot of them and they multiply like mosquitoes," Rajim said. "Nicki and I killed those three with stones. Could've had more rabbit too but she didn't want to waste ammo."

"Grouse, the lost valley's chicken," Nicki said.

The companions built a fire and roasted Nicki's kills until they were charred and cooked through. They ate the rabbit and packed the cooked grouse.

"Do you think we need more food?" Nicki asked.

Gill shrugged. "There wasn't much meat on the birds. If we're in that tunnel for more than a day, we'll run out."

"I'd rather not hunt again," Rajim said.

"He's right. Every time we go in those woods we're taking a risk," Nicki said.

"We can go get some meat from my *spinosaurus* kill," Gill said. "Unless animals of the valley have feasted on it."

"How far we talking?" Nicki said.

"Not far. Half a mile, maybe, and I know the way," Gill said.

Rajim sighed in frustration.

"What?" Gill said.

"Are we making this more complicated than it needs to be again? I want out of the valley ASAP," Rajim said.

"I'll go with you, Gill," she said.

Rajim sighed again. "Not happening. You wait here, and Gill and I will go."

"You gonna shoot this time if I need you to?" Gill said.

Rajim didn't answer. He shouldered his rifle and stalked off into the trees. Then realizing he had no idea where he was going, stopped and waited for Gill just inside the tree break.

Gill and Nicki exchanged a "why is this guy such an asshole" glance. "Keep the fire going, we'll be back in a half hour."

It was cooler beneath the tree canopy, and the smell of rot pervaded the air. Rajim leaned against a tree and waited for Gill to pass. He said, "Why you gotta bust my balls? Make it seem like I'm afraid to fire my gun?"

"We've been in some tight spots and you haven't fired, and I want to know why. Has nothing to do with trying to embarrass you in front of Nicki. You seem to be doing that just fine all by yourself." Gill knew he should have left off that last part.

"I've got eight bullets left, and when you're throwing rocks I'll still have eight bullets and you can kiss my ass."

"And your wife?"

"Leave Nicki out of this," Rajim said. "You know she feels sorry for you, right? If it weren't—"

They'd stepped from the trees and the *spinosaurus* corpse lay in the center of a clearing. The corpse looked undisturbed.

Rajim stumbled forward, eyes the size of quarters. His mouth fell open a crack, and his head twitched like he'd been shocked. "I need a minute." He disappeared into the trees leaving Gill alone.

Gill pulled his knife and stripped skin off the dinosaur's breast. The dead animal was laying on its side, and Gill cut from the top of the carcass, slicing off thin strips. The meat smelt earthy and good, and when he had a few pounds he packed it in the plastic wrap from Rajim's sandwich.

Rajim returned and said, "You sure the meat is OK?" His tone had shifted. His eyes burned and he wore a smirk that reminded Gill of a little kid who had stolen candy or successfully hunted down Christmas presents.

"Yeah," Gill said. Why did he even bother with the guy?

"Just more bullshit?" Rajim pressed.

"No, not bullshit." Gill pointed. "I took the meat from up here. The blood has been draining for the last two hours. You know, gravity and shit?"

Rajim said nothing.

"I got three or four pounds. Let's go get it smoked so we can get out of this valley. In the meantime, keep your mouth shut."

Rajim raised his jaw, but said nothing.

"Let's go," Gill said. He was happy for the quiet. Rajim required so much patience Gill didn't know much more he had. That fight was on the horizon, as sure as it would snow come November.

Three turkey sized birds watched as they entered the woods, but when Gill moved they fluttered away. He felt a bit like Bambi when she emerged into the forest for the first time. He was an oddity. A creature that had never been seen in the valley.

He stepped over a stone and the lump in his pocket bit into his leg. Brian's sneaker. With all the problems, arguments and tasks of survival, he hadn't thought about his son, the reason he'd come here. The reason they'd all come.

Now it was down to Nicki, Rajim, and himself, from nine. He hoped Belinda's wound was healing and that a rescue team was on its way to find them. They'd get a helicopter. Climbers. Drones. All the things they should've had before they started the search for Brian. Gill told himself that maybe if they'd had all those things Brian wouldn't have been killed, but he knew that was bullshit. He'd done everything he could. It had been his son's fate to die in these mountains in the jaws of a prehistoric beast. He couldn't make sense of things any other way.

If anyone said it was God's plan, or the will of God, he might end up in jail for murder. He didn't want thoughts and prayers. He wanted his boy back, and no God, real or imagined, could bring him back.

Wind pushed through the trees and Gill turned Brian's shoe over and over in his pocket, the pain eating him up, burning his stomach. Then came the rage. The hatred. The willingness to give his life to exterminate every last living thing in the valley.

Ahead, the mountainside loomed above the trees, and Gill saw his rope dangling from the lowest cave mouth. He wondered if they were three separate caves or if the three tunnels connected inside the mountain. It was time to find out.

Nicki stood huddled against the cliff face, drinking water and filling their water pouch from a thin trickle running down the mountainside. Gill got a chill, and he didn't like the look Rajim gave him.

"Yo, got some solid meat. Not t-bones, but they'll do," Gill said.

"Thanks," Nicki said.

"No worries. We're good for a while now," Gill said.

"Mr. Provider," Rajim said. "The man." His eyelids hung half closed and his shoulders slumped.

Gill put the *spinosaurus* meat on tree branches and smoked them over the fire. When they were done he cut the dried meat into chunks and put it in the empty beef jerky bag. The process killed another hour. He kicked dirt onto the fire, closed-up his pack, filled his water bottle, checked the M16 and grabbed their bundle of supplies.

"You guys ready to roll? We're losing daylight." The sun was almost past the lip of the broken ice ceiling, and soon grey dusk would settle over the valley. They couldn't lose another day. Gill was sure that if they waited until the next day to enter the cave some other circumstance would prevent them.

"You first?" Rajim said. "Our fearless leader."

Gill slipped the M16 strap over a shoulder, trussed his pack, and started to climb.

21

Gill and Nicki waited for Rajim. He struggled up the mountainside, the rope twisting and jerking as he fought his way to the cave mouth. The party's footprints in the dust and dirt from their prior incursion trailed into the darkness, and a fowl breeze of rot and sulfur pushed through the tunnel. Gill shifted on his feet. His legs hurt. He'd done more walking and running in the last ten days then he'd done in the past ten months, and without enough food and water, or the valley's magic gas, his body was rebelling. Cramps, the bottoms of his feet stung, sharp pain in his neck and back, all contributed to his brooding mood.

"Hey, snap out of it," Nicki said. "If I lose you, I'm toast."

"Lose me?"

"You seem like you're on the verge of checking out, and Rajim and I can't handle this alone. I can't handle him alone in here."

Gill said nothing. On some level he knew Nicki no longer loved Rajim, but that didn't mean she loved him, and it certainly didn't mean she was going to leave her husband. Things were complicated when children were involved, and if Gill knew Nicki as well as he thought he did, she would never do anything to hurt her kids. If there was one certainty in the world, it was that when parents got divorced the children paid the price.

There was also Reserve to consider. In many ways their small mountain town existed in another era, away from the modern world and the trials and tribulations it brought. At its core, Reserve was a catholic town, and religious folk didn't hold well with divorce, and Nicki was an elected official. His parents had been forced to get an annulment after nineteen-years of marriage to remain in the church, essentially saying their nuptials didn't exist. Did that mean he shouldn't exist?

"Are you OK?" She brushed hair away from his eyes, then realized what she'd done and pulled her hand away and stepped quickly back.

Gill smelled her sweat and the scent of her fading perfume. They were a foot away from each other in the cave mouth. He was sweating, the heat between them undeniable, but it had to be denied.

Rajim struggled over the lip of the tunnel mouth and rolled onto his back, breathing hard. "I don't ever want to do that again," he said.

Gill and Nicki each took a step back. Rajim didn't appear to notice.

"Let's go," Gill said. "I want to make some progress today."

"Go ahead. I'll catch up," Rajim said as he coiled the rope and put it in his pack.

"No," Nicki said. "We're not splitting up."

"Fine." Rajim made a show of getting up, hoisting his back and whimpering with pain.

This wasn't the man of an hour before. Rajim's confidence was gone. The feeling returned that Rajim was hiding something. Something his wife didn't even know about.

"Let's go," Nicki said. She bent to help Rajim to his feet, but he brushed her off.

"I'm fine," he said.

They walked for hours in the dark, Gill's flashlight beam lighting the way. The cockroach bugs scuttled about, and Gill saw a rat or two, but there were no other dangers. The cave was damp, and the sound of dripping water echoed through the tunnel, though the party came across no water.

The tunnel twisted and turned, rose and fell, and Gill had no idea what direction they were traveling in. When they'd entered the cave they'd been heading south, but now he couldn't even guess.

The veins of gold and silver ended, and the cave walls were a dull grey-black that didn't alter in color or texture.

"You think this is an ancient lava tube?" Nicki asked.

"How could it be?" Gill said.

"I don't know. Maybe from when the mountains formed?"

"Maybe," Gill said. He stopped walking to take a drink of water and handed the bottle to Nicki.

It was then they noticed Rajim was gone.

"Rajim! Rajim!" Nicki called.

"Yeah," Rajim said. He came into the light, a smile painted on his face.

"You need a rest?" Gill asked.

"No. You?" His voice was sarcastic and tinged with anger.

"Just keep up, will you?" Nicki said.

"Sure thing, boss."

A tingle ran up Gill's spin.

The tunnel made a sharp right turn, and plunged downward. Gill and Rajim slipped on the steep floor and tumbled down the tunnel together. Nicki managed not to fall, but tripped over the two men as they lay tangled.

"Shit on me," Rajim said as he got up and brushed himself off.

"Gladly," Gill said.

"Man, you really are—"

"Look at this," Nicki said.

She clicked on her flashlight and panned it over the cave wall revealing intricate drawings.

Gill shined his light on the wall and whistled. "Dang, so there were people in here at one point."

"So it would seem," Rajim said. "So what?"

Nicki and Gill ignored him as they examined the cave drawings.

They were primitive, but extremely detailed scenes that spanned many years. "It looks like a timeline," Gill said.

"Yes," Nicki said.

There were eleven drawings. The first a grouping of stick figures walking toward what looked like a sunset. White lines shot from a circle like sunrays. Then a picture of stick figures climbing a mountain, and another of the stick figures fighting.

"Looks like they had a disagreement on how to move forward," Gill said.

"Notice how there are less figures in the next scene?"

Gill and Nicki moved down the tunnel, leaving Rajim in darkness.

The next four scenes showed tents in the valley, and various gatherings that appeared to be ceremonies. Then a drawing showing the stick figures fighting what looked like the T-rex or the *spinosaurus*. The next few scenes were unclear, but it was the last image that made Gill scratch his head.

Stick figures stood in the center of a clearing surrounded by crude drawings of trees. The figures were holding up their arms and some were bowing. In the center of the scene was an object with lines like sunlight shooting from it.

"Praying to their God?" Nicki said.

"Maybe," he said, but Gill didn't think so. Whatever the ancient inhabitants of the valley were worshiping, it didn't look like a person.

"Can we go now?" Rajim said.

Gill glanced at his watch. It was 4:51PM and there was no end to the tunnel in sight. "Yeah," Gill said.

They walked for five more hours as the tunnel twisted and turned through the mountain. Gill's feet hurt, and blisters stabbed his heels. His watch read 9:59PM. "I'm almost done. You want to eat and hunker down to rest?" Gill said.

Nicki looked scared in the flashlight beam, the dark bags beneath her eyes standing out. She looked around for Rajim and found him gone again. "What the hell is it with him? Why the—"

"Right here. You need something?" Rajim said. As before, he slipped from the darkness, a smile on his face like he'd caught Gill and Nicki in some uncompromising position.

"You ready to rest?" Nicki asked.

"I'm hungry, I know that. Where are we gonna sleep? On the ground?" Rajim asked.

"We've got all our gear. We can setup our tents if it makes you feel more... secure," Gill said. He had to stop poking the man, because eventually Rajim was going to deck him.

"Piss off," Rajim said. He dropped his pack and leaned against the cave wall, his face disappearing into darkness as he leaned back out of the flashlight beam.

"Righty oh," Gill said. He dropped his pack and broke out the food rations and passed a strip of dino meat to Nicki, then Rajim, both of whom accepted the meat and ate greedily. Gill's piece was tough, and tasted like ass, but he forced it down. When he was done he put up his tent and unrolled his sleeping bag.

"Where should we... umm... you know?" Rajim said.

"No, I don't know," Gill said.

"Where should I take a shit? That plain enough for you?" Rajim said.

Nicki said, "Head back up the tunnel the way we came."

"Make sure you go a long way, I don't want to smell it all night and who knows what creatures might be stirred by your rank crap," Gill said.

"Either of you got any leaves?"

Gill sighed. The man was an infant. "I do." Gill went to his bag and retrieved two green leaves. He'd brought a stack just for this purpose along with a tiny bundle of kindling in case they needed a fire. He'd also packed a few sticks that could be made into torches at need.

Rajim took the leaves without so much as a thank you and stormed off into the darkness.

Gill said, "What's going on with him? His mood swings are worse than an infant's."

"I'm not sure... but something's up. Maybe just his reaction to the trauma we've been through? We spend all our time surviving, so we forget we watched Clint get eaten and we're in a situation we might not get out of. That kind of stress takes a toll."

She stood next to Gill and heat rolled off her.

"Doesn't appear to have affected us," Gill said.

"You're stronger than he is, Gill. You've been through so much. Dealt with so much pain. The worst thing Rajim has had to deal with is..." She paused to think. "Being here, I guess."

"Which is bad," Gill said. "What is it with you two? Seems you can't stand each other."

She sighed. "There was an... incident."

Gill's eyebrows rose.

"I've never told anyone. I..." Tears welled in her eyes, and she took a step closer to him.

He rubbed his hands together and coughed to hide his discomfort.

"It's just... I feel like I can tell you anything."

Gill said nothing.

She blurted, "He hit me." She looked at him, trying to appraise his thoughts by the expression on his face. She flinched, not liking what she saw there.

"Hit you?"

"It's not as bad as it sounds. We'd had a really bad fight, he'd been drinking, and he slapped me. He cried like a baby after."

"Jesus."

"Yeah. Things haven't been the same since, but things hadn't been good for a long time."

Gill said nothing.

"Do you ever wonder... I mean, do you ever think about me?" She turned away. "I'm sorry. I mean, do you think..."

Gill took her hand and she faced him. "I think I know what you're trying to ask, but I'm not comfortable answering."

"Why?"

"You're married, and Abigale has only been gone six months. I feel like... like..."

"You'd be cheating on her?"

"Something like that. But..." He took her other hand and pulled her close. Gill looked over his shoulder to make sure Rajim wasn't there, then said, "I do think of you. Too much, I'm afraid. We can't—"

She pulled him in and kissed him. Gill wrapped his arms around her, lost in the fantasy he'd had many times.

The sound of Rajim coming down the tunnel broke the spell, and Nicki and Gill pushed away from each other as he arrived.

"Now I feel better." His smile was back, and his red eyes gleamed.

The party crawled into their respective tents and slept. Gill heard Rajim's snores and the faint puff of Nicki's breathing. She'd kissed him. What did that mean? What did he want it to mean? These thoughts brought a smile to his face, and for the first time in a long while he slipped into his temporary death content.

Gill's watch alarm went off five hours later, and though the valley was still under the cover of night, that didn't matter inside the tunnel where it was perpetually dark. They ate breakfast, broke the makeshift camp, and continued on.

The party walked for several hours as the cave turned sharply downward and to the left. They'd seen no other side tunnels, not even cracks that bugs could crawl through.

Gill's watch read 10:19AM when the companions came around a bend and a wedge of light marked the tunnel's end.

Gill jogged in his excitement, then ran.

Nicki was the first to arrive at the exit, where Gill and Rajim found her with her mouth hanging open. Evergreens filled the hillside before them and above a broken ice sheet covered half the valley. Gill pulled out his binoculars and found their precipice.

The tunnel had taken them around to the opposite side of the valley.

22

Gill took a deep breath, then screamed as he balled his fists and jumped up and down like a toddler. Every decision he'd made since Brian was taken by the raptor had gone wrong. All the preparation, the planning, the climb. All for nothing.

"Calm down," Nicki said.

"We've been trapped in this valley four days—seven out from Reserve—and we haven't accomplished shit except basic survival," Gill said.

Rajim chuckled. "Laughing with you, Gill. How the hell did we go in a half circle?" he said. "We just can't get a break."

"Understatement of the century. Look down there," Nicki said.

There was no ledge or outcrop of stone jutting from the mountainside at the end of the tunnel like the precipice they'd enjoyed upon arrival in the valley. The sheer cliff face plunged seventy feet straight down and ended in a pile of stones half submerged in the still lake that ran to the cliff face's base on the northwestern edge of the vale.

From their new vantage point the party had an excellent view of the entire valley. The flat lake reflected the blue cloud-filled sky and the broken ice roof. Evergreens packed the valley floor, with an occasional open patch of dirt or grass. Gill drew out his binoculars and examined their precipice, and he wondered if the emergency radio was charged. No large animals or dinosaurs could be seen stomping about below. All was quiet.

"We'll have to climb down and skirt the edge of the lake," Rajim said.

"You sure about that?" Gill said.

"Why? You think there's something in the water?" Rajim said.

Gill eased to the end of the tunnel and examined the lake below. The water was clear, and nothing could be seen swimming within, yet his nerves jumped like he had spiders crawling all over him.

Rajim picked-up a pebble and dropped it in the lake. There was a faint *plop* and tiny ripples arced across the lake. Nothing surfaced or showed itself.

"You fool. Throw yourself in next time," Gill said.

"Besides the disturbance, what were you thinking?" Nicki said.

Rajim put his arm around his wife's waist and smiled at Gill, but said nothing.

Nicki shook him off.

"If there is something lying in the deep, do we want to disturb it? Shouldn't we be as quiet as possible?" Gill said.

Nicki nodded.

"Or we could go back," Rajim said.

"That your vote? Waste another day and half?" Gill said.

"We got nothing but time. Why risk it?"

Gill rolled his shoulders and flexed his hands. "I think we should climb down, quietly, and work our way along the cliff's edge. Take our time. Go slow and be silent. Should take less than an hour to get to shore if we're lucky."

Nicki laughed. "Lucky? You didn't just say that."

"But I did." Nicki and Gill laughed, and Rajim put on his sour face.

"I say we go back the way we came. Finish circumnavigating the valley from there," Rajim said.

It would be Nicki's choice then, which put her in a difficult position. Side with Gill and piss-off her husband, or side with Rajim. She didn't hesitate. "I think we should climb down. We've wasted too much time already and we're running out of food," she said.

Gill smiled at Rajim, and the man returned a glare.

"Of course, you do," Rajim said. He stalked back up the tunnel and disappeared into the darkness.

"What the hell does he do off by himself?" Gill said.

Nicki said nothing.

Rajim had left his pack so Nicki went through it and retrieved the coil of rope. The cave walls were smooth, and there was nothing to tie-off the line on. "How we gonna do this?" Nicki asked.

"I'll have to hold the rope for you and Rajim, then free climb," Gill said.

Nicki peered over the ledge. "Looks tough. There's a few footholds, but there's no place to tie off a safety line as you go down."

"What? Superman can't handle it?" Rajim was back and his mood had improved.

"Look folks, an asshat in its wild habitat," Gill said.

Rajim laughed loud and crazy, and Gill and Nicki exchanged lifted eyebrows.

"You sure you can hold our weight?" Nicki said.

"I can handle you easy enough," Gill said.

Rajim either didn't hear Gill, or ignored him, because he picked-up his pack and put it on, but said nothing.

"OK, then," Nicki said. "Let's do this."

She handed Gill the rope and he played it out through his fingers, letting the cordage slip down the rockface. When the end hit the boulders below, Gill said, "About thirty feet left, which means it's only seventy feet down."

"Only?" Nicki said as she stared over the lip of the tunnel mouth. "That's a six-story building."

"Don't fall then," Gill said. He tied a follow-through knot and slipped the loop around his waist, then braced against the wall. "Nicki, you're lightest, so why don't you go first so I can get a feel for this. Also, having Rajim around if things go bad isn't the worst thing."

Nicki nodded. Rajim leaned in for a kiss, but she turned away. Daggers shot from Rajim's eyes, and inwardly Gill smiled. If they got out of this alive, Rajim's life was going to change.

Nicki sat with her legs hanging over the edge, and she turned and laid on her stomach, the rope beneath her. She grabbed the line with both hands and inched off the ledge.

Gill slipped, but held her weight as the woman belayed down the side of the mountain. Rajim watched from the cave mouth, and Gill felt the tension in the rope ease when Nicki reached the bottom.

"All good," she yelled.

"You ready?" Gill said.

Rajim went to the cave mouth and peered down at his wife. "Be down in a minute, babe," he said. He turned on Gill. "While we have a moment alone, I just wanted to say something to you."

Silence in the tunnel save for the breathing of the two men.

"Back off my wife."

"Rajim, what—"

"Shut it, OK? I see you two. Guinevere and Lancelot. You and I will settle this when we're out of this mess, but for now, stay away from her." The man's eyes glowed red and his cheeks were flush with anger.

"Whatever," Gill said. "You ready to do this? I barely held her weight, so you might want to try and climb. I'm not going over the edge for you."

Rajim harrumphed, slung his rifle over his shoulder, grabbed the rope, and went over the edge.

Gill had an urge to untie the knot tethering the rope to him and let the man fall to his death. Gill didn't think Rajim would be missed, but then he remembered Kiki and Fred. They'd miss him, and it wasn't their fault their father was an ass. And there was the fact that he wasn't a murderer.

Rajim lurched on the rope as he half climbed, half belayed down the mountainside. After a minute the line went slack.

"He's down," Nicki said.

It was his turn. Gill undid the loop from around his waist and dropped the line and his pack down to Nicki and Rajim. He strapped the M16 over his back and got down on his belly, dangling his legs over the edge, and began working his way down the cliff face, going slowly.

He was only half way down when his hands and toes cramped. Most of his weight was on the tips of his toes and fingers as he found purchase in the smallest cracks. He slipped, and his heart hammered as he slid ten feet down the mountain face before his foot found a crack in the stone.

One movement at a time, he inched down, deliberate and calculated.

"Come on. I thought you said you could climb." Rajim's voice echoed off the stone.

"Shut up. Can't you see—"

"What's that?" Rajim said.

Gill looked down and saw Rajim and Nicki staring out at the lake, but he saw nothing in the clear water.

He had thirty feet to go when the pain in his fingers became so intense his muscles locked-up and he started to slide. He grasped vainly at the stone and fell, pushing off the cliff face with his feet at the last instant in an attempt to avoid the rocks directly below. He plummeted toward the lake, his reflection staring up at him from the still water.

Gill crashed into the lake and went under. He hit the bottom hard, the water at the lake's edge only three feet deep. Pain lanced his shoulder and hip, but he sat up and flexed his arms and legs.

Nicki was by his side, helping him out of the water onto the pile of stones at the edge of the lake. "You OK? That looked nasty."

The right side of his body stung, but nothing was broken, and he wasn't bleeding. "I think I'm alright," Gill said.

"Smart the way you pushed off as you fell, or you'd probably be dead," Nicki said.

"Yeah," Rajim said.

A miniature tsunami fanned out across the lake.

"So much for staying silent," Gill said.

"Can you move?" Nicki said.

"Yeah," Gill said. He got to his feet, dripping wet as pain ran through him. "Everything hurts."

Other than a few birds flying overhead, nothing appeared to have noticed the commotion and the three companions worked their way over boulders around the lake's edge. It was slow going, and Gill had to stop and rest several times. He had a nasty bruise on his hip, and his knee was screaming, but everything worked. Water dripped down the cliff face in several spots and the party stopped to drink and fill their bottles and eat some dino-jerky.

Gill couldn't stop glancing at the flat surface of the lake. Not so much as a shiner had shown itself in the clear water, and he'd never seen anything drink from the lake. The party had gone halfway to shore when widely spaced ripples rolled across the lake. The birds fled, and a hollow hum rose like a lighthouse warning signal.

"What's that noise?" Rajim said.

The ripples on the lake's surface grew larger as something rose from the depths. Water lapped against the boulders, and Nicki slipped. Gill grabbed her and stopped her plunging into the drink, but she didn't have a chance to thank him before Rajim was there, pulling them apart as he tried to assist his wife.

The awkward moment left Rajim and Gill face-to-face, each holding one of Nicki's arms. Gill looked into the man's red eyes and saw desperation and… something else.

"I've got her," Rajim said.

Gill let go of Nicki and straightened, and it pained him to do so. He felt alive when he touched her, as if she imparted some of her life energy to him every time they connected. She was another man's wife, and again he pushed his feelings deep and wondered how long he could keep this up? Living a lie and with Nicki so close. Guilt washed through him. Abigale had been dead less than a year.

The ripples in the lake became waves, and they snapped and popped as they broke on stone. The hum became louder and more consistent. Somewhere a great beast wailed as if in warning. Gill thought it sounded like momma T-rex. They still had a mile to go before they reached the shore, and he was already exhausted.

"Gill," Rajim said.

Gill ignored him and said nothing.

"Gill!" he repeated.

"What!" Gill hadn't meant to yell, but there it was. He turned to see what Rajim wanted.

The man gazed out on the lake, where a knot of water rose from the surface and rolled toward them.

23

Gill looked to the shore, but there was no way they'd make it in time and there was no going back. He gazed up, searching for climbing footholds, but there was nothing but the slick grey stone of the cliff face. There was nowhere to run and that meant they needed to make a stand.

"Guns at the ready," Gill yelled. He pulled the M16 from his shoulder and braced himself against the mountainside.

Nicki pulled free her Colt, but as she moved to brace herself, she slipped. Her hands shot out to stop her fall and the gun fell from her grasp into the lake. "Shiitttttttt," she yelled.

"No worries, Nicki," Gill said.

"Maybe you and I should try and hold the thing off while Nicki tries to make it to shore?" Rajim said.

Gill liked that idea. He and Rajim could distract the beast, whatever it was, with gunfire while Nicki got away. "OK."

Nicki looked to Gill, who nodded slightly. Rajim stared at her, but she didn't meet his eye. "Fine," she said.

With Nicki gone, Gill turned his attention back to the lake. The fist of water had doubled in size as it motored across the lake like a rising submarine. It was still five hundred yards out, but Gill thought he saw a white mouth filled with teeth just below the surface.

"Should we try and get a better position?" Rajim said. The man's mood had shifted yet again, and he looked scared and lost.

"Like where?" Gill wasn't far behind Rajim on the panic scale.

Rajim worked his way back along the cliff face the way they'd come until he reached one of the larger boulders, and began to climb.

The rock wasn't huge, but it would put him above the water. Judging by the size of the rolling mound coming at them he didn't think it would matter, but standing still and doing nothing certainly wouldn't help. So as he'd done more times than he'd like to admit, he followed Rajim.

The sun passed the lip of the broken ice ceiling and the grey of dusk settled over the valley. Gill watched Nicki struggle over stones, slipping and falling as she climbed in a panic. She was moving fast and had put a half mile between them. She might make it if he and Rajim could distract the beast for a few minutes. A crazy thought flitted through his mind, the adrenaline flooding his body: what would Nicki do if he and Rajim were killed? She'd be on her own. No gun. No supplies. His heart ached at the thought of her struggling to survive.

Three-foot waves crashed and Rajim and Gill got soaked. Gill watched Nicki as the waves pounded her. She grasped at the mountainside, but there was nothing, and she slipped and plunged into the water.

The knot of water adjusted its course and headed her way.

"Shit," Gill said.

"What?" Rajim asked.

Gill pointed and watched Rajim's mouth fall open a crack. "What do... what should we..." Rajim straightened and threw his head back. He lifted the rifle to his shoulder, sighted, and fired. The crack echoed off the mountainside and hit the lake with a *snap*.

A guttural wail rose from the lake and the mound of water doubled in size as the creature below writhed.

"Nice shot. Seven bullets left now, eh?" Gill said.

Rajim didn't answer.

The sea monster had shifted its course yet again and was locked on Gill and Rajim.

"Now what? Doesn't seem like the slug hurt it much," Rajim said.

Gill spared a glance for Nicki, who was climbing from the water, not looking back. She'd make it now, thanks to Rajim. That he hadn't been the one to save Nicki sat in his stomach like bad shrimp.

"Gill? You with me?"

"Yeah," Gill said through a fog. He was with him, but he didn't know for how long. Something in him screamed to let go, to let the monster take him to the abyss where he could finally rest, but then he saw Nicki struggling over stones and knew he had one more task. A purpose to live. He had to get Nicki back to her children.

With newfound confidence and purpose, he checked the M16 as he aimed at the mountain of water that rose ten feet from the lake's surface. He spared a glance for Nicki, who'd almost made it to shore.

The sea creature was two hundred yards out.

The beast's flat white head surfaced, mouth half open, teeth gleaming. Two opaque eyes stared forward, the rest of the animal's body submerged.

"You ready?" Gill said.

Rajim didn't even look his way.

The creature was a hundred yards out, its long white body torpedoing from the lake.

Gill hadn't prayed since Abigale's wake. He'd never been a religious man, but as a creature from another time came at him he begged God for a second chance. Just a little help. Nothing big. He knew his prayers would go unanswered, and he often wondered if his nonbelief was the reason why. Did you have to believe unconditionally for the mighty one to favor you with his assistance?

The beast screamed as it launched from the water, jaws snapping. It looked like a giant white crocodile with black scales, twenty feet long from the tip of its long tail to the front of its snout. Stubby legs were thrown back, cold eyes focused on Gill as he brought up the M16 and screamed with wild rage.

Gill fired three bursts of three, peppering the monster with bullets. The beast crashed into the mountainside, its jaws missing Rajim by five feet. The man screamed, put his rifle to the beast's head, and pulled the trigger.

Nothing happened. He'd forgotten to reload the gun.

The beast slid back into the water and roared, whitewater pounding the mountainside and knocking Gill and Rajim into the lake.

Gill struggled in the surging water and was thrown against the cliffside, and all his bruises and cuts throbbed. He saw white and bubbles as he was tossed in the tumult.

His chest hurt from holding his breath, and tiny stars blinked before him. He stroked hard, trying to surface, but instead hit bottom, his nose smacking a rock. Blood filled the water as Gill twisted and pushed off the lake bottom and surged upward. He broke the surface and realized he could stand.

Rajim surfaced just as the creature vaulted from the lake again, this time zeroing in on Rajim, but he was too fast. Rajim dove behind a boulder as the beast's jaws snapped closed behind him, and he wedged himself between two large stones as the dino-croc clawed and bit at the boulders, trying to get to its prey.

Gill remembered the M16. It had been underwater for a few seconds. He worried it might not fire, and he only had two bullets left. He aimed at the creature's head as it attacked Rajim's hiding place.

A shrill cry rose above the chaos. Nicki had screamed. She'd made it to the shoreline, but was being chased by a snake that looked to be fifty feet long and two feet thick. She shrieked again as she ran across the grey rock beach, her hair flying behind her. Why doesn't she shoot it? Gill thought, only to remember she'd dropped her gun in the lake.

The giant gator thrashed and heaved, giving up on Rajim and diving back into the shallow water, sending a deluge into Gill.

Gill scrambled over boulders, searching for a hiding place.

The beast circled. It was so large it walked on the lake bottom, the shallow water nothing more than a puddle. It threw its narrow head back and wailed, eyes rolling, seven-inch dagger-like teeth filling the open jaws.

Gill wedged himself in a crack in the mountain face, rifle before him. The creature came at him, and Gill aimed inside the beast's mouth and fired.

The dino-croc roared in pain and missiled at Gill only to miss and smash into the mountainside. Rocks fell, the lake erupted, and Gill was splattered with blue blood. The great beast twitched, but didn't roll over and die. It eased back into the water, watching.

More screams from Nicki as she ran across Gill's line of sight. The huge snake lifted its head and struck, trying to take a bite of Nicki, but the woman was being smart. Like the snake, she didn't move in a straight line, but instead zigzagged across the hardpan, throwing the snake off her trail.

Rajim was still in his hiding spot and Gill couldn't see him. The creature lay motionless in the lake, not dead, but watching. Blood filled the water, and for an instant Gill thought the animal might die where it lay.

Hearing his wife's screams, Rajim emerged from his hiding spot, sighted the snake and fired twice. Two puffs of dust rose next to the snake. He'd missed, but the giant serpent had stopped pursuing Nicki. It raised its head and stared out over the lake, and then went to the ground looking for her, but she'd disappeared into the forest.

Gill took a deep breath. Nicki was safe, and he found that was really all he cared about. He did love her, despite the numerous reasons he shouldn't.

Croczilla inched back from the mountainside, and blood clouded the water as it slipped deeper into the lake.

"Rajim, let's go. This is our chance," Gill said.

"Did you kill it?"

"I don't know, but I got it pretty good."

"If it's not dead, I'm not leaving my bunker," Rajim said.

Never? Gill thought. He said, "Your call. I'm going to find Nicki." Gill figured that would jolt the man into motion, and so it did. The two companions struggled over the piles of stones as fast as they were able, which wasn't very fast. Gill didn't want to end up in the drink again. He was bruised, hungry, and tired.

On shore the giant serpent was nowhere to be seen, but neither was Nicki. Gill looked back over his shoulder, but saw no sign of croczilla. The lake had gone still.

"Smart shooting."

"I missed," Rajim said.

"I know, but you bought her time to escape," Gill said.

Rajim looked away and said nothing.

Gill wanted to think of Rajim as a fool, a dullard, but the man was smart. It was a shame he was such an asshole.

They reached the shoreline without further incident and both men called for Nicki, well aware that it might bring unwanted guests. They called, and they called, but Nicki didn't answer.

24

The grey of dusk settled over the valley as Rajim hunted and called for his wife. The rocky shoreline stretched around the lake, and Gill saw no footprints in the patches of silt between stones. He sat on a rock and let his head fall into his hands.

His head jerked up when water lapped on the shore, and memories of croczilla rushed back like the tide. Gill got up and backed away from the water. Crocodiles were amphibians and Gill assumed dino-croc could walk on land, though he saw no signs of the beast along the shoreline.

"Nicki! Nicki!" Rajim yelled.

It was only a matter of time before his crooning brought company, and Gill didn't think he could handle any more fighting without some food and sleep. What the hell were they going to fight with, anyway? The M16 had one bullet left, Nicki had lost her handgun, and Rajim, if Gill's count was right, had stayed true to his plan and had five shots left. What would they do? Make spears and bows and arrows? He sighed. Did it really matter? The guns had been wet and bullets didn't have enough punch to put down the big boys anyway.

"Gill," Nicki said as she strode from the forest. "Is that thing gone?"

In all the commotion he'd forgotten about the serpent. "I... I don't know. Are you OK?"

"Yeah. You?"

"I'll live I suppose."

"There you are," Rajim said as he approached. He put his arm around Nicki and kissed her on the cheek and she didn't move away. It was amazing what a little trauma could wipe away.

"You alright?" she asked.

"Fine now that you're OK," Rajim said.

"Who fired that shot that saved my butt?" she said.

"Me. I missed, but we got lucky," Rajim said.

"He's being modest. They were good shots from that distance," Gill said. "Where'd you learn how to shoot?"

Rajim said nothing as he shifted from foot to foot and stared at the ground.

"We should find a spot to rest up and eat," Nicki said. "There's a conifer in the forest with wide bows that droop to the ground. We can hide under there. Nothing will find us," she said.

But what can they smell? Gill thought, but he said nothing.

Without discussion the three companions picked up their stuff and headed for the forest. The trill of birds and buzz of insects had returned, and creatures big and small chuffed and wailed from within the forest. Dusk was deepening, and soon it would be dark and their fifth day in the valley would come to a close.

The woods were thick, and the party pushed through branches and around scrub pine and hemlocks, the tiny needle-like leaves poking and tearing at them as they passed. Gill occasionally saw one of Nicki's footprints in the dirt, and it wasn't long before they reached the tree she'd spoken of.

"This will work," Gill said as he bent beneath the bows of the giant evergreen.

Nicki and Gill pushed through the foliage to their hiding place. Rajim didn't follow them.

"Where's Rajim?" Gill said.

"I'm sure I don't know. You want me to put a bell on him?" Her tone was accusatory, and again Gill was struck with the idea that Nicki's encounter with the giant snake had somehow changed her perspective on Rajim. So much for the better. This way he didn't have to deal with the man's passive aggressive behavior. But these disappearing acts. What was he up to? Gill didn't trust him, and worried that whatever the man was doing, whatever he was hiding, would somehow put himself and Nicki in more danger.

"I'm going to find out once and for all what he's up to," Gill said.

Nicki's face twisted, and she huffed. "I'll come with you then."

The forest grew quiet, and that made Gill nervous. There was one universal truth among all wild things that lived in forests. When danger was on the way, a warning was given, and that alert was silence. The insects and birds had gone still, and the ground trembled gently beneath their feet.

Rajim stood with his back to them, hunched over as if examining something in his hand. Gill put-up a hand and he and Nicki paused, watching.

Nicki shifted on her feet and stepped on a twig. It snapped, and the sound filled the silence. Rajim spun around, his hand going to a jean's pocket.

"Hey," he sputtered.

"Whatcha doing?" Nicki asked in a playful voice.

Gill turned to look at her and she didn't meet his eye. She felt guilty for their kiss, that was obvious, and her near death experience had probably reminded her of her life's goals and responsibilities.

Rajim smiled, his mood having shifted again from strident asshat to congenial nice guy. "I'm good."

"What were you doing just then?" Gill said.

"Nothing."

"Bullshit. We saw you."

A cloud passed across Rajim's face and he looked to his wife, who was also staring incredulously at Gill. "Piss off. I don't owe you shit."

"Really?" Gill said. "I think you do."

"How's that?" Nicki said, defending her husband.

Gill looked at the woman who an hour before had been his fantasy, his dream, and she'd kissed him, gave him affection he desperately needed. Now they were back where they'd been.

Rajim shook his head and walked away. Gill's hand shot out and grabbed the man by the arm as he passed.

"Get off," Rajim yelled. He jerked his arm free and threw an elbow that just missed connecting with Gill's face.

Gill stepped forward, twisted Rajim's arm behind his back, and drove him forward into a tree trunk. Rajim struggled and bucked, but Gill held him fast.

"Gill, let him go," Nicki screeched.

Gill stuck his free hand in Gill's pocket and pulled out a clear baggie containing a substance that resembled brown sugar. He released Rajim and pushed him away, holding the baggie up for Nicki to see.

Nicki looked sad, and she held out her hand but didn't touch the bag. "What is that?" she said.

Rajim said nothing.

"What is it!" She yelled so loud Rajim jumped, his eyes burning red, shame spreading across his face.

"It's brown tar heroin. How long have you been snorting this stuff?" Gill said.

"Heroin! You do this in our house? With our children around?" Nicki shouted.

"Honey, wait, I—"

"Don't honey me." Nicki stepped beside Gill, her allegiance having shifted again. "Answer me, Raj. Now. How long has this been going on?"

"Since college. OK. You happy now, Gill? You piece of shit. Just couldn't mind your own damn business."

"Since college?" The betrayal Nicki felt was clear in her voice, the disappointment and sorrow slashing across her face.

"Nicki, you don't understand. It started when I played—"

"You're making excuses now?" She sounded incredulous.

Realizing he wasn't winning the battle with his wife, Rajim turned on Gill. "Give me my shit."

"What?" Nicki stepped forward in shock, then stepped back. "Don't you dare give that to him."

Gill sighed. Under normal circumstances Rajim's addiction wouldn't be his problem. Wouldn't even be his business, other than to feel sorry for Nicki and the kids. But out here, in the lost valley, everything each of them did affected the others. What if he was needed and was wasted? His decision making had been affected judging by his mood swings, but could the man quit cold turkey? Gill had a cousin who'd been hooked on smack, and it had taken him the better part of five years to slay the beast, which never fully died. The withdrawal symptoms had been horrible. What would the party do if Rajim got sick and couldn't walk and fight?

"I don't know what to do," Gill said.

"What the hell is going on with you? This is simple. We throw the stuff away, so he can't hurt himself anymore." Nicki stepped forward to take the baggie from Gill's hand, but he pulled it back.

"This might not be the best time for him to quit, Nicki. We need him functional right now," Gill said.

She appeared to consider this, her gaze shifting from Gill to Rajim. Her husband's face had grown red as he did his best to contain his anger.

"You two done deciding what's best for me?" Rajim said. "Give me my stuff. Now. It's not yours, and I'm not your responsibility and what I do is none of your business."

"Rajim, I don't—"

Rajim charged and Gill had no time to react. The two men went down in a tangle, wrestling on the ground. Nicki yelled as Rajim fought to pull the baggie from Gill's hand.

Gill swung and connected with Rajim's jaw, the crack and spray of blood causing Nicki to scream louder. The two men clutched at each other, ripping each other's clothes, throwing wild punches, half of which didn't land. Rajim shook his head, recovered from Gill's blow, and lashed out with a brutal kick that landed on Gill's ribcage.

Pain ran through Gill, and he let go of Rajim and rolled away, vaulting to his feet.

Rajim wasn't as fast. He staggered to one knee and looked up as Gill's roundhouse kick connected with the back of Rajim's head and he crumbled back to the ground.

Nicki shrieked, but Gill was gone, lost in his rage, everything that had happened the last few days spilling from him as he jumped on Rajim and pounded him.

Rajim wasn't done. He bucked, lifting Gill off him and tossing him to the side. Rajim got to his feet, swaying like a drunk on a three-day bender, but his fists were up, and his eyes glowed with hatred, his face twisted. "Come on, bitch. Let's go."

Rajim stepped forward and threw a punch, but Gill easily sidestepped it. He could have easily countered and taken the man's head off, but Nicki's wails were starting to break through his rage. If he hurt the man, Nicki would be pissed, and they'd have an injured man to deal with as they tried to escape the valley.

Gill's chest hurt from where Rajim had kicked him, and he wondered if he cracked a rib. The men circled each other, blood dripping down Rajim's face, Nicki shrieking for them to stop. He wouldn't stop. Rajim had this coming and it would be him who delivered the justice, but Rajim would have to explain to his kids what had happened to him and Gill wanted no part of that.

Rajim swung and Gill danced out the way, bouncing on his toes, fading in and out, playing with the man.

Gill rabbit punched Rajim in the face, snapping his head back. So much for going easy on him. Nicki rushed forward and grabbed Gill's arm, and as he shook her off, she fell.

Rajim screamed, rushed Gill and tackled him. The men clawed and punched at each other, their situation forgotten, days of frustration, fury, and jealousy spilling over. Gill was landing punches, and Rajim covered up, blocking the blows as best he could.

Nicki tugged on Gill's arm, begging him to stop. Gill paused and looked at her, and Rajim kicked him in the balls. Gill made a hollow *pssfftter* sound and crumpled to the ground.

Seeing his opportunity, Rajim jumped on Gill, but there wasn't much behind the blows. Hungry, tired, wounded, thirsty, pain paralyzing him—they'd both had enough. Gill covered up and let Rajim get out his aggression. The man was losing steam fast, and this way he didn't have to hurt him, despite the nagging impulse to kick his ass.

"To hell with you both," Nicki said.

Gill and Rajim stopped fighting and watched her stalk into the forest.

25

Night was coming on fast, the sun having long passed over the valley. It was chilly, but sweat rolled down Gill's back and across his forehead. Rajim held onto Gill's shirt, and the two men stared at each other, deciding if they should continue their fight. With an unspoken agreement, they untangled from one another.

The forest erupted with life as birds and animals were stirred by the commotion. The evergreen forest swayed and shifted in the growing darkness, and shadows hung under every tree bow and behind every stone. The ground trembled, and a mighty roar boomed through the valley. Dead pine needles and leaves covered the ground, and Gill dusted himself off as he got to his feet.

He felt like he should apologize. That's what you did after a fight, but Rajim didn't deserve an apology. You can't act like an asshole and not expect to catch some hell. Yet Rajim had a valid beef. His drug habit and marriage were none of Gill's business.

"You OK?" Gill asked. That was as far as he could go.

Rajim nodded, but said nothing. Instead he turned his back on Gill.

"Here," Gill said. Rajim turned and Gill tossed him his drugs. "When we… if we get back, you need to deal with this, man. You've got kids."

"Piss off," said Rajim. He opened the baggie and pinched some of the brown tar heroin and sniffed it. The man breathed deeply, and a smirk spread across his face.

"All better?" Gill mocked.

"Screw you."

"Shouldn't you have looked for your wife before you got all lit up?"

"Not that it's any of your business, but I don't get 'lit up'. It takes the edge off, nothing more."

"Like aspirin?"

"Gill, don't be a dumb shit, and if you don't stop getting between me and Nicki, I'll…"

"What? Try and kick my ass? How'd that work out for you?"

Rajim stepped forward and got in Gill's face. "Next time will be different."

"There isn't gonna be a next time."

Rajim winked and walked away.

"You hear that?" Gill said. He thought he heard yelling.

Rajim lurched to a stop and turned back to Gill. "Yeah. It's Nicki." He pushed through the trees in the direction of the noise.

Gill followed close behind, and Nicki's voice got louder and clearer as they went. She was calling to them to come to her.

Rajim picked up his pace and tree branches whipped Gill as he tried to keep up. They exited the forest into a small clearing. Nicki stood with her back to them, examining a large pile of pine needles, leaves and debris.

Rajim ran to her. "Are you OK?"

She said nothing, and if glares could freeze, Rajim would have been an icicle.

"Gill," she said. Her stare shifted to Rajim, then back to Gill. "What do you make of this?"

Rajim laughed. "A pile of leaves gathered by the wind."

Gill wanted to ask the man if the sugar made him stupid, but decided against it. He was done fighting with Rajim. He was done fighting period. He'd made that commitment to himself before, yet it had never stuck. When danger came, and his life was threatened, he found he wanted to live. The trick was feeling that way when the adrenaline wasn't running. He looked at Rajim, suddenly understanding the man better.

"Don't know," Gill said. He walked around the mound of leaves and noticed nothing unusual with the exception of large claw tracks all around the pile.

Ignoring the shade being thrown his way, Rajim said, "Could something be hidden in it?"

Gill started. That was actually a good question. Perhaps Gill had things backwards. Rajim seemed sharper than he had half an hour prior. Perhaps the junk did him good? He knew heroin was used for many treatments back in the day—many modern pain killers are heroin in pill form or worse—and perhaps he'd been wrong to condemn Rajim so quickly. The man was right. Who the hell was he to tell anyone what they could and couldn't do?

"Good question," Gill said. He dropped to a knee and eased his hands into the pile, searching. Seeing Gill, Nicki and Rajim did the same.

The ground trembled and they all paused. The insects still trilled, and the birds sang, so they continued looking.

"I think I've got something," Nicki said.

Nicki pulled away leaves revealing three large blue and yellow eggs.

"This makes sense now. Scientists believe dinosaurs may have built nests like this. The eggs are in the leaf pile in the open so the sun can warm them," Rajim said. Nicki and Gill stared at him, and Gill wondered what the hell was in that heroin.

Nicki said, "How the hell do you know that?"

"Channel eight-one, National Geographic," he said.

It had grown dark, and moonlight streamed through the broken ice roof filling the valley with ethereal shadows. In the darkness the hemlocks and evergreens appeared to take the shape of dinosaurs, and they shifted and swayed in a gentle breeze that brought the scent of flowers, dino scat, and the ever-present stench of rotten eggs. Shadows danced, and Gill's hackles rose. He was exhausted, and he couldn't shake the feeling he was overlooking something.

Nicki picked-up one of the eggs, caressing it. "It feels warm," she said.

Rajim pulled a flashlight from his pack and held it up behind the egg, revealing the fetus of a tiny dinosaur that looked like a premature piglet. "Damn. That's amazing."

"Should we take one with us?" Nicki asked.

Gill chuckled. "Sure, just what our messed up world needs, dinosaurs running around."

Nicki took it as intended and laughed, but Rajim's face went cold.

The ground trembled and this time the shrill forest symphony ceased.

Gill realized what he had overlooked. "We need to get out of here. Now!"

"What? Why—" Nicki said.

The ground shook, a pounding that sounded like mortars going off in the distance. The same sound they'd heard many times in the valley.

Rajim said, "Shit. Mom or dad."

"Or both," Gill said. He took the egg from Nicki's hands and placed it gently back on the pile, and brushed leaves and debris over it. "Let's go."

The sound of the approaching dinosaur was thunderous, and Gill couldn't figure what direction the beast was coming from.

"Should we hide?" Nicki said.

"Yeah. Hide," Rajim said. He scrambled toward the woods, but when he realized Gill and Nicki hadn't followed, he stopped. "Come on!"

His command spurred Nicki forward and Gill followed. The three companions hid behind a stone partially covered by the bows of a dense evergreen, and they peered through the thick branches at the clearing.

The rumble of the creature's approach grew stronger, and the trees across the clearing swayed and parted.

Gill had been expecting the T-rex, or the *spinosaurus*, but the beast that pushed through the trees into the clearing was unlike anything he'd ever seen.

The brown beast walked on four thick legs and was ten feet tall. Its armored head had two long curved horns that pointed forward, giving the creature the look of a devil. Black eyes rolled as the dinosaur searched the clearing. It threw its head back and wailed, telling anything near to clear-out. Its broad armored body melted into the darkness, but Gill saw its massive tail snaking behind it, and his nerves jumped.

The clearing went dark as a cloud slid over the valley. In the blackness Gill saw the outline of the giant beast as it stepped into the clearing, turning its massive head side-to side.

Gill heard the tinkle of a bullet being inserted into metal, then the snap of a rifle bolt being slid home. Rajim had loaded his gun.

Gill whispered, "What are you going to do with that?"

"What do you think?" he rasped. "Shoot the damn thing if it comes at us."

Gill was going to tell him to hold his fire, but said nothing. If Rajim had proven anything to him, it was he knew when to fire his weapon. But in the dark?

The dinosaur walked around its nest, the ground shaking as the beast sniffed at its eggs and nudged the pile with its snout. It paused and threw back its head, and the sound of rushing air filled the clearing as the beast let loose with what sounded like an exasperated sigh.

The ground trembled, but the creature hadn't moved.

Gill said, "Umm. Sounds like parent number two is on the way."

"Should we split now? It won't see us in the dark," Nicki said.

The rumble got closer and louder.

"Maybe we should," Rajim said.

Branches cracked and creaked behind them and Gill spun around to find a giant armored head with curved horns sticking through the vegetation.

The companions ran through the trees into the clearing, and both dinosaurs roared. In the dark it was hard to see, and Gill followed Rajim, who followed Nicki. They ran past the first dinosaur as it stood over its nest and bolted for the forest on the opposite side of the clearing, away from the newcomer.

Jurassic mom had a different idea. The massive animal swung its thick tail, just missing Nicki and Rajim, but catching Gill on the back of the legs, cutting him down. He face planted and slid into the nest, disappearing within the leaves and pine needles. He felt an egg crack beneath him, and closed his eyes and waited for death.

Instead, the dinosaur chuffed and stomped its feet, sticking its snout into the nest, searching, but not snapping its massive jaws. Why hadn't the beast stomped him? Then it dawned on him: the eggs. The beast didn't want to hurt its eggs.

Gill army crawled from the pile of debris and worked his way toward the forest. A brief flash lit the night. Nicki letting him know where she and Rajim were. He crawled toward them, the creature's tail swishing back and forth over his head, its giant claws scraping the ground. Dirt and pebbles cascaded over him, but he crawled on. The tree break was close, a dark black line at the clearing's edge.

Something slithered across his legs and Gill jumped, and a squeal escaped his lips.

Both dinosaurs went still.

Gill got up and ran. He crossed the forty feet between the nest and woods at a full run, and when he was halfway the ground trembled as the beasts pursued him.

He reached the woods and didn't stop. Branches smacked him, and rocks and fallen trees threatened to take him down. Nicki and Rajim fell in behind, and the three companions ran blindly through the forest.

Gill ran headlong into a tree and bounced backward into Nicki and Rajim. The three lay tangled and silent, hoping their pursuers would pass them by. Seconds passed. Then a minute. Then two. There were no sounds of pursuit. The ground had stopped trembling.

"You think they gave up?" Nicki said.

"Can't find us in the forest," Rajim said. "Especially in the dark."

"Oh, yeah? How the hell did that second beast find us then?" Gill said.

The party quietly untangled themselves and got up, brushing themselves off. "What now?" Rajim said.

"We find a place to hunker down for the night and get some sleep," Gill said.

"Let's get away from here. Those things are too close," Nicki said.

"Aye," Gill said.

The forest thinned, and Gill heard the lake lapping against the shore to the north. Stars blinked through the hole in the valley's ice roof, and moon glow lit their way, the clouds having passed.

"Everything we do here leads to danger," Nicki said.

"We've been incredibly lucky so far," Gill said.

"Lucky? Lucky? You been hitting my stash," Rajim said. Nicki shot him a look, and Rajim lowered his head.

Gill smiled inwardly. No, dude, she's not over your drug habit nor will she ever accept it. If Rajim couldn't see that he wasn't as smart as Gill thought he was.

The party walked on for several more minutes and came across a depression in the ground with a group of stones at its bottom.

"I say we crawl down there and set up our tents within those stones," Gill said.

Rajim stuck out his chin and looked into the hole. "It's not that deep. Those things can stick their noses right in there."

"We'll keep watch. I'll go first," Nicki said.

They climbed down the incline into the depression, and set up their tents, ate the last of the dino-jerky, drank the last of the water, and settled in for the night.

"I've got to drain the main vein," Rajim said. He hid himself behind a large round juniper bush.

"Sure you do," Nicki said. "Night, Gill."

As Gill crawled into this tent, he said, "Until tomorrow then."

26

Water lapped against Gill's face as he jerked awake. Rainwater ran through the mesh door of his tent, and there was three inches sloshing around, small waves breaking on the neoprene walls. He got up, his sleeping bag soaked, and unzipped his tent flap and went outside.

Rain ran off the ice shelf above, and a waterfall cascaded into the valley, filling the small dell they camped in with water.

He yelled for Nicki and Rajim, and the two stumbled from their tent like drowned rats as they rubbed sleep from their eyes.

"What the he…" Rajim started to say, but when he saw the waterfall cascading down from the ice roof above, he whistled. "I hadn't realized in the dark we were directly under the lip of the ice shelf."

"I don't think it would have mattered if you did. I would never have thought about the effects of rain," Gill said.

"Easy to see how this depression was formed now," Nicki said.

The rainwater cascaded onto a pile of rocks, spattering about the clearing.

"Explains why there's no animals about," Rajim said. The man tossed his head side to side, rolled his shoulders, and flinched. "I've got to hit the head."

Nicki and Gill exchanged glances, but said nothing. Did Nicki know he'd given Rajim his junk back? What would she do if she did? He reminded himself that it wasn't his business and he pledged—again—to stay out of it. His feelings for Nicki were irrelevant. She was her own person and would have to deal with her husband as she saw fit.

"How the hell are we going to dry all this shit out?" Gill said.

Nicki shrugged. "We've got bigger issues. We're out of food, though I guess water isn't an issue." She grabbed her water bottle, strode to the waterfall and stuck her bottle under it. It was full in moments, and she drained it and filled it again.

Gill joined her, and as they drank their fill, he said, "We'll have to go hunt some grouse. Can't afford to waste any bullets."

"Yup, but how the hell will we cook without a fire?"

He hadn't thought of that. They'd have to find a sheltered spot and some dry wood. He looked to the sky, rain beading on his face. It felt good, and Gill closed his eyes and sucked in a deep breath. He said, "Maybe we can get something going under the bows of an evergreen."

"Might work. Let me go see if Rajim still has anything in his pack while he's gone," Nicki said.

She left Gill with his thoughts. The rain was letting up, and the waterfall grew thinner as less rainwater spilled into the valley. The ice sheet above caved inward toward its center, directing the entire ice sheet's water flow into a narrow channel. The water was up to his knees, and he sloshed toward his tent and began dismantling it.

Nicki joined him. "He's got nothing." She broke down one of the long fiberglass poles that supported Gill's tent.

"What, you didn't believe me?" Rajim stood behind them, his black curly hair matted to his head, eyes red as cinders.

Nicki sighed and shook her head. Gill said nothing.

Rajim said, "Whatever." Then he started breaking down the other tent.

"What day is it?" Nicki asked.

"No idea. It was a Wednesday when we left, right?" Gill said.

"Uh huh," Rajim said.

"We're nine days out from Reserve, so that would make it a Thursday?" Nicki said.

"I think so. Why do you need to know?" Gill said.

"I don't... it's just..."

Rajim piped up. "She's upset because we're going to miss Fred's recital at school today."

Nicki nodded.

"I wonder what everyone's saying back in town?" Gill said.

"You think a rescue party has been sent out yet?" Nicki asked.

"I hope so, or we're screwed," Rajim said.

Gill had focused so much on his own situation that he'd failed to consider what it must be like for Nicki and Rajim to be away from their children, to constantly be worrying about them and the pain of knowing how scared and concerned they'd be about their parents. He stuck his hand in a pocket and grasped Brian's little sneaker. The rubber and fabric brought him comfort, and as he held the shoe he thought of his boy. Gill's heart ached, and a tear slipped down his face.

Seeing this, Nicki said, "Oh, Gill, we're sorry. I—"

"No worries," he said.

They wrung out their stuff as best they could, but with a light rain still falling it proved difficult. Once they'd packed, the party drank more water, filled their bottles, hoisted their packs, and struck out to look for food.

Getting out of the depression proved difficult. Wet mud lined the side of the dell, and Gill slipped several times as he climbed. When the three adventurers had escaped the depression, each looked like a pig that had been rolling around in a sty.

Nicki took out a towel and they wiped their faces and hands.

Finding grouse was easy. Several of the fat birds rested beneath the bows of a tall Douglas fir with wide branches, trying to stay dry. Nicki made a slingshot with a branch and some elastic string from her backpack. She was an excellent shot, and she easily took out three grouse.

"We can light a fire here, no?" Rajim said.

Gill searched for dry wood as Rajim and Nicki gutted and plucked the birds. Soon the grouse were roasting over an open flame surrounded in stones, and the three companions sat beneath the tree, drops of water working through the tree canopy, damp belongings hanging under tree branches.

The rain stopped as they ate, and the sound of rushing water ceased. Sunlight streamed into the valley as the storm passed, and a rainbow stretched across the valley.

Seeing the rainbow made Gill reach for Brian's sneaker again, memories of the day he was taken flooding through him.

"What the heck is that?" Nicki said, pointing.

Beyond the forest to the east a bright multicolored light shot errand rays of color in every direction.

"Never seen a rainbow like that before," Rajim said.

"That's no rainbow," Gill said.

"What then?"

"Don't know. Finish eating, and we'll go find out." Gill was surprised Rajim hadn't protested as he did whenever Gill decided for the group.

The forest thinned, and to Gill it felt as though he walked through a Christmas tree farm. Evergreens grew in ordered lines as though planted that way, and they all appeared of the same size, and of perfect shape. The valley's edge loomed up before them, but there were no tunnel holes in the cliff face of the valley's western boundary.

"What do you make of these trees? Looks like they're all the same age," Gill said.

"Probably a fire. This could be new burn growth," Rajim said.

"Or just new. We have no idea how long ago the ice shelf collapsed," Nicki said.

The ground was muddy, and all footprints and tracks had washed away. The animals of the primeval valley ventured from their hiding spots now that the rain had stopped, and the forest filled with screeches and wails of wildlife fighting for food. Clouds streamed by overhead, but patches of blue sky peeked through. When was the last time he'd seen the sun? It seemed a long time ago.

"Ok, that's new," Rajim said.

The trees ended, and a clearing of purple heather and juniper stretched to the mountainside. At the far end of the area a large translucent stone stood like a sentinel, the clear rock clouded with patches of black and brown mineral deposits. Water dripped from a precipice above, the brown liquid landing atop the giant stalagmite.

"So, a liquid version of the gas?" Rajim said.

"Could be," Gill said.

"How?" Nicki said. She ran her fingers through her short blonde hair and cracked her knuckles.

"Maybe the water is running over the same mineral deposits as the gases, and as the minerals get broken down they're incorporated into the gas and water," Gill said.

"Look at Mr. Wizard," Rajim said.

"You need to go take a piss?" Gill said.

The giant crystal looked like a low grade, cloudy diamond with no clarity and so many imperfections one could say it was half river stone.

"Look here," Nicki said. She'd walked around the edge of the crystal and was staring at a chiseled carving in the stone.

The picture revealed stick figures standing before an object emanating light.

"Looks like the cave drawings," Nicki said.

"And we mistook this huge standing stone for the sun," Gill said.

Sunlight streamed into the valley, and despite the cloudiness of the stone, daggers of multicolored light knifed from the crystal. Animal and dinosaur footprints covered the area and many of them were fresh.

Gill dropped to a knee. "Why do you think the beasts come here?"

Nicki and Rajim said nothing.

The party examined the stone from all angles, yet there was nothing unusual other than the carving.

"Why do you think we haven't seen other formations like this one? There're plenty of spots where water runs down the mountain face," Nicki said.

"Aye, but maybe this mythical mineral deposit that Gill thinks explains all this is in one spot. You know, like a meteor or something."

Gill opened his mouth to reproach the man, then shut it.

"But we saw and smelled the gases in the tunnel we came through to get here," Nicki said.

"Yeah, and we also walked a tunnel that took us in half a circle. The water dripping here could originate on the other side of the valley," Rajim said.

"Possible," Gill said.

The party fell silent. The day was getting on and the forest symphony was in full swing, the insect buzz so loud all Gill heard was static. With nothing left to investigate, the companions worked their way around the valley to the south, away from the lake and back toward their starting point.

"Look at that," Rajim said.

Gill followed his pointed finger and saw a bird sitting on the edge of the broken ice ceiling. It was huge, and when it flapped its giant wings he saw it was an eagle. The bird stared down into the valley, turning its head to look in Gill's direction.

"That's a big boy. Ten-foot wingspan at least," Rajim said.

The beast dropped from the ledge and took flight, disappearing over the ice sheet into the blue sky.

The sound of trickling water soothed Gill's nerves, and not for the first time he wished he had a drink.

Nicki stopped and leaned against the cliff face, her head falling into her hands. "What time is it, Gill?"

"My watch says 2:38PM. Why?"

Nicki burst into tears, sobbing uncontrollably.

Gill didn't know what to do. Nicki'd been fine two minutes prior. He looked to Rajim, thinking her husband might have the crucial clue, but Rajim looked more perplexed then he felt.

Nicki looked up at Rajim, tears streaming down her face. "Fred's concert just started."

Rajim tried to put his arm around her and she shook him off, but to his credit he kept trying. "Honey, he'll understand. When we tell him this story, all about what we've been through, I think he'll be OK with it."

"What if I'm not OK with it?" she said.

Rajim and Gill said nothing.

"We need to get the hell out of here. Now. What are we going to do?" she said.

"I've got an idea," Gill said.

27

"Let's go back to basecamp and see if the emergency radio is charged. If it is, we'll try and send an emergency signal to mark our position," Gill said.

Nicki looked away from the mineral deposit, gazing across the valley. "I think I can see the precipice to the southeast, but..." Gill handed her binoculars. "Yeah. I see it."

"How far do you figure it is?" Gill said.

"Depends. We going in a straight line? Or are we following the valley's edge?" she said.

Rajim said, "What happened to getting out as fast as we can?"

Nicki looked to Gill, who said, "We don't really know which way will be faster because we have no idea what we'll meet along the way. Staying at the edge of the valley means we'll have water, and it should be easier to avoid larger creatures. Cutting across the valley through the forest is shorter, but faster? I just don't know."

"How long do you think it will take to walk the edge?" Nicki said.

"I hate to say it," Rajim said. He looked at the ground and sighed. "We haven't searched this section. Could be caves."

"True, but who cares? After walking in circles, we need to reevaluate our plan," Gill said. "You know what? I think we should take the riskier path. Head straight across."

"Really?" Rajim said. "You want to take a risk?"

"Not want. The longer I think on it the more I worry following the edge of the valley could take a long time. We can cut across in a day and a half. Maybe less."

Nicki said, "Straight line it is then." She reached into her pack and pulled out a slingshot for Gill. "I had some elastic band left so I made you this."

"Thank you. Can't imagine my hunting knife will be much use as a weapon here on out," Gill said.

"Let's hope not," she said.

"You have a gun with more than one bullet," she said.

"Yeah. I do. Hopefully it will fire. It got wet."

Nicki hefted her pack, turned away from the giant crystal deposit, and walked into the Christmas tree forest.

Rajim followed.

Gill stood alone. He put the slingshot in his back pocket and ran his hand over the dirty colored crystal, tracing the stick figures in the carving. Who were those people? Where had they come from? If they'd been primitives, they might have worshiped the crystal because of its light. Gill started. What role did the crystal play before the collapse of the ice roof?

He pulled his backpack straps tight, cracked his neck, and followed Nicki and Rajim.

Noon approached, and sunlight still angled into the valley. It was warm, and the scent of rotten eggs had faded, replaced with flowers and earth. Gill caught up with Rajim and Nicki, and the three companions threaded through the woods. Animal paths and forest cover let them move fast, and they made good time as the slight downward grade brought the party to the valley floor.

Gill pulled his slingshot and pressed a stone in the cradle.

A blue glow radiated through the forest ahead. The party veered northeast, moving off their line, but heading for the anomaly. The Douglas firs grew tall and broad and were packed close together. Gill pushed through the thick branches; spiders, insects, and birds fleeing before him.

The Douglas firs ended, and a spattering of Colorado Blue Spruces filled a thin clearing separating one forest from the other. The trees filled in as the party pushed on, the spot of color a welcome change amidst the endless evergreen of the valley. The Colorado Blue Spruces had scaly grey bark with yellow-brown branches, and waxy grey-green leaves on curved shoots that supported brown cones five inches long.

"The blue spruce is the state tree of Colorado," Gill said.

"Well la di da," Rajim said.

"How is it you didn't get fragged, Rajim?" Gill said. He knew the man had served in some military, though not in the US.

"Speak English," Rajim said.

"He means how weren't you killed by your own troops?" Nicki said.

Rajim turned to her, opened his mouth to say something, then thought better of it and turned back to Gill. "My soldiers feared me, grunt."

"I was no grunt, but that's no insult," Gill said. "Without grunts there's nothing, dipshit. And fear you? You shitting me, snowflake? I guess I'm not surprised you'd be a rule by fear guy."

"I'm sure you were everyone's favorite," Rajim said.

Gill stopped walking and turned to Rajim, who almost bumped into him. The two men stood face-to-face, anger coming off them in waves.

Nicki sighed and dropped an arm sarcastically between them. "Oh, stop, please stop." Gill didn't think she could sound less interested.

The men looked at her, but said nothing.

"Yeah, you two are worse than two teenage girls fighting over a scrunchie," she said. She pushed past them into the blue forest.

Gill felt like a fool and took a step back.

Rajim looked at the ground.

Nicki led them through the thickening trees. When Gill caught up, she asked, "Where did you serve, Gill? I seem to remember you telling me you were Army."

"I was a Chief Warrant Officer specializing in cyber weapons," Gill said.

"Another piece in the puzzle," Nicki said. "I never knew that's how you became a techie."

Gill harrumphed. "I learned to be a techie from the big computer companies who preferred I didn't have my military experience."

"Makes it harder to train you," Rajim said. "They prefer clay."

"So doing home service of basic computers for Reserve was your plan?" Nicki said.

"No, that was never the plan," Gill said. "I hadn't planned on meeting Abigale, either."

Birds chirped and in the distance two creatures screeched at each other as they fought. Gill saw nothing but the grey-green of the forest that packed them in on all sides.

"I'm sorry, Gill," Nicki said.

"For what?"

"Picking at a scab. I wasn't thinking," she said.

"Good. I want you to talk to me. Not think," Gill said.

"How sweet," Rajim said.

"Little insecure, are we?" Nicki said.

"It actually helps sometimes to talk about Abigale. Helps keep her memory alive," Gill said.

"How did you meet?" Nicki said.

"Total random chance. That's one of the things that made it so special. I was on leave in Los Angeles, sightseeing. She was in town with a sorority sister taking a break from her last year of graduate school. I was on Hollywood Blvd, checking out the walk of fame, taking a selfie with Alfred Hitchcock's star, when this beautiful woman stumbled across James Cagney. I caught her, still frame, eyes meet, I ask her to have coffee, the end. So corny it's true. Just like a rom-com."

"A boring one," Rajim said. He rubbed his eyes. Baby clearly needed his formula.

"There any other kind? But it's the only one I've got," Gill said. "She wanted to come home to Reserve, and be a town doc. It was her dream since childhood. Sooooooo…"

"I don't think it's boring," Nicki said.

"You just play on computers or did you see battle?" Rajim said.

"I was deployed in a variety of attack scenarios and though my primary responsibility wasn't tactical, I served—"

"Sssshhh." Rajim stopped walking and held up a hand. "You ever kill anybody?"

Gill's first instinct was to rabbit punch the guy. Hard. Rotate his hips and twist on the balls of his feet, directing all his muscle and energy to one blow, his arm stone.

Instead he closed his eyes, breathed, and reminded himself that Rajim was baiting him, and an outburst was exactly what the man wanted. Gill cracked his neck, and the *pop* was loud in the confines of the packed forest. "I don't know," Gill said. "Yes, I have shot to kill, but I don't know if I was successful."

"How very convenient for you," Rajim said. He turned and continued working his way through the trees.

"What's your story?" Gill said.

"Gill, that's not—" Nicki said.

"It's OK. OK. Really. I asked him, so I have to be prepared to answer as well." Rajim looked over his shoulder so he could make eye contact with Gill. Then he looked away and said, "I have killed."

"You sound upset?" Gill said.

"Gill, I—"

"Nicki, it's fine. Really it is. Promise," Rajim said.

"This is some serious drama, huh?" Gill said.

"I believe killing another human being is a crime against nature. But there are times when one must do what one must. In my country you were the hunter or the hunted, and there were no game wardens."

Rajim was from India, and from what Gill'd heard around Reserve, his father was still a prominent business man there.

The center of the valley was damp and lush, and dead plants and trees pocked the vibrant landscape. "This place looks like it's going through major upheaval," Gill said.

"As moist as it is here, I think it might be drying out because of the ice shelf being gone," Nicki said.

"All the dead plants. You're right," Rajim said.

"Our screwed situation aside, this place is amazing," Gill said.

"One in a million," Rajim said.

"One in a googolplex," Gill said.

Nicki laughed and Rajim sighed.

Ferns with thick leaves and giant flowers with firework tops filled in the landscape as the blue spruce forest broke up. They'd made good time and were half way to the opposite side. The sun eased past the lip of the ice shelf and the eight-hour dusk settled over the valley. Gill was starving, but there was nothing for it. They'd managed to avoid the wildlife, but the smaller animals had avoided them, which meant no food. He had a little water left, and their backup supplies were full, but the hunger pains were getting bad.

The flat land at the bottom of the valley started to climb, and the familiar forest of Douglas fir engulfed the companions.

"A little further up is where Clint and I were attacked by the T-rex," Gill said. "And... close to where we found Brian's finger."

"Strange that we haven't heard or seen big T, no?" Nicki said.

"I don't think there's many of them in here," Gill said.

Animal paths wound through the evergreens and the party slipped quietly through the forest. "We made the right call," Gill said.

"You did," Nicki said.

"No. We discussed it and heard the sides. That's how you make decisions. Not based on fear," Gill said.

Rajim didn't reply to the jab. His eye sockets were red and dark bags hung beneath his eyes. He couldn't afford to lose the man right now, so he threw him a bone. "Let's take five. I've got to pee."

The party split up and Gill opened his jeans and urinated. There wasn't much there. He zipped up and headed back to the rendezvous point and found Rajim in a much better state of mind.

"You think we can make it up there by nightfall?" Rajim said.

"Naw, but by lunch tomorrow. We're gonna have to camp down here tonight," Gill said.

"Lunch. Very funny," Rajim said.

The man had a point. They needed food, and it didn't matter if they weren't inclined to take the time to catch and prepare it.

Gill froze. He'd felt something.

The ground trembled, and Nicki grabbed Gill's arm. Like the Earth's heartbeat quickening, the valley shook. Tree branches cracked, and the three companions stood frozen in the evergreens unable to see what was happening around them.

"It's like the thing knows we've stepped on its lawn," Rajim said.

A mighty wind rushed through the forest and the ground shuddered. Gill flinched as a great wail reverberated through the woods.

28

"Let's hide here and wait it out," Rajim said.

"That's what Clint and I did, and the thing still found us. Bit the tree off right next to us and we were hidden well," Gill said.

"It can smell us?" Nicki said.

"This is crazy," Rajim said.

The ground trembled harder and faster as the great beast approached. Gill was unsure what to do, and he was tired of deciding. The companions huddled beneath the great evergreen, cowering like little children hiding from their mother.

Sweat dripped down Gill's back, and his head pounded. Hunger pains knotted his stomach, and his mouth was so dry he thought his lips might crack. He brushed hair away from his face and turned to Nicki. She watched him, waiting for their next move. Rajim stood sullen like an empty bag, eyes staring at the ground. Gill sure could use some of the man's smack at the moment. His nerves were jumping so hard his hands shook, so he stuffed them in his pockets and felt Brian's sneaker. The smooth rubber sole, the course canvas fabric, the tiny shoelaces with plastic tips. He longed to take it out. Smell it, rub it on his face. It was the last thing he had of his son.

"Which way is it coming?" Gill said.

Nicki's eyes darted about. "Everywhere," she said.

It did sound like the booms were coming from more than one direction, but they needed to get moving so they might throw the beast off their trail. "Stay close to me," Gill said.

He pocketed his slingshot and pulled the M16 from his shoulder. He racked the slide, inserting his last bullet into the firing chamber. He hoped he didn't need to use it.

He'd been saving it as a last resort for himself.

That dark idea worked into him like a worm. He'd thought all along that if things got too bad, he'd eat a bullet. The idea had dominated his thoughts after Abigale passed, but Brian had driven it from his mind. He was a father. Someday might be a grandfather. He wouldn't leave his son alone in this world. That had been his justification, and then Brian went and left him alone.

Sorrow washed over him, the energy draining sick feeling that reminded him none of this mattered. His life didn't matter, but what did matter were the lives of Fred and Kiki. They needed their parents.

Gill moved stealthily through the evergreens, easing past branches, dipping under bows, and avoiding open areas. The ground shook beneath their feet, but less violently. Gill thought they'd done right, and he breathed a sigh of relief.

A great rending and cracking ahead brought the party to a halt. Before them the forest opened up and standing amidst the Douglas firs was a young T-rex. The beast was twice the size of the *utahraptor* that had taken Brian. Its glassy eyes rolled toward them, tail smacking the ground. Dust clouded the air, and the beast squeaked its version of a roar, and Nicki chuckled.

"That what we're running from?" she said.

The young T-rex opened its jaws, and white teeth shone in the grey dusk. The beast raised its head and wailed, the thin cry almost comical. "No," Gill said. "That thing isn't big enough to shake the ground. No, where there's junior there is sure to be mom and dad, remember?"

"Aye," Rajim said. He'd been quiet and trailed behind. His red eyes studied Gill with derision.

The T-rex bent low and charged, head hovering just above the ground as it wove between the trees, eyes locked on its prey.

The ground vibrated, and Gill turned to flee only to find a full-grown T-rex sneaking-up behind them.

"Shit," Rajim said.

The bigger beast roared, and this stopped baby in its tracks, as if mom was telling its child no snacks, we'll be eating dinner soon.

Trapped between the two beasts, Gill got low, aiming the M16 back and forth between the two animals.

"What now?" Nicki said.

"They definitely see us," Gill said.

The big T-rex came on, jaws snapping, slime dripping from its open maw.

"Run!" Gill yelled. He didn't know where the words came from. He'd yelled without thought, his primal survival instinct taking over and pushing him forward when his rational brain wouldn't. Flight or fight, the most basic of human decisions had been made for him.

Nicki and Rajim followed, and the three companions ran through the forest, heading south away from the baby T-rex and its pissed off parent. The smaller beast squeaked like an infant whose toys have been taken away, and momma wailed in fury, lowering its head and pursuing the party.

Gill zigzagged, dodging around trees, juniper bushes and boulders. He'd been told once that's how you ran from an alligator. It threw them off and messed with their eyesight. Gill only hoped these big lizards had some of their ancestor's tendencies.

A third T-rex pushed its head through the trees. Daddy. The beast's black leathery skin was striped with yellow and green, and dark eyes rolled as its head moved up and down and side to side like a bird. It lumbered through the forest, stepping on junipers and snapping tree branches.

Dad T-rex snapped its jaws at Gill, who changed direction and avoided the beast. The T-rex swung its tail and Gill dove to the ground to avoid it. Nicki leapt over him, but Rajim stopped to help him up and the two men ran on.

Baby T-rex cut them off. It clicked and chuffed as its head darted forward, jaws snapping. Gill brought up the M16, stuck it in the beast's mouth as it bit at him, and pulled the trigger.

His last bullet blew out the back of the creature's head. Blood and bone sprayed the ground and the baby T-rex toppled over. Dust clouds filled the air and bought Gill and his companions the time they needed to escape.

Gill changed direction again, and headed back the way he'd come, trying to throw mom and dad off the trail. A gust of wind tore through the clearing, driving away the dust, revealing the dead baby T-rex.

There is one certainty in the world: moms protect their young. Upon seeing its dead offspring, momma T-rex bent forward and sniffed the corpse, its mouth opening in what looked like a smile. Then it lifted itself up, narrow head turning, eyes searching for the killer.

Dad T-rex threw back its head and screamed, and the painful wail put Gill's nerves on edge. The beast stomped, its tail whipping, breaking trees and sending waves of dust over the forest.

"Let's get moving," Nicki said. She grabbed Gill's shoulder and spun him around, shaking him. "Gill! Snap out of it."

Gill stood still, his mind far away. He fingered the sneaker in his pocket, saw Brian's face in his mind's eye, thought how nice it would be to see his son again. To have peace.

Nicki slapped him across the face and Gill blinked.

"We've got to go," Nicki said.

Gill nodded.

The thick evergreen forest to the south could provide cover, so Gill headed for it. Animal paths twisted through the dense woods, and Gill realized these were the same paths he and Clint used to flee the T-rex when they'd first entered the valley. The precipice and radio weren't far if they could shake the fifteen-ton lizards chasing them.

Gill hit a wall of trees and could go no further. The evergreens wove into each other like a fence, and there was no way through. Branches cracked and the ground shook, mom and dad T-rex not far behind. The beasts nosed through the trees like anteaters plucking ants.

To the left, the forest fell away down a gentle slope back to the center of the valley. To the right, the grade continued upward, trees, bushes and boulders filling the landscape. They couldn't go back, so Gill whirled to face the T-rex. He pulled his slingshot from his pocket, loaded it, then laughed. What the hell was a stone going to do when 9mm parabellums had no affect?

"Rajim, you ready with that rifle? It's all we got," Gill said.

Rajim didn't respond.

The ground had stopped shaking, but the sound of cracking trees persisted as the T-rexes nosed through the evergreens like cows grazing on grass.

"They're gonna find us in a second," Nicki said.

"They're really pissed," Rajim said.

"You would be too if some stranger killed your baby," Nicki said.

Gill's heart pounded. He had killed their baby, but what choice had he had?

Before Gill could speak, Rajim defended him. "Gill just did what he had to do, Nicki."

She said nothing.

The forest canopy disappeared as jaws filled with razor-sharp teeth tore the top off the tree next to Gill. The great beast shook its head and tossed the evergreen from its mouth and roared. The dinosaur lowered its head, preparing to take a bite of Rajim.

With no choices left, Gill ran at the beast. The others would have to decide for themselves what to do. His days of leading and giving advice were over. He bolted directly beneath the dinosaur, juking left as the creature's tail swung at him.

The T-rex stomped, and tried to turn, only to run into its mate who had pushed through the trees. Mom and dad chuffed and stamped, confused, and that gave Gill an idea. "Split up," he yelled. "Split up."

Nicki ran left and Rajim went right. Both dinosaurs paused and tracked their movements, and that ten seconds probably saved their lives. Nicki blended into the forest, but Rajim wasn't so lucky. The trees on the hillside were sparse, but the dinosaurs didn't follow either of them.

The T-rexes struggled to turn around, their tails smacking each other and taking down trees. Gill ran on, legs pistoning, head thrown back. The ground shook as the beasts pursued him, but Gill was possessed, and as he put more distance between himself and the dinosaurs his thoughts turned to Nicki. She'd gotten away, and so had Rajim.

Gill came upon a pile of stones not unlike the one Brian had used to hide from the raptor, and he searched for a crack or hole. Once tucked neatly between two standing stones, he waited. Tiny stars of light danced before his eyes, his chest ached, and the bottoms of his feet burned like he'd just walked on hot coals barefoot.

The T-rexes passed him and stopped. The female screeched, and turned to the mate, jaws snapping in his direction. There were some universal truths that spanned not only mankind, but all living things, and females blaming their mates for things they had no control over was as common as devil's grass and just as painful. The two beasts circled each other, roaring and chuffing. Gill had destroyed a family, and it didn't make him feel good.

The beasts jawed with each other, posturing and nudging, but after ten minutes they lost interest and separated, mom heading east and dad west. Gill sighed. They needed to go west, and now he had pissed off *tyrannosaurus-rex* parents roaming around. Could things get any worse?

Then they did.

29

The male T-rex attacked the rock pile where Gill hid. Black skin with yellow and green striations flew past his field of vision, then he saw six-inch teeth below two softball sized eyes. Slime dripped onto him as the dinosaur bit at the stones, and a dark tongue lashed out. Rage baked off the beast like heat, its corded muscles tense. The T-rex's short arms clawed at the stones, and smaller rocks tumbled off the pile, but the boulders Gill hid between were too large for the dinosaur to move.

When the T-rex broke a tooth, the beast wailed in pain, throwing its head back, eyes rolling back in their sockets. The five-inch broken tooth landed on Gill's head and fell to his feet. He stared down at it, mouth hanging open. He wanted to pick it up and examine it, but he couldn't bend down in the narrow confines of his hiding place.

The T-rex circled the stone pile, braying and chuffing, the ground shaking.

The beast paused, and looked to the east, then jerked its head back as a stone struck it on the snout. Gill smiled. Nicki was firing stones at the creature. Had to be her.

The dinosaur took a step toward the forest and another rock hit it on the nose. It roared and lurched into motion.

Gill's chest hurt, but as he sucked air, the pain eased. His heart pounded, ears ringing, lower back throbbing. He was chilled, yet sweat dripped down his back and across his forehead.

The ground stopped shaking and a faint tremble ran through the land.

"Psst. Gill? You OK?" It was Nicki.

"Can I come out?" he asked.

"Yeah, Rajim is leading the beast away from here," Nicki said.

"That's mighty Christian of him," Gill said.

"No, not Christian, Nickian," she said.

He smiled. Through all the chaos and heartbreak. Through all the pain and suffering, the loss and confusion, she'd been there for him. He wished he knew a way to repay her, and the idea that jumped into his mind was so evil he wouldn't allow himself a second to think on it.

He wiggled out from between the two boulders, covered in dirt and slime.

"Thought I'd lost you that time," she said. "What were you thinking?"

What had he been thinking? He knew very well, but how could he tell her he had a death wish? That his emotions swung like a pendulum from life to death and back again each second? How could he tell her she was the only reason he carried on? Tell her he was trying to save her by drawing the beasts after him? He said, "You know how it is when the adrenaline gets flowing."

She nodded, but said nothing.

"I see you made it. Joy." Rajim joined them.

"Mission accomplished?" Nicki asked.

"For all their strength these creatures aren't very bright," Rajim said. "I led it in a circle and it got so pissed it stomped off." He giggled.

Nicki and Gill exchanged sidelong glances.

"Let's go get our packs and get going. The sooner we're off the valley floor the better," Nicki said.

The companions backtracked through the evergreens to where they'd dropped their packs when they ran. They were out of water and food, and the party was in desperate need of both. Dusk grew thicker as the sun, long passed the lip of the ice shelf, started its descent to the horizon in a world Gill no longer felt was his own. They were nine days out from Reserve, but it felt like a year since he'd eaten a proper meal, slept in a real bed, and sipped a drink by the fire. Those peaceful things were nothing, however, to the loss that still burrowed into him like a disease. How could he feel sorry for himself when Brian was dead?

They hoisted their packs, and Nicki said, "Keep your weapons at the ready in case we see some game. Do either of you have any water?"

Gill and Rajim shook their heads no.

"That's priority one. Find water," Nicki said.

"That brackish puddle is around here someplace," Gill said.

"I'd rather die than drink from that," Rajim said.

"That might come to be," Gill said.

"Do you think we'll make the precipice before dark?" Nicki asked.

"I think so. Doesn't look very far," Rajim said.

"I disagree," Gill said.

"Surprise, surprise," said Rajim.

Gill sighed. "No way we'll make it today. I can't see the sun, but this day is waning, and it will be dark in three or four hours. We've still got a ways to go through difficult country, and I don't know about you guys, but I'm exhausted. Every muscle aches, my mouth is like paper, and the hunger pains are so bad I can barely walk." Showing weakness before Rajim wasn't what he'd wanted, but there it was.

Rajim coughed. "Tough it out. You can do it." Rajim slapped Gill on the shoulder and plunged into the forest.

Nicki raised her eyebrows, but said nothing, and she and Gill followed.

Birds sprayed from the Douglas firs as the party drove through the thick forest, sharp spike-like leaves poking and scraping at them every step of the way. Clouds rolled in overhead, making the valley even darker. Gill pulled his flashlight, but the battery was dead, and he heaved the light into the woods.

"What'd you do that for?" Nicki said.

"You got batteries?" he asked.

"No," she said.

Gill threw up his hands as if to say that was why.

"Someone will find that flashlight someday and wonder where the hell it came from," Rajim said.

"Too bad about the baby rex," Nicki said. "Not that we've explored the entire valley, but there doesn't appear to be many T-rex families in here."

"Could be that there's only one," Rajim said. "And Gill might have wiped it out by killing the youngling."

"The dinosaur population is small, I'll grant you, but there has to be more than one family," Gill said.

"Maybe," Rajim said.

"Maybe?" Gill said.

The exasperation in Gill's voice made Rajim smile. He said, "All I'm saying is we don't know anything for sure. For all we know the collapse of the ice roof triggered a thaw and the genesis of new life."

Nicki and Gill said nothing. Rajim had a point, no matter how farfetched. "Guess we'll never know," Gill said.

"No, we will," Nicki said.

Gill and Rajim stopped walking and turned to look at her.

"We're going to get out of here, and when we tell everybody what we've seen, scientists will come running from all over the globe," she said.

"Tell everyone? If we do get out of here, we'll need to decide—together—what we should say of this place," Rajim said.

Gill noticed the gleam in Rajim's eye and wanted to press the point, but didn't. It was a useless argument. If they escaped the valley, which was looking like more of a longshot with each passing second, they'd worry about it then.

The forest thinned, and the companions saw Gill and Clint's footprints in sand patches that dotted the needle-covered floor like pockmarks. Gill stopped, getting his bearings. He felt Nicki and Rajim's eyes on him. They were near the spot where they'd buried Brian's finger.

Gill bent and touched his dead friend's footprint in the sand. Clint had died helping him. Another friend gone, another debt he could never repay.

Gill rose and went east, threading through the trees until he came upon the cross made of evergreen branches sticking from a pile of sand. Gill knelt, feeling the sneaker in his pocket.

Nicki and Rajim joined him. "It's not your fault he's dead," Nicki said. "There was no way you could have foreseen any of this."

"Aye, but that doesn't make me feel any better about it," Gill said.

She nodded, but said nothing.

A snake with a wide bump at its center slithered through the forest and Gill jumped.

Rajim laughed, "You afraid of snakes?"

"No, but…"

"Looks like it ate a mouse or hedgehog," Nicki said. "What kind of snake is it? Looks like a smaller version of the one that attacked me by the lake."

Gill had forgotten about that beast. With creatures of the valley challenging their every step, he'd pushed the giant snake from his mind. Dinosaurs could be heard coming a mile away, but that snake… It could attack without warning. "No idea what type it is, but you're right. It sure looks like the big boy."

The companions went on, the gloom of dusk thickened, and it grew colder and harder to see where they were going. Gill tripped over a root and stumbled, and it occurred to him how screwed he'd be if he broke a bone or sustained an injury that hampered his ability to walk. He went forward with new care and concern, another worry seeping through him like sewage.

"I think we should stop for the night," Nicki said.

"You read my mind," Gill said. "One of us is going to get hurt if we continue."

"We've still got no water, no food," Rajim said.

"Indeed, it's going to be a miserable night," Nicki said.

They found a large conifer with wide bows and made camp beneath it. Then the party set about breaking branches and leaning them against the tree bows to make walls. Within minutes they were tucked inside the makeshift structure, preparing for bed.

"I've got to hit the head," Gill said.

"Me also," said Rajim.

Both men pushed out through the tree branches and set off in opposite directions.

Gill found a spot and unzipped his pants. He stared into the gloom, searching the mountainside in the distance for the precipice and the basecamp, but in the darkness, he couldn't see it. The night creatures scuttled and chirped, but nothing approached him as he squeezed out a trickle of dark yellow urine.

He zipped up and headed back to camp. The sky above had cleared, and Gill gazed into the heavens, hoping to be hit with a great idea, some revelation that told him what to do should the radio gambit fail, but nothing came. The wind whistled, and the faint scent of scat wafted over the valley.

His eyes drifted to the dark forest, half closed as weariness took him. Out of the corner of his eye he saw a light in the sky and he looked up.

A white light followed by a red light glided across the sky. It wasn't that high, and it moved in a straight line as it crossed over the valley.

He needed to start a fire. Do something to get the pilot's attention. It could be a search helicopter and soon it would pass the valley and be gone.

He ran back to camp and found Nicki and Rajim chatting. He quickly told them what he'd seen, and the companions searched the sky together.

"There!" Gill said, pointing. "We need to send a signal. Light a fire. Anything." Gill frantically searched the area for dried wood.

Rajim said, "You want to signal that plane?"

"Yeah, what other?"

Rajim laughed, long and hard. "That plane?" He chuckled and got himself under control. "That's most likely a commercial jetliner traveling at five hundred miles per hour. They wouldn't see a bomb explode in here."

Rajim turned and headed back to camp, muttering and laughing as he went.

Gill felt the fool. Rajim was right. He hadn't thought things through.

Nicki put a hand on his shoulder. "Don't let him get to you," she said.

"It's just... we haven't seen anything from the outside world for so long. I kind of lost it a little," Gill said.

"No worries. Come back and go to bed. We've got a long day tomorrow."

"Sure, in a minute," he said.

He saw the white teeth of her smile in the darkness. Gill searched the sky, but the aircraft was gone.

30

The next morning dawned bright and warm. The three companions broke camp and were off in search of food and water a half hour after sun up. Though he'd slept well, hunger pains and thirst nagged Gill's every step. His stomach ached, his mouth dry of saliva, knees and feet sore, lower back pulsing with muscle spasms, nerves jumping. He was a mess, and if he didn't get some food soon he didn't know how much longer he could go on.

Rajim did a good job of hiding his discomfort, but it was clear he was hurting. He wheezed with each step, eyes downcast, face sullen. Nicki looked worse. The bags beneath her eyes were black as night, her hair flat with grease. She walked like a doomed prisoner, putting one foot in front of the other, head down.

The ground trembled and the party came upon a fight between two *spinosauri* who appeared to be competing for a female, who stood off to one side watching the bout. The travelers traversed the skirmish, and soon they were climbing up the gradual grade that led up to the cliff face.

Gill pushed through a thick stand of trees, and he recalled the place where he and Clint had been attacked. There'd been no sign of the T-rex parents, and Gill wondered how the large animals slept. Did they lay down? Seek shelter of some kind? Or did they sleep standing up like elephants?

When the party came free of the tangled forest the precipice loomed above.

"We missed our mark a bit," Gill said. "We'll have to head south until we find our way up."

"It's not far," Rajim said. "I recall this spot from…"

One of your drug jaunts? Gill thought.

The companions walked on and the land fell away to the west. To the east a gentle rock-strewn slope led up to the precipice.

Rajim was in the lead, and he froze and put up a hand. "Nicki, you got your slingshot ready?"

Nicki eased before her husband, weapon at the ready.

Gill didn't see what had caught Rajim's attention until Nicki fired and her stone struck what looked like a jacked-up squirrel. The rock hit the animal in the head, and it keeled over.

"Yes," Rajim said. He raised his hand to high-five his wife, but she only stared at him and left him hanging.

The beast was mostly muscle with little meat, but once they got back to basecamp they could light a fire, get water, and make a stew or soup using the entire animal. It would taste like ass, but beggars couldn't be picky.

Nicki cleaned and gutted the kill and stored it in her pack. "The path that leads to that good water spot is up here on the right. Should one of us head up there now and we can meet back at camp?" she said.

"Makes sense," Rajim said. "Why go all the way to camp and then have to backtrack? I'll go." His lips drew into a thin line and he shot Gill a dirty look. No doubt in his rush to be alone so he could snort some horse, he'd forgotten that he'd be leaving Gill and Nicki alone.

"Unless you want to go?" Rajim said, trying to correct his error.

Gill smiled. "Naw, you can do it," he said. Then for extra emphasis, "And I don't think I'm up for that climb." Gill handed over his water bottle.

Rajim sighed, pulled Nicki's bottle from the side of her backpack, and without a word to his wife, started the climb up the incline.

Nicki and Gill continued on, and when Rajim was out of earshot, Gill said, "You knew nothing about his drug use? Never saw any signs?"

Nicki's brow furrowed, lips narrowing, eyes like knives. "No, I didn't," she said. Then realizing the harshness of her tone, she softened. "I think he balances things a bit better at home, so the mood swings aren't as pronounced."

"There have never been any incidents? Things that now make more sense? Issues with the children?"

"No. Nothing. Rajim is great with the kids," Nicki said. "It's obvious he doesn't like you much, though."

That was no surprise. That's what happened when a husband discovered his wife had eyes for another.

Gill and Nicki passed through two large boulders and found their supply of firewood and saw their ring of stones. Gill said, "I'll get the fire going while you find a stick to roast that thing on."

"Aye," she said.

So it was that when Rajim returned their stew was ready for cooking in the turtle shell bowl, and the sweet aroma of charred meat stole over camp. "Look what I found," Rajim said as he handed his companions their water bottles. He held an uprooted plant.

"Oregano?" Nicki asked.

"Thyme, I think," he said. "It has a wonderfully sweet taste with a hint of pepper. Should I toss it in?"

"Pull the leaves off, rip them and then toss them in," she said. "I'll add water."

Gill and Nicki drank deeply as Rajim put the herb into the stew. "You check the radio?" Rajim asked as he worked.

Gill laughed. "I'd almost forgotten, we've been so busy cooking. No, it's up yonder on that big boulder. As soon as we're done eating we'll get it."

The three companions passed around the turtle shell, each slurping in meat and liquid. When the stew was done, Nicki said, "That barely put a dent in my hunger. I'm still famished."

"Me as well, but it was better than nothing," Rajim said.

Gill didn't speak. He stared up the incline at the large boulder atop which sat the tiny solar panel. What if the battery hadn't charged? What would they do? He had several ideas, but none of them were easy or fast.

After the companions broke their fast, they retrieved the radio.

"The red light is on," Gill said as he picked up the radio's battery. "It's got three dots out of five."

"You think we should try it or let it charge more?" Nicki said.

"It's taken days to get this far," Rajim said. "We must try it now. We have no choice."

There is always a choice, my friend, but in this situation, Gill believed Rajim to be correct. "Yeah, we've got to give it a go." Gill pulled the wire he'd rigged to connect the battery to the solar panel. Then he snapped the battery into place. "Drum roll, please." Nothing. Rajim and Nicki stared at him like he was nuts. "Drumroll? You guys never seen Lampoon's Christmas Vacation?" They stared blankly at him. "Jeezus."

He twisted the control knob. The radio beeped, a burst of static, then nothing except the occasional rip of interference. "Here goes." He turned the channel selector to the emergency channel, and said, "Mayday. Mayday. This is Gill Philips, and I'm with Sheriff Nicki Sande and her husband Rajim. We are in need of assistance. Anyone copy?"

Nothing.

Gill activated the emergency beacon signal and repeated his distress call into the radio. Minutes flew by, and when Gill pressed the small button to check the battery strength he saw that it was down to two red lights. "Shit," he said. He raised the radio to throw it, but Nicki put her hand on his arm and brought it down.

"Don't go doing something y—" Nicki said.

"H... l....too," burst from the radio. The companions stood stunned, staring at the device as if it had magical properties.

Gill brought the radio to his mouth to respond, Nicki stopped him. "You'll step on their transmission."

Seconds passed with only an occasional burst of static.

Rajim said, "Try again."

Gill got halfway through repeating the distress call when static burst from the radio.

"G... l? Do you... Where d.... corn... dents," said a male voice over the radio.

"Shit," Gill yelled, and he held the radio above his head in a vain attempt to get a stronger signal.

"Did he say coordinates? That they have our coordinates?" Nicki said.

"No... I don't know. He could have been saying 'give me your coordinates.' But why? He should be able to get our location from the distress beacon."

"Signal might be intermittent," Rajim said.

They waited, but there was no further communication. Gill clicked off the radio to preserve power. "Where can we get a better signal?"

"I don't know," Rajim said. "But what I do know is we're real close to the cliff face and the signal might be bouncing around up here. If we go down to the valley floor, we'd still be boxed in by mountains, but maybe we'll get better reception."

"That's pretty thin," Gill said.

"You got anything else?" Rajim said. "We saw metal striations in the cave walls, remember?"

He didn't, and he did. Gill checked the battery and saw two red dots. He clicked the device off and put it in his backpack. "OK, let's go," he said.

The companions retraced their steps as they threaded their way through the forest, avoiding the local inhabitants, going slowly and carefully. Morning mist rose from the forest floor as it burned off under the glare of the sun. Gill was sweating, and he took off his jacket and tied it around his waist.

The party was waylaid when they came across a flock of grouse hiding within a shallow hollow, and Nicki and Gill picked-off seven birds in the matter of minutes as the survivors scattered. They gutted and stored the birds for later, drank some water, and pushed on.

The landscape had become dull and stale. Evergreen upon evergreen, scrub pine and juniper filling every crack. He longed for the forest of home, where a variety of trees and plants flourished at the lower elevations. Strange the things you miss when they're taken away.

They walked four hours without resting, and the sun passed the lip of the ice roof and dusk painted the valley grey. When Gill stumbled in his weariness he called a halt.

Nicki sat and drank water while she cleaned the haul of birds. Tonight, they'd have a feast.

Rajim wandered off into the forest and when he was gone, Nicki said, "You might want to make yourself scarce when he gets back."

"Why?" Gill said.

"We're going to settle this drug shit once and for all," she said.

"I'll stay, just in case things get nasty," he said.

She nodded and continued plucking feathers from dinner.

Rajim came back with a big smile on his face and went to get his water bottle.

"Feeling better?" Nicki asked.

"Huh?" Rajim feinted ignorance.

"Didn't your mother tell you if you don't have enough for everyone..."

"Stop. I don't need this right now," Rajim said.

"I don't give a shit," she said. "You're going to stop this craziness. Now. Or when we get home we're done, and I won't let you see the children."

Gill started.

"You would do that? To me?" The betrayal and pain in his voice made Nicki look away.

Without meeting her husband's eye, she said, "You bet I will. I don't want my kids around a junkie, no matter how functional."

Rajim's chin fell to his chest.

Nicki backed off. "It's not too late."

Rajim lifted his head and looked at Gill. "You put her up to this?"

Gill raised his hands in surrender. "Nothing. This is all her, and if I were you I'd listen."

"You're not me, and you have no idea what it means to be me," Rajim said.

"Yes, I know, you have it so rough," Gill said.

"Will the two of you stop it. What? I'm not my own person now, Rajim? Capable of my own thoughts without help?"

"That's no—"

"Yeah, I know."

Birds chirped, the ground trembled, and somewhere a giant beast roared.

"Should we try here? We've come down far enough," Gill said.

"Why not. Give it a go," Nicki said.

31

Gill turned on the radio and held it in the air, moving it around trying to get a signal. Static burst from the device, then nothing. Rajim and Nicki huddled close, all three companions focused on the radio. Another burst of static, then a rhythmic pitter-patter that reminded Gill of driving on a concrete road and the thump of passing over expansion joints.

Gill repeated his distress call three times but got no response. The status light for the emergency beacon function glowed green, so Gill assumed it was sending out their location. There was nothing to do now but wait.

"Well that was a—" started Rajim.

Static, then "We... py," said a voice, broken as the signal dropped out. "W—" A sharp burst of static, then "yee."

"Did you hear copy? He said copy," Nicki said. "Did you hear it?"

"I heard something, but..." Rajim said.

"I definitely heard it. Twice. We copy. Should we 10-4 back?" Nicki said.

Gill lifted the radio and spoke into it. "10-4. We copy. What is your ETA?"

Nothing but static. The party waited. A minute. Then two, and then five. Nothing, not even static. The radio beeped a long mournful death buzz and shut down. Gill saw that the light for the emergency beacon was still green. It should continue to transmit for days as it ran on a trickle charge.

"Well that's that," Gill said.

"Should we charge it again?" Nicki said.

"Why not? What do we have to lose?"

Nicki nodded.

Gill rolled out the solar panel and placed it atop a stone and reconnected the wire to the battery.

"Let's have something to eat," Nicki said.

They'd saved some food from the prior night, and the companions sat and ate grouse and drank water.

"Now what?" Nicki said between bites.

"We wait. What else is there?" Rajim said.

Gill didn't like the man's tone. He hadn't disappeared recently, and his eye sockets were red, and he was jumpy and stressed. Who could blame him after what he'd been through? It was a miracle they all hadn't cracked.

"We could continue our search for a way out? There's plenty of valley edge left to search, though I'm not hopeful," Gill said.

"Nor me. The raptors would have found any way out, and it would be a major coincidence if they found two ways out at the same time after all these years," Nicki said.

"Unless it hasn't been many years," Rajim said. "Does it matter? We've got nothing better to do."

"It does matter because we've almost been killed about ten times since we got here. If we believe we were successful in communicating with the outside world, why not wait for a rescue while staying safe up on the precipice?" Nicki said.

"And if we're wrong?" Rajim said.

"Then we're wrong. So what? If nobody shows in the next few days we'll know," Nicki said.

Gill sat back and listened to the debate but didn't offer an opinion. He wasn't sure what they should do. He thought their emergency beacon had done its job, but what that meant, and the timing were beyond his speculation. He didn't like the idea of traipsing around the forest, especially since he didn't think further searching would yield any fruit based on what he'd seen.

"Gill, looks like you're the tie-breaking vote," Nicki said.

Rajim sighed.

"I'm not sure. Let's make camp in the hollow where we caught the grouse. Get some rest and think on things a bit," Gill said. His companions didn't look happy, but they offered no alternatives.

They'd been trapped over a week and had made little progress escaping the valley. The party was covered in bug bites and cuts, so Rajim and Nicki didn't protest. They worked their way back to the dell, caught a few more grouse and prepared them for cooking.

"The taste of these things is growing on me," Gill said.

"Your new holiday dinner?" Nicki said.

"Wouldn't go that far, but it tastes like gamey duck," Gill said.

Rajim said, "Thanks for that. Now I know I never need to try duck."

"You've never eaten duck?" Gill said.

"No!" Rajim snapped. He drew into himself like a deflating balloon, aware of the intensity of his response.

Nicki said, "Do you need to go to the bathroom?"

Gill braced for an angry retort, but instead Rajim took his wife's hands in his. He held them up to his mouth and kissed them. "Nicki, I've heard you and there's no way I'm going to lose you."

Gill's heart ached. He didn't want to hear this.

"I love you, and Kiki and Fred. I don't know what I'd do without you," Rajim said. He went to embrace his wife and she pushed him back.

Rajim reached into his pocket and drew out the baggie of heroin. There wasn't much left. "I haven't had any since... since you gave me your ultimatum."

"Look, I said what I said because—"

"No, it's OK, honey, really it is," Rajim said.

Nicki looked to Gill and he saw her question there. "Is this really a good time to do this?" he'd said. He'd warned her. "You clearly need medical help with this. It's nothing to be ashamed of, so if you need a little to get you through this we'll tackle it when we get out of here."

"No, there will be no counseling," Rajim said.

"How do—"

Rajim ripped the baggie and let its contents fall to the ground, and he pressed the brown powder into the dirt with his foot. Then he dropped the baggie.

Gill smiled. First piece of litter. He was proud of the man despite their problems. It took guts to slay your demons, and Rajim had taken the first step.

"Oh, Rajim," Nicki said. She threw her arms around him and they kissed, Gill forgotten.

Dusk deepened as the day faded, and the three companions rested under a conifer. Gill's stomach gurgled. He'd eaten nothing but meat since the last power bar, and his body wasn't used to it.

Rajim was having a tough time. He shook uncontrollably and three times he'd had to run into the forest to puke. He looked half dead, but was remarkably upbeat. Nicki tended to him, and he'd sent no malicious vibes Gill's way since Nicki had recognized the sacrifice he'd made. What we do for our families, thought Gill. Then he remembered he no longer had a family, and the now familiar heat of sorrow rushed over him and he hung his head.

"You alright, cowboy?" Rajim said.

"Just not feeling great," Gill said.

"Why don't you hit us with those escape ideas you have?" Rajim said.

"If you feel up to it," Nicki added.

"I'm fine," Gill said. He shifted his position because something was digging into his leg. He removed the offending stone. "If we can't go under or through the mountains, then we have to go over them."

"We've been through this," Nicki said.

"Give the man a chance," Rajim said, and Nicki turned to him in amazement.

"I'm not talking about climbing over them. I know we can't do that, not unless it was our last resort."

"What resort are we at now? Club Primo?" Rajim said, but his tone was jovial.

"We could attempt an ascent, but maybe there's another way over," Gill said.

Nicki and Rajim waited patiently and said nothing.

"We could make a balloon, a glider, or kite to reach the top of the mountain peaks. If getting over isn't possible, a signal fire could be lit up high," Gill said.

"How would we make such things?" Nicki said.

"I think the balloon would be the easiest to construct. We could make the balloon itself using parts of our tents, or animal bladders or skin, although obtaining the latter would take time and require great skill and luck," Gill said.

"And what? You're gonna blow them up like it's your birthday?" Nicki said.

Gill chuckled. "We might be able to capture the gases from the thermal vents or the bubbling tar pit we saw. The tar itself could help seal the balloon."

"That sounds like ten kinds of crazy," Nicki said.

Rajim said nothing.

"You really think we could make something strong enough to carry all three of us?" Nicki said.

"No, only the lightest among us could go," Gill said. "And that would be you, Nicki."

At this, Rajim perked up. "No way, Gill. I won't allow it."

Nicki turned to Rajim and it seemed to Gill that all the goodwill the man had managed to garner from his wife dissipated like a puff of smoke. "You won't allow it?" she said.

Rajim's eyes fell to the ground. "I mean... sorry," he said meekly.

"So that's it? Make a glider out of who knows what, or try and make a balloon? That's all you got?" Nicki said.

Gill felt like telling her not to take her anger at her husband out on him but thought better of it. They were all stressed beyond normal capacity and tensions were running high. "No, I have a more practical idea." Gill paused, then said, "We could light a huge barn fire and throw wet wood on it. Smoke-out the entire valley. That would mark our location and perhaps someone would see the smoke, especially if they're already searching for us."

"Really? It took a couple of days to get folks to look for a three-year-old boy. Reserve could think us dead in the tunnel collapse. Especially if Kate didn't make it out. For all we know that radio transmission started the process."

There was Rajim and his rational points again. "Agreed, and there's no guarantee anyone will see the smoke, or care. We're at fifteen thousand feet above sea level."

Rajim said, "And burning down the valley with us in it might not be the smartest play. Things could get out of control, and what if we're stuck in here for a long time?"

Silence fell between them, and darkness settled over the valley. The fire felt good, and they cooked more grouse and drank the last of their water. The night symphony was going full tilt, and it was hard to hear anything other than the trill of insects. They saw no dinosaurs, but several squirrels and chipmunks approached camp to examine the travelers.

When they'd eaten, Gill said, "Rajim, how you holding up? Most people get a little help, drugs and stuff, when they go through something this hard."

Rajim lowered his head in the darkness. The man hugged himself, and he shook like he had the chills, but for the first time since Gill had known him, Rajim didn't seem angry with him. "I feel like shit. Thanks for that, by the way," he said.

"Rajim, I—"

"Oh, stop. I'm just busting your stones. Actually," he said as he turned toward his wife, "I owe you both a thank you. I'd been doing the shit for so long I didn't even think about it. I didn't even enjoy it anymore. I just did it because I always did, and I was afraid of the person I might be without it."

"All very common, honey," Nicki said.

Honey. That didn't take long. Amazing what a bit of honesty and humility could achieve. "You're one strong bastard. You know that?" Gill said.

Rajim laughed but didn't respond.

Blackness filled the valley, starlight providing the only light outside the fire's glow. The dark shapes of trees swayed in the gentle breeze, and the whisper and sigh of pine needles rubbing together accompanied the constant chiming of insects.

The ground rocked and what sounded like a massive explosion made Gill vault to his feet.

"What in all that is holy was that?" Rajim said.

The ground didn't shake, but the forest grew silent.

Another explosion split the night, and the sound of falling rocks was like an earthquake.

"I don't know what it is, but I know it's not a dinosaur," Gill said.

"Ground's not trembling, and that sure sounded like an explosion," Rajim said.

"Rescuers!" Nicki yelled. "Maybe they're trying to open the tunnel so we can get through?" Nicki said.

Gill stared toward the western mountains where he thought the sounds had come from, but saw no flashes of light, no fire. "Maybe," he said.

32

The valley woke. Creatures of the night mixed with the beasts of the daylight, and the ensuing chaos left Gill and his companions exposed at the center of it all. Beasts big and small fled the area as an avalanche tumbled down the mountainside to the west, flattening trees and reshaping the landscape. Dust and smoke clouded the night sky, and a great braying and screeching rose above the static of the insects.

Gill drew his slingshot, realized it wouldn't do much against the apex predators of the valley, and put it away. "Rajim, get that rifle ready."

"How many bullets do you have left?" Nicki asked.

"Four," Rajim said. "Thanks to me using the gun sparingly. Hopefully it will fire." Rajim had cleaned the weapon after its dunk in the lake and declared it OK to go.

"That was easy with me taking all the shots for you," Gill said.

Nicki sighed, and Gill looked at his feet.

The party hid within a densely packed section of forest surrounded on three sides by boulders. "How far to the precipice?" Nicki said.

"At least three miles," Gill said. "Should we make a run for it?"

"What? Are you crazy?" Rajim said. "It's pitch-black and we can barely see our hands in front of our faces, and you want to risk moving? With four bullets?"

"What if Nicki's right, and the explosions are for a rescue attempt?" Gill said.

"Then they can wait seven hours until sun up. They'll still be there, and we can travel safer and faster in the daylight," Rajim said.

Gill considered this, but when a young *spinosaurus* poked its head through the trees and roared, the party scattered, running through the woods blindly. A flashlight flicked on ahead and Gill saw it was Nicki. She waited for Rajim and him at the edge of a small clearing.

"Hurry!" she yelled, as Gill crossed the open space with Rajim.

When they reached Nicki, Rajim spun around and brought up his rifle. "You guys go ahead. I'll catch up." He kissed Nicki and dropped to one knee, sighting the weapon on the dark shape of the dinosaur as it came at them in the blackness.

"No," Nicki said.

Gill grabbed her arm. "He's right. Let's go," Gill said, but Nicki wouldn't budge.

The outline of the beast was twenty yards away when Rajim fired. One shot to the head that stopped the *spinosaurus* in its tracks. The dark shape paused, and then the beast let loose with a fart that splattered feces on the evergreens. The creature sputtered and fell over with a crash.

"Where did you learn to do that?" Nicki said, but like all the other times she'd asked this type of question of her husband she got a simple one-word answer.

"Military," Rajim said. He slung the gun over a shoulder and stood up, the thunderous cacophony of the valley's creatures rising to a crescendo.

A pack of cat sized beasts that looked like giant squirrels running on two legs bolted past but paid them no mind.

Rumble. Rumble.

The trill of insects stopped, and a light breeze reminiscent of gunpowder and rotten eggs stirred leaves, and shadows danced under every tree bow. In the darkness the party moved slow for fear of tripping or falling due to an unseen obstacle. Gill led, feeling his way like a blind person through the trees, branches scraping at his face, pain lancing his back, knees and feet.

Rumble. Rumble. Rumble.

"Sounds like mom and dad are on the move," Nicki said.

A familiar clicking sound brought Gill to a halt and Rajim and Nicki bumped into him in the darkness. Stray beams of moonlight cut through the sparse cloud cover, throwing spot lights on the valley floor. A *utahraptor* stood within the light, watching the party.

"It sees us," Gill said. "Rajim?"

"I see it," he said. He had his rifle at the ready. "I've got three bullets left, so until this thing attacks us I'm holding fire."

Fair enough, Gill thought. The beast lifted its snout and sniffed the air, its golf ball sized eyes glowing in the darkness. The dinosaur scratched at the ground, then decided they weren't worth the risk and scampered off into the forest.

The company continued, working through the evergreens, scattering birds.

Nicki stepped on a stone, twisted her ankle, and fell with a yelp.

"Sweetie," Rajim said as he came to his wife's aid. "Are you OK?" He helped her up, but she winced and cried with pain.

"I think it's broken."

Gill ran his fingers through his hair. This was exactly what he'd been worried about. How would they make it now with Nicki being unable to run? "You can't put weight on it?" Gill said.

"Not really. It hurts badly," she said.

"You need to try. We—"

"She doesn't need to do shit. Stay out of this, Gill," Rajim said. Then he turned to his wife, and said, "He's got a point, though. We can't stay here."

"Should we carry her?" Gill said, but as soon as he said it he knew that wasn't a real possibility. The confines of the forest were too tight, and it was hard enough for one person to squeeze between the trees, but two people carrying a third? It would take days to reach the cliffside.

"That will never work," Rajim said before Gill could recant his suggestion. "What about a crutch? We could make one fast from a tree branch."

"It hurts bad, Raj," she said.

As if in answer a roar broke the stillness and was answered by several others.

"You're gonna have to fight through the pain," Rajim said. "Gill, can you find a stick for a crutch?"

"I'll try," he said.

Gill dropped his pack and went searching. In the darkness it was difficult to see anything with clarity, so he took to turning on the one remaining flashlight for short intervals, so he might see where he was going.

He'd stumbled around for ten minutes when he heard Nicki's cry of pain. He backtracked and found Rajim standing over his wife. "What the hell happened?"

"I touched her ankle. I think she's right, it's broken," he said.

"Great, just great." Gill threw up his hands in frustration.

"You fin... ah... branch?" Nicki said through clenched teeth.

"No, I rushed back here when I heard your scream," Gill said.

"I got it covered here, Gill," Rajim said. "Go. Get it done. And fast."

"Yeah," Gill said.

The forest continued to come alive as the beasts of the valley fled the explosions on the eastern mountain face.

Gill found what he was looking for in a pile of sticks that appeared to have been gathered by a flood. It was difficult to tell in the blackness, but Gill believed at one point a large volume of water had flowed this way. Perhaps a chunk of the fallen ice sheet melting? The stick was long with a Y at its end. Gill dragged the branch through the forest.

When Rajim saw the branch he said, "That's perfect."

"How long should I make it?" Gill asked.

"Lay the branch next to her."

Gill did so and was able to break the stick at the perfect point. Rajim helped Nicki to her feet, and she put the Y end of the stick under her arm and took a step forward. She winced with pain but kept going.

"You OK?" Rajim asked.

"No, but what choice do I have?" she said.

Gill and Rajim said nothing. Gill took the lead and Rajim followed Nicki as the party continued their trek through the forest.

"Do you hear that?" Nicki said. She stopped walking and leaned heavily on her crutch.

A faint puffing sound like the exhalation of some giant beast thrummed in the distance.

"No idea. Come on," Rajim said.

The party came free of the trees and a clearing dotted with stones and devil's grass stretched before them.

"You recognize this place?" Rajim asked.

"No, but we better avoid it. Look," Gill said.

Two dark forms crouched low at the center of the open space. The beasts weren't large, but their green eyes glowed in the blackness, and the rumble of growling echoed over the clearing.

"Mountain lions?" Gill said.

"Haven't seen any signs of them yet, but I wasn't looking," Nicki said. "We go around?"

To the north there was a crag in the land filled with junipers, and to the south the ground rose to a line of stones that marked the top of a hill. They could go around the hill or try and sneak past the cats. "I don't know," Gill said. "I guess we should go around because if we're forced to run…"

One of the mountain lions roared, and four green eyes approached in the darkness.

Rajim said, "You think a warning shot will do anything?"

"It might," Gill said.

Rajim brought the butt of the rifle to his shoulder but didn't fire. A hollow boom reverberated over the valley, and the cats bolted.

"Another explosion?" Nicki said.

"Sure sounded like it," Rajim said.

The rhythmic thumping sound returned, like driving a car on a flat tire. Gill wiped sweat from his brow and said, "At least now we can cut across."

With Rajim's help, Nicki hobbled across the clearing, Gill watching their backs.

"What the hell is that?" Rajim said. A white glow was building between two mountain peaks to the southeast.

"No idea," Gill said.

The rifle fell off Rajim's shoulder as he struggled to help his wife. He got frustrated and gave it to Gill. "Only three bullets left, and I reserve the right to take it back."

Gill was astonished. "Thanks," was all he could manage.

"What good is it if I can't have it at the ready?" Rajim said.

The light in the mountains grew, and the thumping sound morphed into the *womp womp* of helicopter rotors pounding air.

"Is that what I think it is?" Nicki said.

"Sure is," Rajim said.

The three companions who'd struggled and fought for each other shared a communal hug. They watched as the searchlight of a helicopter glided through the mountains, its bright light a beacon in the darkness.

"Should we light a signal fire?" Rajim said.

Gill searched the forest. The creatures of the primeval valley didn't care there was a helicopter on the way, and all the dangers they'd faced since arrival were still valid threats and a fire would bring predators like ants to honey. They didn't have enough time to make a big enough fire anyway. "Not yet."

Another explosion rocked the night, and stones fell, and rock cracked.

The helicopter raced over the valley and disappeared over the lip of the ice shelf and was gone, the sound of its rotors fading.

"It didn't see us?" Nicki said. She turned to Rajim. "They didn't see us."

"No signal fire," Rajim said.

"Yes, I'm sure we could have gotten a blaze going in the thirty seconds," Gill said.

Rajim's shoulders slumped and Nicki stared at the ground.

"Chins up. They're looking in the right area," Gill said. "If those were explosions like we think, they've got a decent idea where we are. Let's press on."

Rajim spat and Nicki sighed.

What else could they do? Gill thought. He slung the rifle over a shoulder and led Nicki and Rajim into the woods.

33

In the darkness every shrub and stone was a menace that could take the companions down. Nicki struggled through the tightly packed trees, squeaking in pain with each step. Rajim tried to help her, but it was difficult in the tight confines. If Gill never saw or touched another evergreen again in his life he'd be fine with that, and his happy memories of Christmas trees had been permanently tainted. Moonlight slanted into the valley, the ice roof's broken edge sparkling in the blackness. The constant sound of chaos filled the night and the air was heavy with the scent of rotten eggs again.

Gill froze, and Nicki and Rajim bumped into him.

"Wha—" Rajim said.

"Sssssh!" Gill turned and whispered, "There's something ahead in the trees."

Many sets of glowing green eyes peered through the woods ahead, and the sounds of clicking teeth, grunts and whines filled the forest.

"Gill." Nicki tugged on his arm and he turned. Eyes glowed in the blackness to the north, and all around the party.

Gill brought up the rifle, but firing in the tight confines of the evergreens would be wasting bullets and inviting a ricochet. Nicki couldn't run even if they had the space, and holding their ground wasn't an option because the beasts would tighten their circle and close in. With fleeing and standing their ground off the table there was but one option. Attack.

Gill whispered in the darkness. "Rajim, your job is to help your wife and keep your eyes on me. Stay low and move fast. I'm gonna carve a path out of here using our last three bullets."

"Who are you kidding? You can't hit the side of a barn. Especially in the dark on the run. Let me do the shooting and you..." Realizing what he was about to say, he turned to his wife and said, "It's your call, babe."

Nicki pecked him on the cheek, and said, "Go shoot."

Gill handed over the rifle without protest and Rajim flicked off the safety. "Make sure your hands don't stray," Rajim said, but Gill could see the man's white teeth glowing in the darkness as he smiled.

The dinosaurs were agitated from the explosions and falling rocks and were on full alert, and Rajim moved through the forest like a soldier, clearing the path for his wife as Gill supported her. The companions dropped their packs for added speed as they could be retrieved if the worst occurred and they remained trapped in the valley. Screeches and wails of frightened animals erupted around them and shadows danced under every tree and behind every stone.

The party hit a thicket of juniper and Rajim headed south, then paused to let Gill and Nicki catch up. She was winded, and Gill was breaking down. Tiny stars flashed in the darkness before him, and his head swam as he grew dizzy. Hundreds of eyes packed the forest behind them, but using the thicket as cover, Rajim led the company south.

"Why don't they attack?" Nicki said.

"We're bigger and unknown," Gill said. "They're probably more scared of us than we are of them, but I don't know," he added. He didn't want to mansplain because he was just making an educated guess.

"I don't know," Nicki said.

"You two want tea?" Rajim said.

A blur of teeth and claws flew from the blackness, and Gill pulled his knife and plunged it into a raptor's chest. He kicked the corpse into the darkness and said, "We have to keep moving."

An explosion shook the eastern mountainside and rocks tumbled and dust obscured the moonlight.

"They might bring the mountain down," Rajim said.

"Keep going," Gill said.

The faint light of dawn peeked its head over the snowcapped mountains as another day came to the valley. The Douglas firs thinned, and junipers packed the ground. Rajim dropped to his knees and crawled into the tangled bushes as Gill and Nicki looked on. Gill was going to call out to Rajim, ask him to hold up, but didn't because he realized the beauty of the plan. If Nicki army crawled, or went on her hands and knees, she was off her ankle. "It'll be OK. Come on," Gill said. He dropped to the ground and crawled into the underbrush.

Spiders and insects of all sizes and shapes bit, scratched, and poked at Gill as pine needles and dead leaves filled his hair and slipped down his shirt. He crawled behind Rajim through the junipers, which were getting bigger but more widely spaced.

The party came free of the tangle and a clearing opened before them, the rotted carcass of a beast at its center. Clouds of flies swarmed, and the stench was intolerable. Gill gagged and put a hand over his mouth, but it didn't help. He puked yellow bile and his throat burned.

"You with me," Rajim said, looking back.

Gill thought of Nicki and looked over his shoulder, but the woman wasn't there.

"Where's Nicki?" Rajim said. "For shits sake. I ask you to do one thing and you—"

"I'm here," Nicki said. She slithered free of the thicket, blood dripping from gashes on her cheeks and arms, her face wrinkled with pain.

The companions took a moment to rest, and their pursuers inched from the underbrush and surrounded them.

The beasts were turkey sized and stood upright like humans. Narrow heads filled with teeth sat atop slender bodies the color of mustard. Glowing green eyes stared through the gloom as daybreak spread over the valley. Black rounded talons stuck from what looked like hands and feet. Gill couldn't see how many appendages were on each hand and foot, but the more Gill studied the creatures the more they resembled humanoids, however small.

The biggest of the flock stepped forward and squawked, its head bobbing up and down. It took several more steps, its herd following.

Rajim lifted the rifle and blew the head off the leader. Blood and bone splattered on the creatures following and stopped their advance. The decapitated creature's lifeless body stood still for an instant, its short arms spasming, and then toppled over.

"What the hell!" Nicki yelled.

"He did what needed to be done, Nicki," Gill said. "You see the teeth on these things? Brian doesn't have any dinosaur figures that look like that." The use of the present tense made Gill feel for his dead son's sneaker in his pocket. He gripped it, memories of his boy flooding through him.

The new alpha stepped forward and replaced its predecessor, its flock behind it, yipping and screaming. There was at least fifty of the tiny beasts, and they packed into the clearing and surrounded the party as if their leader's brains weren't dripping down some of their faces.

"I've only got two bullets left, so I suggest you guys get your slingshots out," Rajim said.

The companions stood back-to-back, weapons before them as the creatures advanced.

One of the beasts lunged forward and Gill fired a stone. It connected with the creature's snout, but the shot only seemed to anger the beast as it came on, teeth bared, its low growl-gargle like distant thunder.

"We're going to have to run through them," Rajim said.

"You nuts? They'll be all over us. And Nicki—" Gill said.

"That's gonna happen in a minute anyway, Gill, I think—" Nicki said.

The roar of a mountain lion brought everything to a halt. The creatures froze, heads jolting about, searching. On the western edge of the clearing two cats prowled beneath the junipers. Several of the strange creatures fled, but the remaining beasts gathered together, their eyes focused on the newcomers.

Gill said, "That be our cue. Come on. Quiet now."

Moving as slow as they were able, Gill and his companions moved away from the impending fight, gradually easing to the south.

"Damn, that was some lucky shit right there," Rajim said.

"Seems so," Nicki said.

More roars as the mountain lions moved in and several of the small monsters ripped through the forest. The sound of tearing meat and breaking bone, and the scent of blood filled the forest, but the companions didn't pause or look back.

Rajim led, and Gill stumbled along half carrying Nicki as they struggled through the evergreens, the cliff face with the precipice rising out of the mist to the east.

"We're almost there. Fast as you can now," Rajim said.

Nicki whined and cried as her broken ankle tormented her.

Several of the toothy creatures, fear forgotten, blocked the party's way through the trees. Rajim didn't slow, he shot the two lead beasts and pushed through the flock, using the rifle to knock the creatures aside. They were out of ammunition and were down to knives and rocks.

An orange glow grew above the mountains as the grey of dawn spread over the valley. Another explosion rocked the ground and debris cascaded down the mountainside. A great cloud of dust pushed across the forest like fog and all visibility was lost.

Animals brayed and squawked as they fled, and Rajim paused beneath a giant conifer to catch his breath. "You…. Ys…. K?" he said.

Nicki nodded.

Gill said, "I'm done. I don't think I can run anymore."

"No worries. We'll take it slow," Rajim said. He moved to take his wife's arm and Gill stepped aside. No more shooting to be done so Gill was no longer needed.

"It's not far now. One last push," Rajim said.

They worked their way free of the woods and hit the cliff face. Gill couldn't make out the precipice above, and thought they were still too far north. They followed the base of the mountains, pausing to drink water that dripped down the cliff face.

The low throb of helicopter rotors thumped in the distance, and rocks and debris still slid down the mountainside. The companions came around a boulder and two *spinosaurus* stood facing one another, chomping and spitting as they circled. The beasts didn't appear to notice the party, but there was no way around.

Gill drew back his slingshot and fired a stone above the beasts' heads. It smacked against the rockface and froze the combatants in place.

"Whatcha do that for?" Rajim said.

"Distraction," he said.

The two beasts searched the area, their bulbous eyes rolling, their dispute forgotten. Rajim drew his knife, looked at it, and put it back in its sheath.

"Maybe lash it to the end of the stick? Like a spear?" Gill said.

Rajim looked ready to retort, but then his eyes went wide, and he grabbed a branch that lay at his feet. It was twisted and bent, but better than nothing. Nicki broke off a thin vine wrapped around the trunk of an evergreen, and Rajim did his best to tie the knife in place. He looked to Gill, and said, "I can at least throw it now. Maybe get one of the bastards in the eye."

Sunlight angled into the valley as the sun crested the mountains and the *spinosaurs* were invigorated. They stepped back from one another, their yellow sail-like backs swaying as they shifted their weight and turned.

"Oh shit," said Nicki. She leaned on her crutch, watching the thirty-foot dinosaurs. "They see us."

The beasts fell in side-by-side, now together in a common goal. The bigger of the two lifted one of its massive legs and stomped the ground and the land trembled. The *womp womp* of the approaching helicopter didn't deter the animals as they came at the party who had their backs to the mountainside.

Above, the precipice loomed in the growing light. The tunnel mouth stood undisturbed, but there, standing on the ledge gazing into the valley, was Ant and Squirrel.

34

Gill pressed his back to the cliff face and Rajim put a protective arm around his wife. The larger *spinosaurus* stepped forward, lowering its head to the ground, and its mouth slid open revealing twelve-inch teeth. The beast gurgled and roared. Its breath was like a gust of wind and the scent of rotten meat washed over him.

Gunshots rang out, but the *spinosaurus* didn't stop coming. Gill looked up but couldn't see Ant or Squirrel. They were firing down at a difficult angle, and even if they hit the beasts, all it seemed to do was piss them off, like sticking a bull with a cattle prod.

The second, smaller *spinosaurus* dropped in behind its buddy as the larger beast advanced. They were a hundred yards away and the pounding of helicopter rotors drowned out all other sound. Dust clouds covered the area as tree branches bent and snapped, and a mighty wind tore through the valley as the helicopter descended past the lip of the ice shelf.

Still the dinosaurs came on.

"Let's move. Stay against the mountainside," Rajim said. He and Nicki inched along the rockface, her crutch gone. Blood dripped from gashes on her face, and her eye sockets were so dark it looked like she had two black eyes.

Hunger pains cut through Gill's chest and he doubled over and leaned against the mountainside. Rajim and Nicki disappeared into the fog of dust. The *womp womp* of pounding rotors shook the air and finally the great beasts turned to look.

The Eurocopter AS350 dropped through the dust and mist, and a person manning a machine gun sat in the open side door.

"We need to get out of the line of fire," Gill said. The helicopter continued its descent, and in moments it would open fire on the dinosaurs.

Ant yelled, but the path that led up to the precipice was still a half mile distant. He remembered the spot with the giant boulder and the gnarled tree. It was the only non-evergreen he remembered seeing in the entire valley. A thought scampered across his brain. Perhaps it had been planted there to mark the path?

"Ouch," Nicki yelled. Something had bitten her.

"What?"

"Snake," Rajim said. "It was in the rocks and when she braced herself it got her."

"How bad?"

"Hurts and it's swelling," she said.

"Keep going, the path should be right up here," Gill said.

The helicopter dropped in low above the *spinosauri*, who roared and bit at the copter as it hovered, but didn't come close. The machine gun rattled, peppering the giant beasts with bullets. The creatures spasmed as they were hit, blood spouting from holes along the dinosaurs' heads and torsos.

The gun kept firing, the glow of its muzzle flash faint in the growing light of morning. The smaller of the two beasts yelped in pain and collapsed, its arms and legs flaying about. Dust rose and obscured the battle, and Gill turned and made one last push for the path.

Clouds of dirt swirled like a hurricane, and Gill lost Nicki and Rajim. They weren't his problem anymore. If they stayed close to the mountainside they'd hit the path. The ground shook, and Gill fell, smacking his head on a rock. Blood poured into his eyes as he propped himself against the cliff face, head spinning.

"You OK?" It was Rajim.

"Yeah," Gill said. Rajim helped him to his feet, but he swayed and if not for Rajim grabbing him under his arms he would have fallen.

"Great. Now I've got to carry you both?" Rajim said without malice. Some of the redness around the man's eyes had faded, and his permanent scowl had been replaced with a sardonic smirk.

The valley shook again, and the machine gun fire stopped.

"Both those big boys are down," Rajim said.

Nicki hobbled from the dust cloud and kissed him "They can take us out of here now!"

The sound of helicopter rotors pounding air filled the valley.

"Where will they land?" Rajim said.

"I think we should head up to the precipice. Ant and Squirrel are up there, and they'll know what the plan is. The path is right there," Gill said. He pointed at the large boulder and forlorn tree as the air cleared and the dust settled.

Gill led, not looking back. Nicki whined and cried, her ankle dangling loose from the end of her leg, Rajim mostly carrying her.

The rock wall was to their left, and the land fell away to the forest to the right. Fog hung over the tree tops, and the scent of peat permeated the air. Ant yelled from above, but Gill didn't understand what he was saying.

The party reached the giant stone and turned upward, climbing the slope covered in gravel and sand. Gill slipped several times, and Nicki was having a hard time and making very little progress. Rajim held her, but when the rocks slid in the sand there was nothing to be done except take the ride and start again.

Gill reached the animal path that led to the precipice and he paused to wait for his companions. His heart pounded in his chest, hunger cramps bit his stomach, and every muscle in his body shrieked.

Rajim was behind Nicki, pushing her up the slope as best he could.

Chirping and braying came from the woods below, and two *utahraptors* stepped from the foliage. The beasts cocked their heads, dark eyes watching the climbers.

Rajim slipped and grabbed a stone, then lost hold of Nicki who slid down the slope and came to a stop covered in pebbles and sand.

The raptors moved toward Nicki, tossing their heads and howling.

Rajim leapt down the slope, his makeshift spear pointing outward like a lance. He screamed and put himself between the beasts and his wife.

The raptors were a flash of green and yellow, and they encircled Rajim. Nicki screamed, but the animals were undeterred. They bit and chomped at Rajim, who thrust his spear point at the dinosaurs, but it was almost comical to think a knife tied to a stick could hurt these creatures.

One of the raptors shrieked, throwing its head in the air, and attacked.

Gunshots from above and tiny puffs of dust on the ground. The raptor's head darted in and out, jaws snapping at Rajim as he struggled to fend off the beast. He slashed wildly with his spear-knife, but the raptor's head dodged and swayed, avoiding the blade.

The smaller raptor got hold of Rajim's leg and dragged him down. He screamed, and Gill leapt down the slope, sliding in the stones, knife at the ready. Rajim's right leg was severed and his frenemy shrieked again, blood spurting from the wound.

The larger raptor moved in, and Rajim pleaded for help, but Nicki was down and out, and Gill was still twenty feet from the fray. The raptor's head knifed forward, its jaws clamping down on Rajim's midsection, breaking him in half. Blood flew from his mouth as what was left of Rajim was bitten and torn apart.

Nicki yelled and cursed, tears streaming down her face. The raptor eating Rajim's leg fled into the forest, but the other beast wasn't going to give up its kill as easily. It dropped Rajim's remains, blood dripping from its smiling mouth, fat and skin stuck between its teeth.

Gill charged, all rational thought gone, letting loose with a primal scream that tore at his vocal chords and set his throat on fire. The raptor was unfazed. It barked and reared-up, knocking Gill to the ground, and returned to devouring Rajim's corpse.

Rajim's head disappeared into the creature's mouth, and the resounding *pop* as his skull was crushed brought the tears Gill thought would never come.

The raptor fled with what was left of Rajim, leaving Nicki sobbing like a child.

Gill didn't know how long he sat there, staring at the blood-soaked ground where Rajim had been. Nicki lay in the fetal position, weeping, her head in her hands.

"Gill! Gill!" It was Ant, and the big man had his hand on Gill's shoulder.

"Ant?" Gill said from his daze. "Ant? What are you doing here?"

Ant lifted Gill to his feet. "Come on now. We've got to go."

"But... Rajim. What about Rajim?" Gill said.

"You saw it with your own eyes. He's gone," Ant said.

Squirrel tried to help Nicki up, but the injured woman was lost in her grief, and she struggled and fought.

Together the three men and one woman climbed the slope and ran the narrow path through the boulders to basecamp. Dust and smoke curled from the cave entrance, and Gill heard the echoes of voices within.

"You blasted through?" Gill said.

"Barely. There is so much ice most of the tunnel collapsed and what's left is unstable," Squirrel said. "We need to hurry."

"What?" Nicki said. Dirty rivers of mud formed on her face as she wept, her red eyes filled with tears. "Why can't we take the copter? My ankle is killing me."

"Too small, and landing in the valley would be a challenge. Now that we've found you, they want us to take the tunnel out," Ant said.

"They?" Nicki said.

"We hired a heli-ski copter to look for you, and Fire Chief Perry and Kate are running things in the tunnel. We called the staties as soon as you went missing, but as you might've predicted they felt the situation would remedy itself and wanted to give things a few days."

"Kate and Belinda are OK?" Gill said.

"Fine. Everyone is fine," Ant said.

Not everyone. Gill fingered Brian's sneaker in his pocket. "You know about Clint?"

Ant nodded.

A gust of wind tore across the valley, swirling the smoke, dirt and dust. Dinosaurs wailed. It was time to leave, but Gill felt unsure. So much had happened, and there was so much in this place he didn't understand. Now that he was almost free, his mind turned to coming back.

Nicki sat on a stone, head in her hands, weeping uncontrollably. "What am I gonna do? How do I tell Kiki and Fred?"

Gill wanted to tell her there was no good way to tell children their father was never coming home. There would be confusion, denial, desperation, and finally anger. Anger that would be directed at her because the children would have nobody else to dump their fears on. Gill wanted to tell her to hang in there, that time helped, but he said nothing and stared up at the broken ice roof and cried, knowing he was part of the reason Rajim was dead.

The pounding of the helicopter's rotors faded.

35

Gill stuffed his face with trail mix and drank two sixteen-ounce bottles of water. The company had halted to rest and eat in a section of tunnel undisturbed by the cave-ins and explosions. Darkness trailed away to his right and left, and Kate, Ant, and Squirrel sat on the ground in a circle with him. Several other people milled about, some Gill knew, others were new to him. The town had put forth considerable effort once Belinda and the others returned and told their stories.

Most of the people in the rescue party didn't look Gill in the eye, as if they felt a collective town guilt for not believing him when Brian had first been taken. Now that time had passed Gill understood Brian was probably dead before Nicki found Gill unconscious in the forest, so in the end the delay probably hadn't mattered.

Nicki sat in a ball off by herself, back against the cave wall, head bent and resting on her knees, which were held tight against her chest. This was a problem. Gill blamed himself for Rajim's death, and it was only a matter of time before his wife came to that conclusion. Gill had tried to talk with her, but Nicki hadn't spoken since they'd entered the tunnel. She was in shock, and hadn't eaten or had any water, and Gill worried for his... the word friend popped into his mind. Were they friends? What do you call two people who've had inappropriate feelings for each other, and have kissed and gone through an ordeal so intense they're forced to bond?

"You got our beacon signal?" Gill said.

Kate said, "Yeah, but we already had a plan, but it was good to hear your voice and know your exact location."

"What of you? We didn't know if you'd made it. When the cave collapsed we called out, but you didn't answer," Gill said.

"I took a beating," she said, and held up her right arm which had a blue cast from elbow to wrist as evidence. "Everything works, but it was a painful climb out. Lydia found me and strapped me to Rhubarb and we went back to Reserve. No idea if you guys were alive or dead. I worried the roof had fallen on you."

"How did you convince them to search for us?" Gill said.

"Our story. The monsters. But most of all, I think it was the fact I was alive. If I survived, it was certainly plausible you had," Kate said.

"Plus, Squirrel and I had been back two days, telling everyone who would listen about what we'd seen. When Lydia came into town with

Kate strapped to Rhubarb it was like a movie. People started to believe, and the adventurers and sportsmen started to show interest."

"And the copter? That had to be big money. And who in the shit was firing that heavy artillery?" Gill said.

"You know Bill Haskel, he piloted his copter for cost of fuel and we all chipped in twenty bucks. No biggie. As for the crazy bastard in the copter, that was Bill's son, Chester. He's home on leave. You lucked out, the kid's a Marine."

Gill sighed and looked at Nicki, who hadn't moved. "All a little too late," Gill said. "Please don't take that the wrong way. You did everything you could, I just feel like it was all for nothing. Brian was gone, everything after that is my fault. Belinda's injury, Clint and Rajim's deaths, Kate's arm. All because I couldn't accept the truth."

Ant said, "Not true. You.... We did what had to be done."

"And I appreciate that more than you know."

Squirrel said, "I know you feel bad, but you were trying to save your boy. You should feel no guilt over that."

"He's right," Ant said. "Those beasts scratched their way free. That's what caused all this. Not you. If we ha—"

A screech echoed up the tunnel.

All conversations stopped, and everyone froze. The seconds ticked by, then another screech followed by a wail.

Chief Perry said, "Let's go. Prepare for an attack."

Gill scrambled to his feet and was handed a shotgun. The creatures were coming from the valley, and Ant and Kate went back down the tunnel toward the commotion. They stopped about twenty feet up, their silhouettes barely visible in the darkness.

The *velociraptors* came at them, bouncing off the walls and screaming in fury, jaws snapping, dark eyes rolling in narrow heads. Ant and Kate fell back, and the party open fired on the raptors as they bounded down the tunnel. Flashlight beams lit the cave, and Gill fired at the glare of teeth in the blackness.

Gill flashed back to the first time he'd been attacked by these creatures in this same cave. The ceiling had come down and Clint had died, but this time there were more guns. More people picking the beasts off as they drove forward. Gill's ears rang, and he ran out of ammo. Amidst the chaos he searched about him and Chief Perry directed him to the ammunition box. He stuffed shells into the shotgun and turned back to the fray. Dust and white smoke filled the air, the *crack* and *pop* of guns echoing through the tunnel. Bullets hit bone, and the beasts yelped and cried as their flock was thinned, but the survivors came on, dodging around the tunnel.

The lead beast reached Ant and lunged feet forward, like an eagle attacking. Ant squeezed off three shots and the side of the creature's head slid off its skull. The corpse came to rest at his feet.

Two more raptors bounced off the ceiling and one caught Ant's arm. The beast raked its talons across his back and blood spouted from the gash as Ant dropped to his knees. The beast came on and Gill lost sight of the deputy sheriff as he was covered in raptors.

"Nooooo," Gill yelled, the boom of his shotgun deafening in the tight space.

Ant screamed, but he wasn't done. Help had reached him, and raptors were stabbed and shot, and Ant was pulled free, blood leaking from wounds on his face, arms and back.

A *velociraptor* came from the dark and crashed into Gill, taking him to the ground. The beast chomped and hissed as Gill pressed the tip of the gun barrel to the underside of the dinosaur's head and pulled the trigger. Blood, brain, and bone exploded upward from the top of the raptor's head, and the beast fell still.

More raptors came on, all the animals working as one, their instincts bonding them to their prey. Gill screamed and fired, jacking back the shotgun's slide and firing as fast as he could. When he clicked empty he let the gun fall to his side as the sharp scent of sulfur overtook him.

There were no more shrieks or wails.

The sound of gunfire slowed, the smoke thinned.

A deep growl rolled through the tunnel.

"Let's go, Kate. Ant, can you walk?" Gill said.

Ant nodded.

Gill helped Nicki as the party fled, climbing through the blasted tunnels, over piles of ice rocks, until they were back in the wide chamber with the opening at its top. Several ropes dangled through the hole, and people started climbing.

They heard and saw no other creatures, and the question that had been gnawing at Gill since they'd entered the tunnels wouldn't leave him be. When they were free, what should they do? Guard the tunnel entrance or seal it?

"You're up, Gill," Chief Perry said.

Gill looked around for Nicki, but didn't see her.

Up Gill went and when he got to the top he pulled himself over the rim of the ice sheet and rolled over in the snow. The chill felt good.

Above, the sun floated past noon.

36

The discussion about whether they should seal the tunnel didn't last long, and within an hour of the party's escape from the cave, charges were being set around the edge of the ice field. The intention was to collapse the entire ice sheet, thus clogging the tunnel. Thoughts for the future would come later, and concerns about the chunks of ice melting and revealing the tunnel opening were also for another day. Climate change was increasing the Earth's temperature fast, but not that fast, and local mine blasting could be put on hold.

"You alright?" Nicki said. Her face was covered in cuts and bruises.

"Yeah. You?" Gill said.

Nicki shifted on her feet. She looked at Gill with eyes that showed desperation, fear, uncertainty, and something else.

"Go ahead. Spit it out," Gill said.

Nicki stared at the snow-covered ground. "How do you do it? I feel like I can't breathe. Like facing my children is going to be the biggest nightmare imaginable."

Gill knew how she felt because to some extent he still felt that way. The void never went away, it just hid and waited for the perfect time to spring out and bring you down. That's why people build walls around themselves, that way they're always prepared for the enviable betrayal. "It gets better with time, but it will never go away. At least that's my opinion. You and Rajim weren't two separate people, you were one. Problems aside, you relied on each other in ways neither of you fully recognized and now all those things are going to feel like a ton of worry and fear on your chest every day, but you have to fight it. Not let it get over on you. Always keep Kiki and Fred in the front of your mind. They are your entire life now."

"The kids. What do I say? How..." She let her head fall in her hands and cried.

Gill gathered her in his arms and she didn't resist. "How about I tell them with you?"

Nicki's head snapped up. "You would do that?"

"For you and the kids. It's important they understand the finality of the situation, but we don't need to hit them over the head with it. Would you consider a lie until they get older?"

"Like what?"

"Telling them he's sick in a special hospital. Write them letters from him, and slowly ease them into the loss and then tell them the truth when they're a bit older."

Nicki's face tightened.

"Or we tell them the truth, and make sure they understand their dad died a hero saving their mother's life," Gill said.

"I think that's what I want to do. I'm done with secrets," Nicki said. "Thanks for everything you did for me in there, Gill. I don't know if I would have made it without you."

"Heads up," a man yelled from across the ice sheet. "Step back from the depression, please."

Silence fell over the ice field.

"Ten to blasting," the man yelled.

"Wait," Gill said. He put up a hand and everyone stared at him.

"Gill, what are you doing?" Nicki said.

"You have to let go, so it's time I did as well," Gill said.

He walked across the ice, Kate, Nicki, Ant, Squirrel, and a host of others watching silently. When he got to the hole that led down to the tunnel he pulled Brian's sneaker free and turned it over in his hand. He caressed the blue fabric, felt the dimpled rubber sole. He brought it to his face and gave it one last sniff. "Bye, buddy," Gill said. He held the sneaker over the hole, wanting to drop it, but something gnawed at him. A voice in the back of his mind calling out to him. He put the little shoe back in his pocket.

Gill trudged back across the ice and joined the group.

Nicki put an arm around Gill. "When you're ready. Not before."

Gill nodded.

"Blasting in ten, nine, eight, seven…"

Gill closed his eyes and shuffled through the pictures of Abigale and Brian in his mental album. The ground shook as the charges detonated, and the *pop* and *crack* of rending ice thundered over the plain as the ice sheet collapsed, sealing the tunnel.

***

The hike back to Reserve was depressing and miserable. It rained constantly, but it got warmer as the party descended and they had plenty of food and water. Gill nudged up to Chief Perry as they walked. He was curious about his opinion about what should be done with the valley. Nicki followed him everywhere like a puppy, as if Gill was going to drop some nugget of gold that would get her through the difficult days ahead. Gill didn't mind. He didn't mind at all.

"So, Chief, what do you make of all this?" Gill said.

Chief Perry shook his head. "I wouldn't have believed it if I hadn't seen it with my own eyes," he said.

"I hear that, and you didn't see the half of it," Nicki said.

"I know, Gill has told me," the chief said.

"What do you reckon happens next?" Gill said.

"The state police are going to want statements from all of you, of course. There will probably be cause of death investigations, but given the number of witnesses, that will be a formality, I would think."

"And the valley?" Nicki said.

Gill smiled. He was going to ask that. The minute he'd climbed from the hole onto the ice shelf his thoughts had gone to returning to the primeval valley.

"It's in our county, so I figure we'll have some say in who studies it," Chief Perry said.

The party came down from the mountains and crossed Clear River, and for an instant Gill was back there, fly fishing with his boy, Brian's death nothing but a dream. They were greeted in town with cheers and condolences, but the festivities quickly turned sour when Rajim and Clint's deaths were reported.

"I need a drink and a shower," Gill said.

Nicki stopped walking and stared at her children, who were waiting with a neighbor in front of the candy store. Fred was licking a huge lollipop, and Kiki ate chocolate—her father's favorite.

"Come on. We'll take them home together," Gill said. A drink and shower would have to wait.

Nicki nodded and blinked.

After going home with Nicki and dealing with two hysterical children for two hours, Gill was asked to stop at the courthouse to approve the memorial arrangements for Brian, Rajim, and Clint, which would be held the next day. There were no remains to deal with, and headstones could wait. They needed to put everyone to rest for the sake of their families. The sooner that was done, the sooner everyone could try and move on.

After a phone call with Nicki, who was despondent, Gill finally headed home as darkness fell. He poured three fingers of Jack Daniels and collapsed on his couch. The house was silent. Brian's bedroom fan wasn't on, no clocks ticked. Outside a gentle breeze stirred leaves and rattled the screen door.

He cried then. Months of sorrow gushing from him. When he was done wailing, he lay on the couch and fell into a fitful sleep filled with images of Rajim's body being torn to pieces while he stood and watched, unable to help him. Brian's lifeless body staring up at him from the placid surface of a lake. Clint's arms and legs being torn off.

He woke sweating in the darkness.

***

The next day dawned beautiful and bright. The memorial was held at the cemetery where eventually tombstones would be placed marking the gravesites of Brian, Clint, and Rajim. Seeing Nicki and her kids cry broke Gill's heart, and the sympathy he received hurt like a knife twisted in his chest.

Most people wanted to know about the valley. What he'd seen. Was it true there were dinosaurs there? He and Nicki had agreed to withhold the details of their adventures until they gave official statements to the authorities. The chief's speech about the formality of a cause of death investigation had stuck with Gill, and Sheriff Nicki had reminded him they had very little proof to support their story. Their dead cellphones with pictures on them were in their backpacks, which were in the forest back in the valley. Kate and Squirrel and the helicopter pilot and gunner, plus Lydia had seen the raptors. It was enough proof, but there was little physical evidence and prudence was always the wise road.

When the service was done, a fast meeting was held at the hall, and all agreed to return the next day at 8AM to decide on the town's next steps. They'd sent a preliminary report to the staties, but hadn't heard anything. A state investigator was due in the next day or two. People had strong opinions about who should be allowed to visit the valley. It had been Gill that reminded them if the staties or feds wanted in, they would be in.

With Abigale and Rajim recently deceased whatever feelings Gill and Nicki had for one another seemed inappropriate and untimely. Nicki said she needed time and space to think things through, make peace with the memory of her husband. Nicki and Rajim had been through a lot, and Nicki said that made it so much harder to lose him. They'd just overcome a major hurdle, and their future had been on the upswing.

Gill struggled with guilt every time he felt anything for Nicki. So he sat in his house, alone, drinking himself into misery and torturing himself with the memories of his dead wife and son.

Shared adversity creates bonds that age differently than normal relationships. Nicki feared, and in truth so did Gill, that their feelings for each other were exaggerated by the shared trauma of the primeval valley.

Three weeks after their return Nicki called to tell Gill she couldn't take Rajim's ghost around every turn, and she was resigning her post as sheriff, taking the kids and leaving Reserve. She said she was sorry, but Gill understood, though it hurt more than he was willing to admit.

Gill and Nicki said their goodbyes, and they never saw each other again.

Isolation and loss ate at Gill, memories of his family tormenting him. He recalled the valley, Brian's finger. The boy's body wasn't found. Gill went into his son's bedroom, which was exactly how Brian had left it. Errant rays of sunlight cut through the pulled drapes, dust motes catching the light like stars. A game of Junior Monopoly he and Brian had started sat half played on a small table. Clothes were piled on the floor, and toys were strewn about. He sat on the unmade race car bed and lifted a fistful of sheets to his nose. Must, flowers from the laundry detergent, and...

He pulled Brian's sneaker from his pocket. Gill never went anywhere without it. He held it up and pictured his son wearing it.

Could Brian be alive?

Gill took a long pull of whiskey and vaulted to his feet. It was possible.

The heat from the alcohol leaked through Gill, and his eyes burned. He'd been fooled. Tricked by cowards who were afraid to continue the hunt. The moment he left the valley he felt it pulling him back, beckoning with mysteries, answers, and his son.

He had to go back. He would go back, and before the feds or anyone else had a chance to stop him.

Gill gathered supplies: guns, ammo, explosives, food and water. Everything he needed to get back to the lost valley. He waited until nightfall to leave so he could slip away unseen. Lights from Reserve glowed in the blackness and stars blinked in the clear night sky as he hefted his pack and slung an M4 carbine over his shoulder. It was time to turn east and head up toward Challenger Peak. If everything went well, he could be with his son by week's end.

Gill looked back at Reserve one last time before he plunged into the forest of evergreens. He didn't expect to see the town again. He felt Brian's sneaker in his pocket, pulled down the brim of his hat, and disappeared into the darkness.

Edward J. McFadden III juggles a full-time career as a university administrator, with his writing aspirations. His novels Shadow of the Abyss, THROWBACK and The Breach were recently published by Severed Press, and his short story Doorways in Time appeared in Shadows & Reflections, an estate authorized Roger Zelazny tribute anthology with an introduction by George R.R. Martin. His other novels include AWAKE, The Black Death of Babylon, Our Dying Land and HOAXERS. Ed is also the author/editor of: Anywhere But Here, Lucky 13, Jigsaw Nation, Deconstructing Tolkien: A Fundamental Analysis of The Lord of the Rings (re-released in eBook format Fall 2012 – Amazon Bestseller), Time Capsule, Epitaphs (W/ Tom Piccirilli), The Second Coming, Thoughts of Christmas, and The Best of Pirate Writings. He lives on Long Island with his wife Dawn, their daughter Samantha, and their mutt Oli.

CHECK OUT OTHER GREAT DINOSAUR BOOKS

PRIMORDIA
by **Greig Beck**

Ben Cartwright, former soldier, home to mourn the loss of his father stumbles upon cryptic letters from the past between the author, Arthur Conan Doyle and his great, great grandfather who vanished while exploring the Amazon jungle in 1908.

Amazingly, these letters lead Ben to believe that his ancestor's expedition was the basis for Doyle's fantastical tale of a lost world inhabited by long extinct creatures. As Ben digs some more he finds clues to the whereabouts of a lost notebook that might contain a map to a place that is home to creatures that would rewrite everything known about history, biology and evolution.

But other parties now know about the notebook, and will do anything to obtain it. For Ben and his friends, it becomes a race against time and against ruthless rivals.

In the remotest corners of Venezuela, along winding river trails known only to lost tribes, and through near impenetrable jungle, Ben and his novice team find a forbidden place more terrifying and dangerous than anything they could ever have imagined.

PANGAEA EXILES
by **Jeff Brackett**

Tried and convicted for his crimes, Sean Barrow is sent into temporal exile—banished to a time so far before recorded history that there is no chance that he, or any other criminal sent back, has any chance of altering history.

Now Sean must find a way to survive more than 200 million years in the past, in a world populated by monstrous creatures that would rend him limb from limb if they got the chance. And that's just his fellow prisoners.

The dinosaurs are almost as bad.

CHECK OUT OTHER GREAT DINOSAUR BOOKS

FLIPSIDE
by JAKE BIBLE

The year is 2046 and dinosaurs are real.

Time bubbles across the world, many as large as one hundred square miles, turn like clockwork, revealing prehistoric landscapes from the Cretaceous Period.

They reveal the Flipside.

Now, thirty years after the first Turn, the clockwork is breaking down as one of the world's powers has decided to exploit the phenomenon for their own gain, possibly destroying everything then and now in the process.

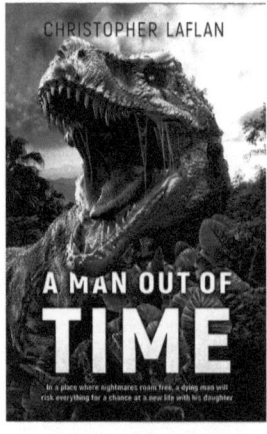

A MAN OUT OF TIME
by Christopher Laflan

Five years after the Chinese Axis detonated an unknown weapon of mass destruction off the southern coast of the United States, Special Ops Sergeant John Crider and the members of Shadow Company have finally captured what they all hope will lead to the end of the war. Unfortunately, the population within the United States is no longer sustainable. In an effort to stabilize the economy, the government enacts the Cryonics Act. One hundred years in suspended animation, all debt forgiven, and a chance at a less crowded future are too good to pass up for John and his young daughter.

Except not everything always goes as planned as Sergeant John Crider finds himself pitted against a land of prehistoric monsters genetically resurrected from the fossil record, murderous inhabitants, and a future he never wanted.

CHECK OUT OTHER GREAT DINOSAUR BOOKS

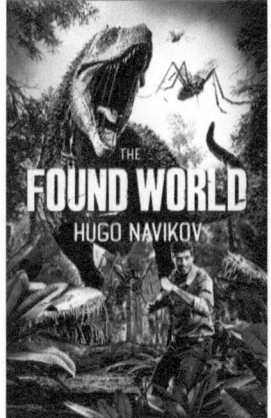

THE FOUND WORLD
by Hugo Navikov

A powerful global cabal wants adventurer Brett Russell to retrieve a superweapon stolen by the scientist who built it. To entice him to travel underneath one of the most dangerous volcanoes on Earth to find the scientist, this shadowy organization will pay him the only thing he cares about: information that will allow him to avenge his family's murder.

But before he can get paid, he and his team must enter an underground hellscape of killer plants, giant insects, terrifying dinosaurs, and an army of other predators never previously seen by man.

At the end of this journey awaits a revelation that could alter the fate of mankind ... if they can make it back from this horrifying found world.

HOUSE OF THE GODS
by Davide Mana

High above the steamy jungle of the Amazon basin, rise the flat plateaus known as the Tepui, the House of the Gods. Lost worlds of unknown beauty, a naturalistic wonder, each an ecology onto itself, shunned by the local tribes for centuries. The House of the Gods was not made for men.

But now, the crew and passengers of a small charter plane are about to find what was hidden for sixty million years.

Lost on an island in the clouds 10.000 feet above the jungle, surrounded by dinosaurs, hunted by mysterious mercenaries, the survivors of Sligo Air flight 001 will quickly learn the only rule of life on Earth: Extinction.